Desiring the Dragon Lord

A Dragon Protectors Novel

Michelle Miles

This is a work of fiction. All characters, organizations and events portrayed in this novel are either products of the author's imagination or used fictitiously.

DESIRING THE DRAGON LORD

Cover Design by Erin Dameron-Hill
Edited by Tina Winograd

ISBN: 978-1-7333887-2-6

Desiring the Dragon Lord

A Dragon Protectors Novel

"Michelle Miles kicks off her new Dragon Protectors series with a bang…" *—4 stars, Amazon Reviewer*

"I read this book in just a couple of days. I couldn't put it down!" *—5 stars, Amazon Reviewer*

"…a wonderful book full of strong minded characters." *—5 stars, Amazon Reviewer*

How far will he go to save the only woman who can tame his inner beast?

After witnessing the brutal murders of his family, dragon-shifter Logan Blake stumbles into the human realm injured and near death. His only goal is to heal and track down the fabled Blood Stone that can restore his dying realm. When a beautiful woman stops to render aid, he's unprepared for the instant bonding he feels to her. Her presence fuels an unquenchable desire and he knows he has to claim her.

Bree Anderson's morning jog is interrupted by the sudden appearance of a sexy, injured man in the middle of Central Park. When he turns up days later at the bar she manages as her father's new bodyguard, she knows he's going to be a handful. She also knows she's up for the job of uncovering who—and what—Logan is. But her de- termination to discover Logan's true identity is put on hold when a vampire mafia kills her father and turns their attention on her.

Logan instantly becomes her fierce protector, until the evil of his past hunts him down in the form of the Drakana—dragon-hunters intent on killing him. The only way he can save Bree from the vamps and the Drakana is to get her as far from the city as possible. But when both factions converge on their hidden location, Logan must make the ultimate sacrifice to save the only woman who can tame his inner beast.

The incessant buzzing pulsed through Logan Blake with a bone-vibrating intensity. It shook him right to the marrow of his dragon bones as he pitched forward into the bright light of the portal. He couldn't keep from looking back to see his father Eli, Chief Magistrate of his clan, shift into dragon form and puff out a breath toward the light. Seconds later, Archer, one of his clan council members, plunged the obsidian-bladed sword through his father's gut and he fell to the ground.

Find the Blood Stone, Logan. It can save the Hidden Lands.

Logan opened his mouth to shout a reply as Eli's powerful Dragon's Breath reached the electromagnetic field of the portal. The brilliant flash of light exploded around him, punching through him with such a brutal force, he flew backward. The ground rose to meet him so quickly, he wasn't prepared for the jarring landing.

As the buzzing subsided, his shallow breathing was the only thing he heard inside his head. He peeled his eyes open and looked up through a canopy of tree leaves. Beyond the trees, the sun brightened the morning sky turning it from deep indigo to a faint pink. He'd made it through the portal and into the human realm but not without great cost.

As he attuned his senses to his new surroundings, he heard traffic in the distance and pounding of footsteps on pavement nearby. He wasn't sure where he'd landed but was grateful he'd managed to get away.

His left shoulder throbbed with a fierce burning pain. Archer managed to stab him, too, with the obsidian-bladed sword before he dove for the opening leaving behind both his dead parents.

Logan grunted as he sat up, running fingers over the wound. They came away dotted with blood. He stumbled to his feet and got his bearings. He was in a park. Beyond the concrete sidewalk was a small lake. And rising around the trees, buildings reached for the sky.

He'd made it to a city. Though, he couldn't be sure which one; he was at least glad he hadn't ended up in some wilderness with no way to get back to civilization. Here, he could heal and blend in quickly with the humans. He had no fear Archer would follow him through the portal since his dying father sealed it with Dragon's Breath after he'd stepped through.

He wavered, his stomach clenching as he bent forward and braced his hands on his knees to clear his head. The poison from the obsidian blade along with the effects of the Dragon's Breath mixed with the electromagnetic field that created the portal hadn't quite worn off.

"Hey, are you okay?"

The female voice startled him into looking up into the most astonishing green eyes fringed in dark lashes he had ever seen. The morning glow lit her delicately carved face accentuating her high cheekbones and full lips. Her hair was pulled into a high ponytail and sweat glistened on her damp skin. She wore running shoes, shorts, and a sports top that clung to her slight but muscular frame.

"I'm…fine," he managed.

"You don't look fine. You're bleeding." She cocked her head to the side and pointed to his shoulder.

Logan straightened with a wince, pain lancing through him. "I'll be all right."

As he said it, she jogged toward him, her hair swinging behind her. Even in the ponytail, the length reached the middle of her back. "Let me help you."

She reached for him but he jerked away. He didn't want her to touch him. Even though he looked human, he wasn't. And the moment she laid a hand on him she'd know he was different. But that wasn't the only reason he didn't want her to touch him—he had just gone through *ka daeko*, the equivalent of puberty in young human males. His hormones worked overtime, desperate for him to mate. If she touched him, he would involuntarily attune to her in an unbreakable bond.

The girl blinked, surprised, and held up her hands. "I just want to help."

"You can't help me," he grunted. He took a step but stumbled and nearly fell forward again.

She wrapped her hand around his upper arm to steady him. The second she touched him, he sucked in a sharp breath. Her delicate fingers on his heated skin left a lasting impression on his newly manifested psyche, imprinting her on him. If he could have anticipated she was going to do that, he could have taken evasive action to keep her away but now the damage was done. That one little touch was enough to ignite his overly-heated dragon's blood to blistering levels.

Her heavy lashes flew upward as a surprise gasp leapt through her mind. He might have missed her expression if he hadn't been looking at her. She quickly masked her shock, though, and made her face impassive as she helped him to a nearby bench.

Even if he couldn't hear her speedy thoughts trickling through her mind, he didn't miss the flutter of her pulse in the long column of her neck or the way she perched on the edge of the bench next to him and swallowed hard as her gaze raked over his body then back to his wounded shoulder.

Damn her. Why did she have to touch him? Even if he wanted to ignore his overactive hormones, he couldn't. Every part of him throbbed with the rhythmic sensation that she was his and he'd kill anyone who tried to come between them. He didn't need that complication. Not now. Not when there was so much at stake.

"You need a hospital."

Was it his imagination or did her voice sound huskier than it did a minute ago? She cleared her throat and tried again.

"I mean, that wound looks pretty bad. What happened?"

"No. No hospitals." He waved away the thought and ignored her probing question.

The last thing he needed was to end up in some emergency room with doctors and nurses poking and prodding him. The second they realized he wasn't human, they would run tests, call the authorities and he'd end up in some testing lab or—worse—dead.

He didn't have time for that. He was on a mission. He had to find Rafe, the exiled dragon knight. He was the only one who could help him now that he'd crossed over into the human realm. He'd know how to heal the stab wound and stop the poison from killing him.

Questions rose into her mind as she looked him over. She bit one corner of her lower lip and glanced around the park. The morning light reflected in her green eyes accentuating the gold flecks making them sparkle.

"Where you in a knife fight?"

"I need to go. Where am I?" He shoved to his feet, ignoring her question because he doubted she could even comprehend what had happened to him.

She rose, her hands on her slender hips as her brows drew together. He could hear her wonder who he was and why he was in the park in dirty clothes with a bleeding shoulder. He wanted to answer her—felt compelled to answer her—but she wouldn't understand the truth. She was human and his dragon troubles were no concern of hers.

His shoulder would continue to fester, the poison spreading through him if he didn't get out of here and find Rafe.

"Central Park West is that way." She pointed to her left.

Relief flood through him, thankful he managed to make it to New York City. That's where he could find Rafe. Was it fate the portal led him there? Or mere luck? Either way, there was hope yet.

"Thanks."

Logan staggered in the direction she pointed. He could still hear her in his mind—damn it—and it took some effort to shut her off. The nausea came back with such force, he clutched his abdomen, and again, bent forward.

Her hand landed on his back and while he *wanted* her to touch him, at the same time he wished she would stop touching him. It had an adverse effect to his hormones. His rational mind wanted to shove her off, push her away, but his irrational mind wanted to take her into his arms and kiss her senseless. Then throw her on the ground, rip off her shorts, and take her right then, right there.

"You need help."

Logan pressed a palm against the side of his head. "Please, stop touching me."

Confused annoyance trickled through her along with a few choice words she called him. He couldn't blame her. From her standpoint, he was an ass.

"Gee, sorry. I'm just trying to help."

"I know you are. But you're…it's…I can't explain. It hurts when you do that."

Her brows drew together. "I hardly touched you."

"I *know* that." He growled the words, impatient. "I need to find someone. I appreciate your concern but I have to go."

He wasn't sure how he could leave her behind. How he could brush past her and never look at her again after he'd unwittingly connected to her. All because she wrapped her hand around his arm. From now until he died, his body would ache for her, want her, need her. He would experience an intense physical pain without her. Even if he had another woman, it would never assuage a raw carnal need pulsing through him on that most basic level. Her very essence had been imprinted on him and there was no turning back.

Logan knew she stood behind him, watching him walk away. Even from the distance, he could smell the faint undertones of her strawberry shampoo and the brown sugar scent of her body wash beyond the salty tang of her perspiration. It did nothing to stop the lascivious thoughts of her naked, presenting her glorious body as a smorgasbord of delectable treats for him to kiss and lick and suck. He could well imagine her honey blonde hair splayed –about her head while she rocked under him, against him, and cried out with pleasure.

Fuck all.

He thought stepping through the portal into the human realm would be his undoing, not the woman out for her morning jog. She was an unexpected distraction, something for which he hadn't planned.

Logan stumbled again, the sickness causing his stomach to cramp and threaten to heave. He clutched his abdomen and fell against a nearby tree with a groan. He could hear her running toward him. The closer she got, the stronger her scent, and the harder he got.

"If you won't go to a hospital, at least let me take you somewhere to patch you up."

He reeled on her, his lips curled back in a snarl about to snap at her when he stopped short. She hadn't flinched when he turned toward her intending to tell her to fuck off. She stood her ground and stared right back at him as though he were not intimidating at all. And dammed if he didn't like her even more for that.

"Stop trying to help me."

"I will not."

He growled.

She propped her hands on her slender hips and stuck out her chest. He could see the well-defined curve of her breasts under her sweat dampened shirt, her hard abs beneath flowing into well-rounded thighs. He tried hard not to look but the synapses in his brain sparked and had other ideas. He *wanted* to look and touch and caress. He clenched his jaw so tight it ached.

Why wouldn't she just go away?

And then it occurred to him she was as much attuned to him as he was her, though she couldn't know why or how. She lacked understanding of what he was and she could no more leave him than he could her. He looked her over and realized with some horror he'd either have to take her with him or experience a deep physical pain at their unconsummated union. He wouldn't be able to think with a clear head.

Logan thought of all the historical information he could regarding *ka daeko*, wondering if there was a way to sever the connection between them. From what little he could remember, the only thing that would calm the savage beast inside him was to sate his carnal desires with the chosen woman with *ka kladou*. He doubted she would be receptive to that idea since they just met.

"My place isn't far from here. Come with me so I can stop the bleeding," she said.

Her place. Right. Like he could be trusted with her alone. He clenched his hand so tightly, the muscles cramped, his nails cutting into his palm. Self-inflicting pain seemed to alleviate the hunger for her naked body flooding through him. And she was right. He did need to stop the bleeding long enough to find Rafe.

"All right," he said at last. He squared his shoulders, determined to get there on his own two feet.

And he hoped it wasn't a horrible decision.

When Bree Anderson started her morning run, she had no idea she would end it with taking a sexy stranger back to her apartment. She didn't know what possessed her to make the offer to him. In fact, she didn't know what possessed her to continue to talk to him or follow him. All she knew was she had to help this stranger who appeared out of nowhere in the middle of Central Park.

The flash of light caught her eye as she rounded the bend and then he was there. She stopped in the middle of the jogging trail while her morning running group went around her and stared in awestruck rapture at the hulking figure on the ground.

She immediately sensed something different about this guy. She could tell there was something otherworldly and ancient about him. Something that made him stand out from others. He didn't possess a telltale aura she was used to seeing in the strange beings that frequented her city. This distinct difference captured and held her attention.

He was freaking gorgeous. When he unfolded his tall body from the ground, she swooned. His black hair was disheveled like he'd been through hell. His striking tawny eyes were impossible not to notice. His clothes were dirty and bloodstained. His face was all hard lines and razor-sharp angles and all she wanted was to run her fingertips over them to see if she'd come away with cuts on her skin.

When she wrapped her hand around his arm, something sizzled between them. At first, she thought it was her overactive, sex-deprived imagination. But she realized it was actually *his skin* burning through the sleeve of his shirt that was so hot to the touch. It was a startling turn on and she couldn't deny the throbbing want pounding through her.

She didn't mistake the sharp intake of his breath when she touched him. Nor did she mistake the sudden urge to wrap her legs around his waist, to feel what was beneath his khaki pants.

God, she was horny.

And stupid. She was apparently stupid for taking him to her apartment. She'd lived in New York her whole life. She knew better than to pick up a strange man in the park. She also knew better than to want to pick up a strange man in the park and *want* to fuck him senseless.

She didn't know him from Adam. All she knew was something drove her to make sure he was taken care of, that he was okay. Had she lost her marbles? Had something fried in her brain when she touched him? Even when she'd touched him again, she still felt that same sizzle. He seemed to have felt it, too, when he growled at her to stop touching him.

It was enough to make her panties melt right off.

With her heart pounding a rapid beat and her pulse fluttering, she crossed Central Park West at 91st Street.

"I'm just one block ahead," she said, pointing.

It took some effort to keep her pace slow enough for him to keep up. He'd refused her help and she couldn't blame him. If she touched him again, she might combust from the heat building under her skin.

The man grunted acknowledgement as they headed up the street. She clenched her fists, resisting the urge to help him. Every time she reached for him, he'd shoot her a glare that told her to back off. He squared his shoulders into a rigid line making her wish she could run her hands along them. She could make out the tapered waist that went down into his lean form, and yes, she did examine his nice round ass.

Bree could tell it took effort for him to keep moving, to put one foot in front of the other. If she offered again to help him, she knew she would be putting his man card at risk and she didn't want to do that. She didn't want to insult his manhood.

They made it to the foot of the steps of her building and she jogged up to open the door. When she turned back, she could see his concentrated effort to get up the stairs, his white-knuckled hand on the concrete handrail as he took one step and then another and made it to the top. His face was bathed in a fine sheen of sweat.

Bree didn't bother to mask the sympathy she had for him. He must be in excruciating pain.

"Stop looking at me like that," he barked.

It took her aback. "Like what?"

"Like you pity me. I don't fucking need that."

"I don't pity you. You look like you're in a lot of pain, that's all."

She shoved open the door and held it for him to slip inside. As he passed by her, she didn't miss the way he brushed against her. The way his sleeve whispered across her breasts. Her nipples instantly went tight and erect, puckering to painful peaks beneath her shirt for all the world to see.

She was grateful there was no one to see.

Except *him*. She wanted him to see but he had ignored it as he passed through the threshold and entered the building.

"I'm on the third floor," she said.

"Of course, you are."

He gripped the banister and started up the stairs in obvious pain. He held his left arm against his side as he pulled himself up the stairs. She could hear his labored breathing and knew it was taking a lot out of him.

All she could think about was trying to soothe him, make him feel better. She wanted to heal him. She wasn't even sure why she was so desperate to help.

At the top of the stairs, she pointed to the door labeled 3B. "That's me."

"Great."

He inhaled a deep breath and leaned on the railing as she unlocked the door and pushed it open. He followed her inside her small apartment the size of a Cracker Jack box. The living room and kitchen combined into one large room with a bathroom and closet between it and the bedroom.

"You can sit on the couch. I'll be right back with the first aid kit."

He muttered something as she trotted off to the bathroom. She paused for a brief moment to check her reflection in the mirror and scowled. She looked like hell. There was no way he'd be attracted to her. She was sweaty from her morning jog and she smelled liked a kid who had been outside all day long.

She tugged down her ponytail and brushed out her damp hair, but it didn't seem to help. It would have to do. Frowning, she splashed cold water on her reddened face—from exertion and embarrassment—and dragged out the first aid kit from under the sink.

Bree took a deep breath and turned back to her bedroom. Through the open door, she saw him shove off his shirt, exposing his long lean form showing off golden skin, a broad chest sprinkled in dark hair and abs she could literally bounce a quarter off.

Good God.

The first aid kit slipped from her hands and crashed on the floor. The bang shook her out of her reverie and she snatched it up, clearing her throat and trying her best to act natural. It was hard to do when her traitorous body wanted to melt into a puddle at his feet.

Bree stood in front of him and got a good look at the wound. It was red and festering. Some sort of white foamy substance oozed from it and it smelled like death. She swallowed hard and tried not to gag.

"Still want to patch me up, princess?" His quiet voice echoed in the silence of the apartment.

He must have known how bad the wound was. Maybe that was why he tried so hard to wave her off, to get her to go away. She should have listened to him. Now she had him in her apartment and she had no choice but to go through with it. She nodded, determined to help him.

"Yes."

She placed the small white box on the cushion next to him and flipped it open. It took several seconds of rummaging with shaking fingers before she was able to grasp the gauze and antibiotic ointment. She also picked up an antiseptic pad. She organized all the items and then gave the wound a cursory glance.

"It doesn't look good," she said.

"It doesn't feel good either." His voice was laced with a hint of humor.

Bree ripped open the antiseptic package and pulled out the small square pad. "This may sting a little."

As she said it, she swiped the wound with the damp pad. He grunted, his jaw clenched tightly and then his hands landed on her waist. His fingers dug into her flesh as he gripped her. She sucked in a breath the second he touched her. His hands were fiery hot, and an image of their sweaty naked bodies burst through her mind.

"Oh!" she gasped.

"Sorry."

He started to remove his hands, but she stopped him. "Don't."

That gaze lifted to meet hers and her mouth suddenly went dry. Her brain emptied of all thoughts. Bree was aware of her ragged breathing as she concentrated on taking a breath in and expelling it.

It was the only sound between them. She couldn't even hear him breathe.

But she could hear the *kathunk* of his heart. Could see it beating against the golden skin of his naked chest. His eyes bored into hers, and for a moment, she thought he could see into her soul. It seemed she, too, could see into the depths of his being. For a brief moment, she saw fiery red scales, the breath of fire, and hear the leathery wings flap against a cold morning breeze. She should have been frightened, perhaps, but instead, she was fascinated.

He blinked, then, and the image was gone. It was the most intense thing she had ever seen. He stiffened, the air tense and hot, and then he relaxed as though nothing happened at all. All that remained was the slick heat between her legs.

"All right," he said. "If you're sure."

They were so close, his breath whispered over her. Gooseflesh rose on her arms and legs and a prickling sensation pierced her. God, she wanted him. She wanted to taste those perfect shaped lips. She wanted to feel his tongue swipe over hers.

"Oh, I'm sure."

Her voice wavered. When the corners of his mouth lifted in a brief little smile, she nearly fainted. She had never been so sexually charged in her life.

"I-I'm going to cleanse it again."

"At least you warned me that time." Mirth twinkled in those eyes.

Bree swallowed, trying to dampen her dry mouth. It was pointless.

She swiped the antiseptic pad over the wound again, cleaning it as best she could. His fingers tightened on her waist again. She delighted in the way he seemed to possess her even though he didn't even know her.

"There. I'll just get this gauze on you and then you'll be free to go."

Bree reached for the antibiotic ointment and the gauze pad. He never took his eyes off her hands as she opened the package and squirted the ointment onto the pad. His hands never moved either.

She held the gauze over the wound and then taped it to his skin, pressing the tape with a gentle hand against him. All the while, heat radiated off his body and into hers, making her wish she had central air conditioning in her old building. She bent slightly over him concentrating on getting the tape just right on the gauze as a tendril of her hair fell over her shoulder.

Bree froze when his hand slid up her side. Her gaze landed on his—that bold gaze that made her want to do all sorts of naughty things with him. A glow sparked deep inside her and she shivered. Not from cold. But heat. Heat that intensified as he looked at her, his eyes lowering a bit as he reached between them.

He seemed to move in super slow motion. She couldn't help but feel like a breathless girl of eighteen. She was entranced by the hard lines of his face and the deliberate way he twined a lock of hair around his forefinger.

A curious swooping pulled at her innards. He remained motionless, merely keeping her hair curled around his finger.

"So soft," he said in a quiet tone. "Like I imagined."

A shudder of desire passed through her. His hand turned into a fist and he tugged her face toward his. His eyes clouded with yeaning and need and lust. Her breath caught in the back of her throat, and for a moment, she thought—hoped—he was going to kiss her. She licked her lips in delighted anticipation.

He blinked, clearing away the fog of desire, as he released her. He nudged her away from him. Disappointed, she dropped her supplies onto the sofa next to him.

"Well. That should do it. You should be on the mend soon."

"Thank you." He tugged his shirt over all that glorious muscle and buttoned it.

"But you should still have someone look at that. I'm no doctor."

She was rambling like an idiot. She clamped her mouth shut as she stepped away and tidied up the trash she'd left behind.

"I plan to."

She closed the first aid kit and picked it up, turning toward the bathroom. He caught her hand, held it.

"Thanks for your help."

It took effort to make her brain form words. "You're welcome."

"I'll see myself out."

She watched him walk away, a sudden pain of loss shooting through her. She pressed her lips together, refusing to call out to him. She didn't want to sound like some desperate female but she didn't want to see him go either.

"Hey," she said.

He paused at the door, his hand on the knob as he turned to look at her over his shoulder with a questioning glance.

"Will I see you again?" She hated herself for asking but she couldn't stop the words from bubbling up and out her throat.

He peered at her a long silent moment before he shook his head. "I don't think so."

As he walked out the door and out of her life, she realized with some horror and regret she hadn't even thought to ask his name.

❦ 2 ❧

It took all of logan's self-control to release the girl and get out of her apartment without ravishing her. And it would have been so easy, too. He had her right where he wanted her—standing in front of him between his legs. He also had his hands on her slender waist. She'd wanted him to ravish her. Despite being able to hear it in her mind, he could also see it written all her over face.

And when he touched her hair, it nearly made him come undone. It nearly made *her* come undone. Her cheeks flushed with color. Her pulse fluttered. Heat emanated off her skin. He could even scent her arousal. All involuntary reactions she couldn't control if she tried.

Sometimes it sucked having enhanced senses especially when there was a female he desperately wanted.

He knew he had to get the hell out of there before he did something he regretted—before she did something she regretted. Even though she gave him those adoring looks and licked her lips like she waited him to kiss her...he couldn't stick around for another second. It was too dangerous. He was too dangerous. His feral emotions would be too much for her.

The strange thing was his shoulder did feel better. He didn't know what she used and he wasn't sure it mattered.

Logan pounded down the stairs and out the door, pausing on the stoop, peering at the street in front of him. The last information he had on Rafe was that he was living in Hell's Kitchen area. He had no idea where or how to get to Hell's Kitchen. He wasn't all that well versed in New York geography, but he was fairly certain he was on the Upper West Side.

Where the girl lived.

The girl destined to belong to him and no other. Too bad she didn't know it.

Logan headed down the street to the corner of 91st and Amsterdam, running through his options. He could hail a cab but he didn't have any money. He could commandeer a vehicle but he didn't want to call that much attention to himself. His last choice was to find the subway system and take a ride. He could easily get over the turnstiles there and jump on a train.

He stepped away from the corner and took a moment to take in the surrounding city. He attuned his senses to the sounds to find the nearest subway station, both aboveground and below. A faint rumbling beneath his feet told him everything he needed.

Logan sniffed the air. The station with the southbound train was several blocks away but within walking distance. As he started forward, the sickness plowed through him again and he had to pause to catch his breath. Even though the wound was cleansed, the poison from the knife was still in his system. He needed it purged if he was to survive.

He found the station at Central Park West and 96th Street with ease. When he descended the steps, he paused and glanced around. There were several transit police filtering through the station, keeping an eye on those who looked unsavory. His height made him a head taller than the average human male. If only he had the ability to blend in with his surroundings like some of his brethren.

He watched several folks as they swiped their MetroCard to get through the turnstiles. That's how he'd have to get through. But with no money, getting a MetroCard would be tricky. He leaned against the wall, propping one foot up, and watched the crowd. He pinpointed a guy who looked like an easy target, and as much as he hated doing it, he had to steal the card to get to the train. He knew he couldn't make it on foot to Hell's Kitchen.

The guy wore headphones, had his cell in one hand, a sack lunch in the other, and a backpack slung over one shoulder. He paused to the side to dig through his backpack looking for his card. He found it a minute later and then stuck it in his back pocket while he juggled the other stuff in his hands.

Perfect.

Logan pushed off the wall and headed for the kid. When he was distracted and didn't see him coming, he bumped into him, making him lose control of his cell phone. He fumbled with it, desperate to keep it from hitting the ground

"Hey, watch it!"

"Sorry, man."

Logan slipped the card from his back pocket with ease as he helped him regain control of the phone and put it back in the kid's hands. He shot him a glare but Logan was already on his way to the turnstile where he swiped the card and was through to the other side by the time the kid realized it was gone.

The train screeched to a stop. People entered and exited. The kid shouted something as Logan jumped onto the train and the doors swished closed. For now, he was safe and moving southbound toward Midtown.

Several people moved away from him, fear and mistrust in their eyes. He couldn't blame them. He looked mean with blood all over his shirt. At least he didn't have to worry about anyone bothering him.

As he took a seat and gripped one of the handrails, the distinct scent of blood and alcohol tickled his nose. He glanced around and spotted the two vampires sitting on one of the benches behind a young woman trying to ignore them while she read a book. They didn't notice him since they were so intent on watching her.

A cold prickling sensation went up the back of his neck as he watched and knew what was about to happen. Perhaps the girl could sense it too because she crossed and uncrossed her legs several times. She slipped her hand into her handbag at her side, reaching for something. At least she was willing and able to defend herself.

When the train stopped, she snatched her purse and tugged it on her shoulder and stepped quickly toward the door. They followed her, elbowing each other with sickening glee.

Vampires. He couldn't stand the likes of them.

Logan stepped off the train behind them. The girl still had her hand in her purse and then pulled something out in her enclosed fist. Probably a weapon of some kind. Even so, nothing could protect her from two vamps with mischief on the brain.

Nothing except Logan.

She made a sharp turn and started up the steps. The vamps followed.

Logan sighed. As much as he didn't want to get involved, he knew he had to. He couldn't let an innocent woman be injured because they wanted to feed.

He leapt the steps two at a time, closing the gap between them. When she made it to the top, she spun toward them with a small spray bottle in her hand. But before she could use it, Logan had reached the two vamps. He collared them both and dragged them the rest of the way up the stairs. She gaped, her eyes wide as Logan shoved them off to the side and dumped them on the ground. He put himself between her and the vamps.

They cowered on the ground looking up at him with shock and bewilderment, wondering what happened.

"You two have a problem here?" he asked.

They exchanged glances. One of them unfolded his lanky body from the ground and stood. He wasn't quite as tall or imposing as Logan.

"We just wanted to say hi to the girl."

Logan glanced back at her. She shook her head.

"I don't think she's interested. How about you move along? Both of you."

The second one got to his feet, eyeing the girl. Logan moved to stand in front of him, blocking his view. They had a momentary standoff before they decided to walk away.

Behind him, the girl blew out a minty breath. "Thank you. Those creeps have been following me since I got on the train this morning."

He turned to her as she put her mace into her handbag. Humans didn't realize there was a thriving subculture that played host to vampires, werewolves, Fae and other supernaturals. Logan was listed as other—a dragon-shifter.

When his father discovered the Hidden Lands was dying and killing the remaining clans, he started the movement from their realm to the human realm. Dragon-shifters seemed to be the most adaptable to human life. In fact, some had already made the transition eons before. Several of those clan leaders managed to integrate into the human world into leadership positions. Everything from royalty to heads of state to leaders of corporations. They had become successful in their own right and they had proven moving out of the Hidden Lands was a viable option. They had learned to live with humans in secret. They learned to adapt to a world that differed from their own and yet similar.

She looked him over, concern flicking across her features. "Are you okay? You don't look well."

He wiped the cold damp sweat from his forehead. He had to find Rafe before there was no stopping the poison coursing through his veins.

"I'm fine. Be careful," he said.

"I will." She smiled and started to walk away.

"Excuse me, miss." She gave him a questioning glance. "Can you tell me how to get to Hell's Kitchen?"

"Hell's Kitchen?" she repeated and her brows drew together in question. It reminded him of the girl he met in the park. "What are you looking for?"

"A friend."

"Do you have an address?" She flicked a lock of hair over her shoulder.

He shook his head. "I'm afraid not. Only a general location."

"Oh, well, it's only a small area on the west side of Manhattan." She rummaged in her purse and pulled out a pen and a small notebook. She drew him a crude map and gave him directions. "Does that help?"

He took the paper from her and studied it. "Yes. Thank you."

"Good luck." She gave him a small wave as she walked away.

And Logan was one step closer to finding Rafe.

The longer Logan walked, the sicker he felt. He knew the poison from the blade was eating through him and he had to find Rafe sooner rather than later.

At least he'd made it into what was known as Hell's Kitchen thanks to the woman's crudely drawn map. He just had no idea where to go next.

The streets were crawling with supernaturals unseen by the humans. Demons passed by smelling like death and rot. More vampires carrying the metallic tang of blood as well as a sharp trace of alcohol. Wolf shifters had an earthy scent to them so strong, it made his stomach cramp. And then there was the Fae—they were nothing like any of the other supernaturals. They carried a bright scent of sunshine with an undertone of a sexy deeper scent reminding him of midnight.

It was sensory overload. A barrage to his olfactory senses making him lightheaded. As if he wasn't already faint enough.

He stopped at a building on the corner, leaning against it and pressing his cheek against the cool stone façade. Loud music thumped from the nightclub or bar or whatever it was and there was a line around the block to get inside.

Upon closer inspection, he noticed those waiting in line were not all human. There was a long line of vamps and shifters waiting for their chance to get in. Logan craned his neck to look up at the red and white neon sign above the place. Bar Inferno. Complete with red and orange flames in neon between the two words.

He had a sudden gut feeling about the place. Either that or he was about to puke what stomach fluids he had all over the sidewalk.

Logan stumbled toward the bar, holding his arm against his cramping abdomen. Sweat dampened his back and armpits. It dripped down the side of his face. He caught the attention of some of the party-goers in line. One girl scowled in disgust at him as he made his way to the front of the line. He knew it wasn't his finest hour but at the moment he didn't give a shit if she or anyone else was disgusted by his looks.

Two vamps staggered out. The bouncer at the front of the line unhooked the red rope and allowed the next two in line inside. The girl squealed her excitement. As the door opened, Logan tried to get a glimpse inside but it was too dark to see.

"Hey! No cutting."

The high-pitched female voice got his attention. She was next in line and glaring at him as if he had done something horrific. All he wanted to do was get a peek inside the place. He wasn't sure why he thought Rafe might be in there but something told him it was a good place to start.

"Back of the line, pal." Her date thumbed behind him—a tall wolf shifter with dark brown eyes.

In his weakened state, Logan knew picking a fight with the guy would be stupid. He would lose that battle. But he still had to find a way inside. He glanced at the bouncer, a tall African-American man. He was bald except for a goatee and arms the size of an aircraft carrier. He wasn't someone Logan wanted to run into in a dark alley. He looked like he could break anyone in half—even a dragon-shifter.

"Say, man," Logan said as lurched toward him.

"You heard the man. Back of the line." He didn't even flinch, blink or look at him when he said it. And his voice was so deep, it rumbled around in his thick chest.

"You don't understand," Logan said, trying again. "My friend is in there."

His glittering dark brown gaze landed on Logan. "Your friend got a name?"

He hesitated. What if he was wrong? And then the poison reminded him he was about to die. He had to take the chance. "Rafe."

One dark brow rose. Logan didn't know if that was a good sign or not. "He didn't mention you."

Logan managed a half smile even though it made him want to hurl. "It's a surprise." When he looked unconvinced, he added, "It's his birthday."

Now he cocked his head to the side with disbelief. "His birthday?"

Logan thought about begging but he didn't want to lose any more dignity than he already had. If he was at full strength, he could kick the guy's ass and go inside. But as things were, he really needed the guy to let him in without incident.

It seemed as though a long eternity passed before the hulking man reached over and unhooked the red rope from the post. He waved him toward the door. The girl shrieked her objection as Logan hurried by before the man changed his mind.

As soon as he stepped across the threshold, bile rose to the back of his throat. It took what little strength he had remaining to keep it down. The place was packed with every kind of supernatural imaginable and they were all drinking and sweating and dancing.

All the odors together didn't exactly present a sweet-smelling bouquet. It was more like an olfactory overload of all foul-smelling things.

A bar lined one wall. Behind it, glass shelves hosting every kind of alcohol imaginable—and some not from the human realm. There were no seats available at the bar and a blonde woman and another girl were busy filling and refilling drinks.

A dance floor hosted swirling couples flirting and trying to find a mate for the night or a lifetime. Packed tables scattered around the dance floor and busy wait staff made sure the food was hot and the drinks flowed.

Logan was out of his mind if he thought Rafe would be caught dead in a place like this. Hell, he was out of his mind for even talking the bouncer into letting him inside. He'd resigned himself to failure and was about to leave when someone clamped a hand around his upper arm. His reflexes being slow, he wasn't able to get the punch off like he would have normally. All he was able to do was clench a fist and give a half-hearted attempt.

"Logan? Jesus. What the hell are you doing here?" He had to yell to be heard.

Logan looked up at the exiled dragon knight, Rafe. He had never been so relieved to see one of his kind in his life.

"You look like shit, man. What happened to you? Never mind. Let's get out of here. This place is too loud."

Rafe took him by the arm and led him out. It took Logan's remaining strength to force his feet to move through the door. When they passed the bouncer, Logan gave him a nod of thanks. Even in his stupor, he didn't miss the look of sheer surprise on the man's face.

"Happy birthday, Rafe," the man said as they passed.

"Happy birthday? What the fuck is he talking about?"

"Tell you later," Logan managed.

Rafe hailed a cab. When it stopped, he hauled Logan into the back and got in next to him. He barked his address. Logan was grateful to be in a moving vehicle and not walking. He leaned his head back on the headrest and closed his eyes.

"What happened to you?" Rafe's gruff voice was in his ear.

"Long story. Obsidian blade…got me."

"Fuck," he said under his breath. He leaned toward the driver. "Hey, an extra hundred if you speed and get us there in five minutes."

It was all the incentive the cabbie needed to get them there. It was the last thing Logan remembered before he passed out.

Logan woke with a start and sat upright on the strange sofa. He glanced around and realized he had no recollection of where the hell he was. Black and white furnishings filled the room. The large space had floor to ceiling windows covered by opaque shades to block out the bright lights of Times Square. Beyond the windows, he could see skyscrapers surrounding them and well below on the street heard cars honking.

"Easy, man. The effects of the poison haven't worn off yet." Rafe handed him a whiskey. "Thought you could use that."

"Thanks." He took the offered glass and downed it, grateful for the amber liquid.

He remembered, though his last recollection was a cab ride. He must have passed out from the pain of the illness. Remembering his shoulder, he reached up and rubbed the spot. A larger bandage covered the wound.

Rafe perched on the chair across from him. "You were lucky. The wound was festering and I had to dig out a small piece of the blade." He pointed to a shard of black glass on top of the coffee table. "You've been out for nearly a day."

Logan set aside his glass and picked it up, running his finger over the smooth surface. No wonder he in such bad shape. He'd lost a day to this fucking piece of glass. He wasn't going to lose any more time.

"Who stabbed you?" Rafe asked.

"Archer." Logan tossed the shard back on the table. "He killed my parents."

Rafe stared at him in mute horror for a moment before he rose, padded across the room to the bar, and picked up the whiskey bottle. He refilled his glass and then came back to refill Logan's.

"I'm sorry," Rafe said.

"So am I. I mean to kill him, Rafe."

"Is that why you came to me, for help?" He laughed, sounding bitter. "You know I can't go back to the Hidden Lands."

"I came to you because you're the only one I can trust. Plus, I hoped you'd have the cure for the poison." Logan held his glass. "I know you can't go back. But I intend to."

"If he doesn't find you here first," Rafe said. "If Archer killed the Chief Magistrate of the clans then he won't stop until you're dead."

"I know," Logan said through gritted teeth. "Don't you think I figured that out?"

Rafe leaned back into the cushion of the chair. "Maybe you should start at the beginning and tell me everything that happened."

"I don't have that kind of time." Logan slammed his glass against the table and then got to his feet. He instantly regretted it. A wave of nausea passed through him, making him lightheaded and he sat again. He rubbed his forehead.

"Yes, you do. The poison is still in your bloodstream. I gave you something to help counteract it, but it won't be out of your system for a while," Rafe said. "It's the best I could do."

"How long?"

He shrugged. "Days. Weeks. Don't know. Depends on you and how fast you heal. It was a pretty deep wound."

Logan's shoulder throbbed and he rubbed it trying to make the pain go away. He hadn't realized how hard Archer stabbed him right before he went through the portal. Everything had happened so fast. The buzzing, the lightning, his father's last Dragon's Breath.

"Start at the beginning," Rafe said.

With a shaking hand, Logan picked up his drink and held it between his hands. Just holding the cool glass gave his burning skin comfort. "The Hidden Lands are dying."

"Nothing new. We've known for a while."

"Yes, but my father wanted to move the remaining clans out of the Hidden Lands and into the human realm."

"You mean abandon the realm?"

Logan nodded.

"And Archer rejected that idea," Rafe said.

"He launched a coup. Killed my father, mother, and two other clan council leaders."

A look of distaste passed over Rafe's face. "Archer wants power no matter the cost."

"Yes, and now he has it."

Logan looked at him from across the rim of his glass. He realized in that moment just how little he knew about the knight. Rafe had been part of the Hidden Lands many years ago. He had been one of the finest knights in the realm. And yet something had happened. Something so dreadful, he ended up in the human realm in exile, forbidden to return to the clans or even interact with fellow dragon-shifters.

He had taken a huge risk coming through the portal looking for Rafe. But when all hell broke loose and things were out of hand, he was the first man Logan thought of. But it wasn't just that. Getting stabbed by the obsidian blade had been an unfortunate accident. There was another underlying reason he wanted to find Rafe, aside from asking for his help to kill Archer.

There was the matter of the Blood Stone but he wasn't sure how to ask Rafe about it. He doubted the man even had it. All he knew were the myths and legends placed it somewhere in the human realm.

"I'm sure he's seized power by now," Logan said.

"How did you get here?"

"I came through a portal," Logan said. "My parents and I intended to come through together but Archer attacked as we were leaving. My father sacrificed himself for me."

Remembering sent a sharp stabbing pain of regret and guilt through Logan. He couldn't help but replay the horrible events over and over in his mind. It made him hate himself a little more because he hadn't been able to save either of his parents when Archer and his Drakana hunters had attacked. It had come as a complete surprise and one for which they were not prepared.

All the more reason to go back and kill Archer. Even if he died trying.

"And you intend to avenge him. Seems noble enough," Rafe said.

"Isn't it?"

"Sure, until Archer finds the portal."

Logan shook his head. "Not possible. It was sealed with Dragon's Breath." His father's Dragon's Breath. His father had been one of the most powerful dragon-shifters in the realm and now he was dead.

He hadn't even had time to grieve for him or his mother. All he'd been able to think about since crossing the portal was finding Rafe and a cure for the poison in his veins.

Now that he'd achieved both those goals, he had to find Archer and get back what was rightfully his—the title of Chief Magistrate as leader of the Council of Five in the Hidden Lands. He also had to find a way to continue his father's work by locating the Blood Stone.

Legend said that eons ago, the stone along with two other mythical relics healed the dying land. In another age when the dragon-shifters had once faced extinction.

"Clever of your father to seal it with Dragon's Breath," Rafe said. "But there are other portals."

Surprise flickered through him. He was certain there were only a few entrances around the realm and those only his father knew about. "How do you know?"

He chuckled. "I've traveled from one side of this realm to the other. There are portals all over the place. Standing stones, for example. The Bermuda Triangle. Ancient monuments and megaliths that have supposed mystical powers in certain geographic locations. He'll come after you if he thinks you're alive. You're a threat to him."

"Then I'll have to be ready."

"You're not going to be anything if you don't heal."

He was right even though Logan disliked hearing the truth. He couldn't deny the impatience tingling through him. He gripped his glass so hard, the crystal cracked.

Rafe scowled. "That was Waterford."

"Sorry." He placed the ruined glass on the table.

"If you want to do this and do it right, then you'll listen to me. You came to me for help and now I'm giving it to you. But you're going to do it my way. Clear?" Rafe said.

"All right fine. I'll do it your way."

"I know someone looking for a new head of security. His last one got knifed by a wolf shifter. I'll recommend you and set up a meeting," Rafe said.

"And then what?"

"And then we wait and see. We'll wait out Archer and his men while you heal and get back to full strength," Rafe said. "What about your powers?"

"Depleted. Going through the portal did something to them."

"Then you'll need to regen, too. In the meantime, I'll do some digging and see what I can find out about Archer and his plans. There are always those who will exchange information for money."

"Who is this guy you know?"

"He's the bar owner at the place you found me. Name's Mario."

"And the hulking guy outside?"

"Oh, that's Bear. He's harmless."

"He doesn't look harmless."

Rafe chuckled. "He is. That reminds me. What was that about my birthday?"

"Nothing you need to worry about." Logan didn't think it necessary to explain to him how he lied his way into the bar/club.

"Right. You got a place to stay?"

Logan shook his head.

"You can stay here. I have another place on the Upper West Side."

"Are you rich or something?" He meant it as a joke but Rafe's serious expression didn't waver.

"Let's just say I'm good at what I do." He gave him a cocky grin. "And don't ask because it's not up for discussion."

Rafe stood and shoved his hand into his pocket. He brought out a key ring and tossed it to him. "Keys to the place. There's a car in the garage you can drive, too, if you know how to drive."

"I may not be from here but I'm not an idiot." He'd visited the human realm enough with his father he knew how things worked. He preferred shifting and gliding through the sky but he knew that wasn't possible since he was in a realm where the people had no idea dragons even existed.

Rafe snickered. "You haven't told me everything but I'll let that slide. Get some rest. I'll get a meeting set up with Mario and let you know when."

Rafe was right about that—he hadn't told him everything. Like the Blood Stone. Logan had a feeling that was something he'd have to find himself.

❧ 3 ❧

After the mysterious man left Bree's apartment, she hadn't stopped fantasizing about him. That had been three days ago. She was still in a dreamy state as she prepared for work that afternoon, combing out her long hair and trying to decide what to wear.

It was like he'd imprinted on her body, mind, and soul. She had a twinkle of hope he would show up at the bar one day, sweep her off her feet, and take her away to ravish her.

But that was silly. That sort of thing didn't happen in real life.

It was hard to get her hazy mind to function. Somehow, she managed to pull on jeans and a flowing off-the-shoulder top in black. It was hard to think about anything or anyone else but the sex god that landed in the park. She still didn't understand why she was so compelled to help him. She was puzzled over the strange flash of light and the way he appeared in the park.

And the way he smelled…he didn't smell like anything she knew.

Oh, her father thought she had no idea supernaturals were part of society. Even though she knew he knew. He thought he kept her safe by keeping her in the dark. Knowing was what made her so good at her job running the bar.

She could tell a wolf shifter from a bear shifter. She also knew the bar was a favorite place for vampires to hang out. Each race seemed to have a signature scent and even an aura.

Shifters had an earthly, woodsy scent and typically had a green or brown aura. Angels sometimes had an earthy scent, too, and sometimes they smelled like the air after a crisp spring rain. Their aura ranged from white to silver to gold to blue. Try as they might to conceal the expanse of their wings behind glamour, she could still see them.

Demons smelled like death and rot, and of course, had a dark deathly aura. And then there were the Fae who were much like angels with their glamour spells and their scent of stardust and sunshine with sparkly silvery auras. Well, the good ones anyway.

But her mystery man did not fall into any of those categories and it puzzled her. She had intuited that otherworldly sense about him. When she looked into those golden-brown, almost translucent, eyes she thought she could see an ancient beast with leathery wings determined to break free of the human prison.

She remembered looking into those eyes and seeing it. For a moment, she thought she should fear him. She didn't though. She was far from afraid and that, too, was something she couldn't explain. He was a stranger and she had taken a big risk inviting him to her place.

Bree sighed as she headed out the door for work. Fantasizing about the guy wasn't going to conjure him no matter how much she wished.

She arrived at Bar Inferno that afternoon to the normal bustle of activity. It wasn't a big place, but it was always crammed to maximum capacity with a line around the block waiting to get in. It had an eclectic appearance—exposed brick on one wall, steel and glass floating stairs leading up to the second floor where there were pool tables and a private security office.

Behind the bar were glass shelves backed by mirrors hosting all sorts of bottles of booze from around the globe. The mirrors were an optical illusion to make the place look bigger. The bar itself was made of mahogany and was the only original piece in the place. Her father had renovated around it, determined to keep it intact.

Meg, a fellow barkeep, was busy cleaning the bar getting ready for the afternoon happy hour. The cooks were in the kitchen preparing their daily dishes. Inferno had some of the best bar grub this side of Hell's Kitchen and had even been featured on a nationally syndicated show featuring bars with unusual fare. It had skyrocketed the little establishment on West 48th Street to fame as a major tourist stop and a must-see.

She could tell New Yorkers from everyone else. New Yorkers would walk thirty blocks in heels to wait in a two-hour line to get into the newest, hippest, most popular place in town. Tourists tend to say, "fuck it" and go somewhere else.

It also had become a major stop for all the supernaturals coming into and out of the realm. That was something she hadn't quite figured out either. Why Bar Inferno? What made it special?

She waved to Meg. "Hey, Meg. Have you seen my father?"

"He's with the new security chief," she said, wiping down the bar. "They're still in his office, I think."

New security chief? She had no idea her father was interviewing someone to replace the last one. He hadn't told her. Which wasn't unusual since her father ran most of the business dealings when it came to Bar Inferno. She was the general manager, so she got to handle the day-to-day stuff. In short, mostly the crap he didn't want to deal with.

Mario's office was on the first floor of the bar behind the stairs.

"He's a real hottie, too." Meg gave a wistful sigh.

She sounded so dreamy, Bree's head snapped around at her. Meg held the damp towel in her hand and absently wiped nonexistent specs of dust and dirt on the bar.

"You saw him?"

"Sure, when he came in." Her lids became heavy as she blinked long and slowly, that faraway look still on her face. "Mario practically hired him on the spot."

"Without talking to him?" Bewilderment trickled through her. That didn't sound like her father.

"He came highly recommended," Meg said.

"By whom?" Bree asked.

Before Meg could answer, the door to the office opened and the two men emerged. Meg sucked in a sharp breath of ecstasy.

Everything seemed to move into super slow motion as first her father exited and then…

God. Oh, God. It was her mystery man. Bree's knees went weak and she landed on the nearest bar stool. Her stomach dropped to her shoes. She had a prickling sensation at the back of her eyes, the back of her neck. First cold then heat swept over her as they made eye contact. Her mouth went desert dry.

Had her wishful thinking come true? Had she conjured the man without knowing? Or was it simply a coincidence?

The man had no reaction. If he did recognize her—and she was certain he did—he kept his face impassive.

"See? I told you he was a hottie." Meg said it low so only Bree could hear.

Mario had a big contented smile plastered on his face as he led the man through the bar directly toward them. It took all her strength not to squirm on the barstool because all she could do was think about that scorching gaze and the way his hands landed on her waist as he touched her, held her between his legs. The way the fine dark hair was sprinkled across his perfectly tan chest.

"Let me introduce you to my daughter. She's the general manager and you two will be working closely," her father was saying.

Dear God. How could he do this to her?

"Logan Blake, this is my beautiful single daughter, Bree." Mario waved to her, sounding and looking so proud, she wished a chasm would open beneath her feet and swallow her whole. Now was not the time for her father to gush about her.

"Dad, we've talked about this," she said.

She hated when he tried to fix her up because it always ended in disaster. The last security guy who worked for the bar ended up dead. Not because of her, but because he was a shifter with a bad attitude.

"She looks like her mother, God rest her soul. The spitting image of her really," Mario continued. Bree blushed to the roots of her hair.

"*Dad.* Stop it."

Bree was certain there was a bemused smirk on Logan's face. He extended his hand to her.

"Nice to meet you," he said.

She hesitated. She knew what that hand would feel like when she grasped it. She knew he would be hot to the touch. She felt his heat radiating over her, through her, into her. Yes, she wanted to touch him. She wanted to grasp that hand and hold on to him forever. But she knew that would be weird on so many levels since they'd only officially just met.

Her mystery man had a name—Logan Blake.

She swallowed the lump in her throat and reached for him, wrapping her fingers around his hand. Just as she imagined, warmth from his touch cascaded through her. His grip was tight, strong, sure. She matched it. He pumped her hand once, twice and then let go.

"Nice to meet you, too," she managed.

"Ah, there, see. I knew you two would hit it off." Her father beamed.

Bree glared at him but he ignored her. Logan, however, gave her a surreptitious once-over. His intense gaze peered at her as though he memorized her. A tingling in the pit of her stomach took up residence and refused to leave.

"Well, Bree, why don't you show our new security chief around?" her father suggested.

"Me, Dad?" She was horrified at the thought of being alone with him.

"I will if she won't," Meg piped up.

Bree shot her a look that said she'd keep her ass behind the bar. Logan cleared his throat.

Her dad replied, "Yes, you, Bree. You're the general manager, right? I have some things I need to do." He clapped Logan on the back. "Nice to have you on board, Logan. I know you'll make a fine addition to the team."

"Thank you, sir."

Sir? He was calling him sir? What a suck up this guy must be. Her father headed back to his office. Meg leaned her elbows on the bar, propped her chin on her fisted hands and gazed up at Logan as though he were a god.

And maybe he was since Bree couldn't get a read on him. He had no aura, either, which she thought strange. But he *did* have that ethereal, mystical scent she'd noticed before.

"It really *is* nice to have you on board," Meg said.

"Meg, don't you have work to do?" Bree snapped.

"It's done." She grinned.

"Maybe you could show me what's upstairs?" Logan suggested, never taking his eyes off Bree.

"Oh! I volunteer," Meg said with a dreamy look on her face.

"You can stay here," Bree said then turned to Logan. "It's nothing but the pool hall and private security office."

And her office, though she didn't add that. She didn't want to think about that yet. Being in the same room with him made her weak.

He glanced toward the stairs. "Will you show me?"

"Sure." But she didn't sound sure. She sounded like she was terrified to be alone with him.

And she was. She'd already seen him shirtless. She knew what was under that sexy white polo shirt he wore. She also wondered how his wound was healing and if she managed to really help him.

And where the hell had he been for three days? Hanging around in the city looking for a job? She didn't dare hope he was looking for her.

"This way." She motioned toward the stairs.

He followed.

She was bundle of nervous energy.

She could hear his light steps behind her on the glass stairs as they headed up. At the top, she paused and turned to her left.

"That's where the pool tables are. You'll find there are certain clientele that spend the entire evening there. They have weekly pool tournaments," she said.

He cocked his head to the side. "What kind of clientele?"

The question caught her off guard. Her first reaction was to tell him the wolf shifters but she bit off that response. He might think she'd lost her mind.

"Oh, you know. The ones who like to play pool." She gave him a nervous grin.

He nodded toward the closed door on the right at the end of the hall. "And that?"

"The security room. It's not much. Dad has a few cameras scattered around but there are still dead zones."

"Dead zones?" he asked.

"Yeah, the places in the bar where the cameras can't see."

She led him to the door. He followed so closely, she was aware of every breath he took. Her hand landed on the knob and she jiggled it but it was locked and she didn't have her keys.

"Oh, I forgot my keys."

"That's all right."

He pressed against her back, bracing one hand on the doorframe beside her head. Intense desire flared deep inside her, burning a hole in her gut. He dipped his head toward her and took a deep breath.

"You smell good," he said, his deep voice a quiet whisper.

"So do you." The words shook as she managed to expel them.

"Turn around."

She could do nothing but obey. When she turned, she pressed her back against the door and met his sultry gaze. Only a hairsbreadth separated them.

"How's your shoulder?" God, she sounded like a weak fool.

"Healing." He leaned closer and brushed his nose against hers.

Why was that the most erotic thing she'd ever experienced? Heat pooled between her legs. She shifted her weight from one foot to the other.

"How did you…find me?" His gaze was like a soft caress.

"I wasn't looking." He cocked a grin. "But I'm glad I did."

Oh, she was, too. She had done nothing but think about him

for days. She had played that morning over and over in her mind, trying to alter the past and change what had actually happened into something she *wanted* to happen. She wanted to slide her hands over his bare chest and press against him. She wanted to kiss him, taste him. The burning need had not gone away and only intensified now that he was so near.

But she hadn't done any of those things. Now was her chance, wasn't it?

With one hand still braced against the door, he lifted his free hand. She stopped breathing. Just held her breath as he reached for her. As his hand slipped across her neck and into the back of her hair at the nape. His fingers tightened in the length, tangling in the locks.

"Oh."

Was that her breathy voice? Bree didn't even recognize it.

"Soft."

"Yes," she agreed.

"Like I remembered."

She wanted to nod but bit her lip instead. The memory of him twining her hair around his finger burst through her mind with such force, she lost all muscle control. Her head fell back into the palm of his hand as a little mewl escaped her lips.

The intensity of his gaze flamed through her but she couldn't look away. She refused to look away. All she could think about was kissing him. Which was crazy because they had met only two minutes ago.

Technically, they had met three days ago. She hadn't bothered to give him her name. He didn't seem too eager to tell her his, either. That situation had been awkward yet intense.

Everything inside her jingled when he dipped his head closer to her exposed neck, lips parted and then…he placed a long slow kiss on her quivering pulse.

When his lips brushed her skin, her eyes fluttered closed as a strangled whimper shuddered through her. His tongue tasted her and his chest rumbled with delight against her and she thought she would come undone. The warm slick heat between her legs pounded with a painful throb that only he could ease. And she so wanted him to.

In her wildest dreams, she had never imagined he would find her. Nor had she imagined he would come to the bar and become the new security chief. She hadn't even imagined she'd be standing with him while he kissed her neck with hot searing kisses that made her head spin.

"You taste good." He whispered it against her, the heat of his breath blistering her damp skin. It made gooseflesh erupt from the top of her head to the bottom of her feet. Her nipples tightened and pressed against the material of her bra.

"You smell good. I've never smelled anything like you before," she said.

His hand tightened and he stiffened, and just like that, the spell was broken. He lifted his head, desire and want and need fading from his gaze and replaced with suspicion and question.

"What do you mean? *Anything* like me before?"

"I-I…" she faltered. What had she said? "I said anyone."

"No, you didn't. You said *anything*." He released her and took a step back taking all the bliss and rapture with him.

She forced a smile. "I did? I didn't mean to."

Hell, she had slipped and he'd noticed. She had no idea how she was going to get out of this one. She really hated the way he looked at her now.

"Maybe you should get your keys so you can show me the security room."

He moved away, out of reach. Even though he wasn't that far away, he might as well be standing at the North Pole for all the frigid air between them.

She nodded. "Right. I'll be right back."

She clutched her hands into fists as she headed for the stairs.

Logan watched her walk away and down the stairs.

The moment he saw her standing by the bar, his thoughts attuned to her and he could hear the shock rolling through her. She hadn't expected to see him. When he interviewed with Mario, he was able to prepare himself a little by taking in the details of the man's office. He had pictures of her scattered about. Her and a woman who must have been his wife. The man's office was tidy and perfect. It also had a distinctive smell of blood—but not real blood. Something synthetic. Something Logan couldn't put his finger on.

When he stepped out of the office and saw her standing there, he hadn't been surprised. He had been overcome with the need to take her into his arms and kiss her senseless. It took every shred of control he had to rein in his emotions and his desires and keep things casual.

As Mario introduced them, he managed to shut off that part of his mind that heard her. He erected a strong mental block to keep her out so he wouldn't pry on her innermost thoughts and feelings. It wasn't right since she didn't know anything about that. Only those who were the most intimate could willingly share their thoughts and feelings.

With Bree, it was an invasion of privacy.

When she said she'd never smelled anything like him before, it took him aback.

Perhaps he was reading way too much into it, but he was certain she meant any*thing* as in creature as opposed to anyone as in a person. What did she mean? Could she scent others as he could? Did she know there were supernaturals here?

It was something he would have to find out later when they weren't in a compromising situation.

He knew he shouldn't have kissed her neck. But when he pulled her head back and exposed the long column, he couldn't resist. He clenched his fists trying to calm his ragged nerves and keep his emotions in check. Now he had the taste of her in his mouth and the smell of her in his nose. Now he would never be able to keep his hands off her.

Now was not the time to get involved even if she had imprinted herself on him. With the threat of Archer looming, he had to concentrate on getting a game plan together and he didn't need Bree distracting him.

Even though she was a spectacular distraction.

Bree returned a few minutes later, color high in her cheeks and her breath puffing out as she took the stairs at a fast clip. She clutched a key ring. He moved aside so she could unlock the door and push it open. She flipped on the light as she crossed the threshold and entered.

In front of him, there were several large monitors that were powered off. He could only assume that was the display for the cameras around the place. There was an office on either side of the room, both with closed doors.

"That's your office there." She pointed to the left.

He nodded to the other one. "And that one?"

"Mine." She practically croaked.

Great. He wasn't sure if he could share office space with her.

"But don't worry. I'm not in there much," she added. "I spend most of my time downstairs overseeing things."

Too bad. He could have easily cornered her behind one of those closed doors—his or hers, it didn't matter.

Actually, it did matter. He wasn't going to do that. He wasn't going to take advantage of her like that. If—and a very large if— they got to the point where he could tell her the truth about how she bonded to him, then and only then would he give in to those desires.

The odds of them consummating was quite slim. The only reason he took this job was to lie low until he fully recovered from the poison and form a plan for going after Archer. He had no idea how he was going to defeat the man with the Drakana behind him but Logan would worry about that later.

Much later.

In the meantime, he had to figure out how to be a security chief for Bar Inferno.

"How do these turn on?" he asked, looking at the controls.

She reached for a remote on the desk in front of the monitors and punched a button. She handed it to him. "There's no sound. Only visual. But you can zoom in and out with that button there to get a closer look at whoever you want."

He peered down at the remote and tested the button she pointed out. Sure, enough the picture on the monitor zoomed into Meg at the bar talking to one of the servers. He saw what Bree meant about dark zones. The cameras didn't show Mario's office, which was located under and to the left of the stairs. Nor did they show who came and went into the bathrooms.

"I can't see Mario's office," he said.

"No," she agreed "And he wanted it that way."

"Why?"

She shrugged. "He's the owner. He dictates what he wants."

"It's not safe," he said. "His office should be monitored, too."

She cocked her head to the side. "Something you know that I should?"

He clenched his jaw. He'd said too much. Mario hired him because he'd been receiving anonymous death threats. Death threats his daughter knew nothing about. And he wanted it to stay that way.

"No," he said. "It's standard protocol."

"Oh." She nodded as though she agreed.

"We should get that taken care of and soon. I need to be able to see who's coming and going."

"All right. I'll call out the security company in the morning and have them install a new camera. But he won't like it," she said.

"He doesn't get a say."

She snorted. "You obviously don't know my father, Logan."

"If he wants me to be security chief, then he needs to trust my instincts."

His instincts never lied.

In fact, his instincts were telling him to kiss Bree again.

"Do you have good instincts?" She spoke in a tremulous whisper.

He turned to her and met her lovely green-eyed gaze. The bright flare of desire and need burned hot there. "Always."

Bree's pulse fluttered against in her throat. "What sort of instincts do you have about me?"

He tossed the remote on the desk. "Good ones."

"I thought about you. After you left." She dropped her gaze as though she were embarrassed to admit it.

His chest constricted. He thought about her, too, and nothing nice. Everything had to do with her naked and either on top or under him. He'd take her either way.

"I can't believe you're here," she said.

"I'm here."

"Tell me the truth. Is this a weird coincidence? How did you even hear about the job?"

"A friend of mine," he said. "So, yes, it's a weird coincidence."

He couldn't believe it himself when he saw her pictures in Mario's office and he knew she was the jogger who had helped him that morning. She was the woman who had inadvertently bonded herself to him. He was in her blood now. A permanent impression that would never diminish. He had become part of her as she had become part of him. She would never be able to get him out of her system even if she tried. Even if they fucked ten ways to Sunday.

"Who is this friend?" she asked.

"I doubt you know him."

She reached for his hand and brushed her fingers across his palm. She left a sizzling trail behind. But it wasn't her hand that was hot to the touch. It was his.

"Bree…"

"I can't stop myself from touching you. From *wanting* to touch you. It's like this burning need inside me."

He understood all too well. He had the same burning need.

"We can't do this," he said.

"We shouldn't do this." She nodded agreement as she lifted her gaze to his. "But I find I don't care so much about what we shouldn't do."

The beast within him flared to life, banging around in his head wanting release. Desperate for release. His heart did a quick punch against his chest, letting him know he was still very much alive. Bree took a step closer to him, the scent of strawberries and brown sugar lingering on her skin at the perfect pulse points he'd fantasized about licking and kissing and caressing.

She made it difficult to resist her. With her imploring eyes gazing up at him full of need and desire. The little breath escaping between her lips. The way her pulse throbbed in her neck.

Fuck all.

He wanted to rip her clothes from her athletic sexy body, shove her naked on the top of his desk and ravage her from head to toe. Right there. Right then.

He doubted she would complain. He sure wouldn't.

His hands were clenched so tightly, they ached. He flexed his fingers, listening to the joints crack as he forced the muscles to relax.

"Kiss me." She pressed into him, her lips parted and ready. To tempt him more, she ran her tongue over her bottom lip. "Kiss me, Logan, please."

Her body brushed his as she leaned in close. So close. She tilted her head back like she had when he'd gripped her hair in his fist and kissed her neck before. Except this time, she didn't want him to kiss her neck.

Logan gripped her upper arms to keep her from falling into him more. That and to keep him from doing something he shouldn't.

"Bree..."

"Don't you want to kiss me? I think you do. I see it in your eyes."

Oh, he wanted to kiss her all right. He wanted to do so much more than that. He was so hard, he had to take a moment to think unpleasant things to make it go away. Trying to think of unpleasant things wasn't exactly easy when Bree stood so close to him looking up at him like that.

It pained him to do it but he gave her a little push away. Then he stepped out of her personal space and backed toward his office door.

"It's not the right time for that," he said.

She stood rooted in place, her eyes wide and her face flushed. He didn't want to hurt her, but he didn't know any other way to get away from her.

"I'm sorry." She ran her hands over her face then and turned away. "I don't know what came over me. I shouldn't have done that. You're right. It's not the right time for that. It will never be the right time for that because we work together now and I'm the boss's daughter and that would be weird. Or something. Wouldn't it?" She glanced at him over her shoulder.

Her nerves must be on high alert for her to ramble so much. He only nodded agreement.

"Okay, well, good to know we're on the same page there." Bree spun toward the door. "I have to get downstairs. Doors open at four. We usually close around four in the morning. You okay with that long of a shift?"

"I'll be fine."

"Great." She pasted on her best smile. "Good luck then. Let me know if you need anything."

After she'd scurried out the door, he turned back to the monitors and focused on his new job.

$\diamond$ 4 $\diamond$

Bree strolled through the bar, the music pounding through her as she greeted patrons. Some regulars. Some tourists. At the bar, she leaned against it, watching the crowd filter in after work, ready to start the weekend with a beer, friends, and gourmet fare. She loved this place almost as much as she loved New York. She'd grown up here. She'd watched her father take it from the dive it had been to the class act it was now.

The regulars knew her and her father. They came for the food, the atmosphere and the fact that a cocktail at a staggering fourteen dollars a pop was considered reasonable.

But tonight, something seemed off. Bear, the bouncer at the front door, had let in an inordinate number of vampires. It was a strange mix with the wolf, bear, cat and other furry shifters that also frequented the place.

Sometimes she hated being able to see those creatures. When she was younger and realized her "gift" for seeing through glamour and scenting supernaturals, she tried to talk to her father about it. She wanted to know if she was somehow a freak. But her father had seemed indifferent, and in fact, had told her to ignore what was second nature to her. By the time she was a teen and seeing more and more of them in the city, she decided she was definitely a freak and didn't bother mentioning it to her father anymore. She thought there had to be something wrong with her.

By the time she reached adulthood, she came to terms with it and decided it was part of who she was and accepted her "gift" for what it was. It had come in handy on more than one occasion.

Except when trying to read Logan.

Or that hot regular patron, Rafe, at the end of the bar. He had no aura, either, like Logan. And his scent was similar. Otherworldly. Ancient. Ethereal. Like exotic soap.

She watched him nurse his beer and wave off the ladies, clearly uninterested. He seemed more engrossed in keeping a watchful eye on the surroundings of the bar than anything else. She often wondered about that—was he an undercover watchdog her father hired?

Bree was aware of the sudden male presence beside her without even looking. His scent gave him away, a scent that reminded her strangely of Logan. The difference between this guy and Logan though, was he radiated a kind of frigidity which was in direct opposite of Logan's fiery emission.

"Hey, sexy."

Annoyance flickered through her as she turned to look at him, taking him in. He stood over six feet tall, dark hair, darker eyes with a striking look about him that might have given her pause if she was interested in his type.

She found it curious this man, like Logan, like Rafe, also had no aura.

What *were* these guys? And why couldn't she figure it out?

"Not interested. Move along," she said.

The smile on his face faded. His hand wrapped around his drink as he all but slithered down the length of the bar. She shook her head.

"Another one bites the dust." Meg chuckled.

Bree turned toward the bar and perched on the edge of the stool. "He's not my type."

"I don't think smarmy is anyone's type." Meg poured her a whiskey, two fingers, neat, and slid it to her. That's what she liked about Meg. The bartender knew what she wanted without ever having to ask.

Bree grinned as she took a sip. "Looks like a busy night. You ready?"

"It's all hands on deck." Meg wiped down the bar with a rag and then tossed it under.

"Good. I know Mario worries about having enough staff on our busy nights." Bree refrained from calling him Dad to the employees, even though everyone knew she was the boss's daughter. She clutched her drink and scanned the crowd.

On the other side of the room, Logan descended the stairs. Her breath caught and her hand tightened on her glass as she watched him navigate the steps with a fluid swaggering grace. His broad chest strained against the material of his shirt. She couldn't stop the memory of his naked chest from going through her mind. The sleeves were rolled to his elbows which did nothing but accentuate the round strength of his biceps and make her even more hot and bothered.

"God, he is so hot." Meg gave a wistful sigh.

"Is he? I hadn't noticed." Bree turned away, pretending he didn't exist.

Meg snorted. "As if. You practically drooled all over him when Mario introduced you."

"I most certainly did *not* drool over him." Never mind her knees weakened at the very sight of him. And her heart did a funny thing in her chest. And there was a quickening of her pulse and a flood of heated desire between her legs.

What the *hell* was wrong with her? She had never had such a strong reaction to a man before, even when she had raging hormones as a teenager. But then, didn't women come into their prime much later in life? Perhaps she was experiencing an early mid-life crisis? Either that or she had lost her mind.

"You did. And you can't tell me you don't want him."

Bree could sense him nearby and knew he walked through the crowd. It helped she could see his sexy form in the mirrors behind the bar.

"I think he's hot for you," Meg said.

"Don't be ridiculous." There was no way a man as sexy, hot, virile as Logan would want her. She was too plain, too boring, not to mention that freakish part of her. How would he feel about that?

He wouldn't care since her instinct told her he wasn't human.

"I saw the way he looked at you earlier today. He's super hot for you."

Bree didn't want to admit Meg could be right. He *had* cornered her against the door of the security office, fisted her hair in his hand and kissed her neck. She expelled a wistful sigh.

"Aha!" Meg exclaimed.

It jolted her out of her reverie and she scowled. "Aha nothing."

"What happened?"

"What do you mean?"

"Between you two. What happened when you went upstairs?" She waggled her eyebrows.

"Please, Meg. Nothing happened. He's not into me. I'm not his type."

"Oh, he is *so* into you. Like I can tell because even though he's wandering through the tables, he positioned himself so he can see you no matter where he is in the room," Meg said.

Bree sat up a little straighter, her heart twisting in her chest. She dared not hope. She couldn't stop from looking at his reflection once again in the mirrored bar. When she discovered Meg was right, she wanted to melt into a puddle of goo. Her heart kicked into overdrive.

Meg dropped to her elbows and leaned close. "Tell me *all* the sordid details. Did you do it in the security room?"

"What? No!"

"Cuz I would. That would be so hot." She came up ramrod straight, her eyes round and wide as she blinked. "Hi, Logan."

Oh, God. He was right behind her.

"Meg."

His deep dark voice rumbled over her and she resisted everything inside her telling her to close her eyes and lean back into him.

A cocktail waitress at the other end of the bar flagged down Meg. She didn't bother to hide the disappointment flashing across her face.

"I gotta go. Duty calls."

Bree's breathing increased exponentially along with the patter of her heart. She forced herself to inhale, exhale with some normalcy but it didn't work since Logan was so near. The roar of the music faded to the background and it was as if only the two of them were in the room, alone.

"Bree." Her name on his tongue was like honey dripping off a honeycomb. "Drinking on the job?"

"It's allowed." Sarcasm laced her words.

"Is it?"

"Sure. I have an in with the owner."

A deep rumble of a chuckle reverberated through his chest to her.

Her gaze flickered back up to the mirrors and she could see his hulking form standing behind her. He wasn't looking down at her—he was looking at her in the mirror, too. Warm tingles erupted over her skin as she watched with owlish eyes as he lifted his hand and placed it on her shoulder.

His warmth pierced her clothes, her skin, and punched right to the heart of her. Pouring into her, spreading through her and touching parts she never knew existed until now. How did he manage that?

If a mere hand on the shoulder elicited that sort of response, what would it be like to kiss him? Or actually have sex with him?

She couldn't even imagine being naked with the guy, yet the image of his bare chest popped into her head again. Bree couldn't stop the whimper that escaped.

Logan snatched his hand back and took a step back. She spun around to face him to keep him from fleeing.

"Don't go."

"I have to. I can't be this close to you and not…touch you."

Oh. "I thought you were mad at me."

A thoughtful look crossed his face. "I wasn't mad."

"Then what were you?" she remarked, pleased at her

nonchalant tone.

His jaw tightened as she looked her over. "What did you mean?"

"Mean?" She swallowed a dry lump in her throat, playing dumb.

She knew what he was referring to—that he didn't smell like *anything* she knew. And he didn't. Which reminded her of Rafe and that dude who just hit on her. She glanced down the length of the bar and spotted him brooding over his drink. A sudden worry gnawed at her.

"What is it?" he asked, as though he could read her.

"Oh…nothing." She waved away the thought, determined not to let some creep bother her. "Sometimes guys like to hit on me."

Logan squared his shoulders, his chest puffed up and it seemed he filled up the entire space in and around them. "What guys?"

"Logan, it's no big deal. It happens a lot."

He looked back at her, his gaze narrowed. "*What guys?*"

"Um." She glanced back down the bar at the poor unsuspecting guy nursing his drink. "That one."

Before she could stop him, Logan stomped away and halted next to Rafe. Oh, crap. He thought she meant him when she meant the other creepy guy. They exchanged animated conversation she couldn't hear.

As they did so, creepy guy turned his head, looking at her and gave her the oiliest smile she had ever seen. He downed his drink, rose and headed her direction. Her heart jumped into her throat as she slid off the bar stool preparing to flee. She wanted to run but where would she go?

"You didn't give me a chance." He leaned closer than she liked. His alcohol-laced breath wafted over her.

"That's because I didn't *want* to give you a chance."

The guy managed to hem her in, making it impossible for her to escape. She realized too late that was his plan all along and now she was stuck. He reached for a tendril of her hair but she batted his hand away. A similar thing Logan had done but she had welcomed him touching her, being close to her. Not this guy.

"I told you I'm not interested," she said. "I thought that was clear."

"It was clear. But I don't give a damn. Besides, I was here first. Not that guy."

He nodded toward Logan as he slipped his hand around her waist. She grasped his wrist, too late, and tried to push him off but he was much stronger. It was clear he wasn't going to take no for an answer. She was about to land a punch when he flew backward and a hand clamped around his throat.

Logan's sudden appearance startled her. "The lady said she wasn't interested." He gave the guy a shove. "Get lost."

Behind the guy, Rafe loomed large and intimidating. The man shot her a glare then Logan. And then he saw Rafe. His face paled as Rafe bared his teeth in a feral grin and collared him. He never took his eyes off the guy when he asked, "You okay, Bree?"

"I'm fine." She blew out a heated breath.

"I'll be taking this one out." Rafe gave Logan a nod and they did some silent communication as he dragged the guy toward the door.

"Thanks." Being in this business taught her how to handle herself, but there were those guys who wouldn't leave her alone. "He was persistent."

"You should take the night off," he said.

"Why?"

"Because I'm here now and I got this." He scanned the crowd taking in everything and everyone scoping out the place.

"I'm the general manager, Logan. It's my job to be here every night."

A vein pulsed in the side of his neck and she could tell she'd gotten to him. He met her level gaze and need curled low and hot in her gut making her senses tingle in anticipation of something she knew she would never have.

"Then I guess I'll have to keep a close eye on you, won't I?"

A deep yearning seared through her, leaving an empty lost feeling with her as he turned and walked away.

❦ 5 ❧

Logan positioned himself in the bar so he could keep an eye on the entrance as well as Bree who continued to sit at the bar. Meg returned and the two ladies chatted. He was all too aware of the flickering glances she gave him as they talked. One thing he knew about women—they liked to gossip.

He shouldn't have touched her. He should have kept his hands to himself but controlling his reactions to her when she was so near was difficult. All he wanted to do was run his hands along her soft curves and kiss her in places to make her beg for more. He wanted her pliant and willing.

It took a lot of self-control to walk away from her but he had done it. He'd been exercising a lot of self-control where Bree was concerned. He hoped it was a sign he was getting stronger in his resolve to keep his hands off her but he doubted it. Even from across the room, he still wanted her. It didn't help she was permanently etched onto his soul.

Rafe returned, scanned the crowd for him and gave him a nod. He made his way over. Despite their short association, they had become fast allies.

"She's not safe here." Rafe took a position next to him, his gaze flickering to Bree.

"She won't leave," Logan replied.

"He'll be back with more, you know." Rafe's tone was conversational, as though they discussed the latest sports recap of their favorite hockey team. "He was Drakana."

"You can't know for sure."

"I do know for sure. I saw the tattoo on the inside of his left wrist."

The starburst of the Drakana was unmistakable. If Rafe said he saw it, then Logan was in a lot more trouble than he thought. The Drakana were hunters—specifically dragon-hunters who went after their own kind. Hired henchmen. Once they were enlisted to hunt and track down a target, they wouldn't stop until that target was caught or eliminated, depending on their orders. Like it was some sort of sick field sport. Logan suspected he was to be caught and kept alive because that's what Archer would want. He'd want the final kill for himself to make sure Logan's bloodline was eradicated.

"The girl has been marked by you. They'll hunt her, too."

His muscles tensed. "How did you know that?"

"You've recently gone through *ka daeko*, right?" Rafe asked.

Logan nodded with a twinge of embarrassment. Rafe was one of his own—of course, he'd know Logan had entered the *ka kladou* phase because of the overwhelming pheromones he emitted when he was so close to Bree.

"I knew that first day. Her scent was—is—all over you. You touched her and she bonded to you."

"*She* touched me." He didn't know why he felt the need to make the correction.

"Doesn't matter who does what. Only that it happened."

"I thought humans couldn't bond to us."

"If you've entered *ka kladou,* any female can bond to you if there is sufficient desire," Rafe said.

A little piece of information Logan never knew. Now that Bree was part of him as much as he was part of her, he should get over it. He glanced at her still seated at the bar talking to the bartender and a few patrons who she seemed to know. The beast inside him rattled around in his head to get her, fling her over his shoulder and take her away from this deafening bar.

"There's no way to reverse it?"

"No," Rafe said, his tone final.

Good to know. He filed it away under "things to take care of later." Bree being one of those things. At least now he could stop fighting it so hard. The only question remaining now was would Bree want him the way he wanted her? She must have sensed him looking at her because she turned her head and met his gaze. Color stained high in her cheeks as she quickly glanced away. To get his mind off her and what they were destined for, he steered the conversation back on track.

"I didn't expect the Drakana to show up here."

"They can scent you as you can scent them. They knew you were here before you knew they were here."

"What I mean is I thought I'd be the one to go to him. I'd be the one to confront him on my own terms. I didn't expect him to send a henchman after me."

"Things never work out the way we think they will." Rafe cracked his knuckles one by one and Logan watched the silvery scars on the back of his hands glisten in the half-light. He idly wondered where he'd gotten those marks. "They won't stop hunting you or her."

"I know."

"What are you going to do?"

"I don't know."

He couldn't leave yet. He hadn't healed. His powers hadn't regenerated. More importantly, he couldn't leave Bree alone. She was an easy target. If they managed to get her, they'd use her to get to him and he would have no choice but to go after them—and her. His carefully plotted plan of vengeance was now all fucked up and he had to figure out something else.

"You better come up with a plan. Before something happens to her…or you," Rafe said, echoing his thoughts.

He turned to look at Logan, his golden eyes nearly translucent in the shadowy bar. Logan could see his restless dragon side flickering in the depths.

"Careful. Your dragon is showing."

Though Logan meant to sound light-hearted he was actually quite serious. The last thing he needed was an angry dragon on his hands. He knew why Rafe was angry—because Logan wasn't ready to go to battle and his life had been threatened. If the Drakana knew about Bree, they likely knew about Rafe which put him in danger, too. Rafe took a deep breath and expelled it to get his dragon side under control.

"Sorry. Coming into contact with Drakana stirs the beast within. Makes me want to fight."

He understood. He wanted to fight, too. It was the only way he was going to get rid of his pent-up energy boiling inside him. He knew Rafe was on his side even though the man hadn't been there when all the shit went down—Rafe had been in the human realm living in exile.

Logan left the Hidden Lands to save his own skin but it was more than merely saving his skin. When his parents had been brutally murdered by a fellow clan leader, he knew the only way to get his vengeance was to get someplace safe while he healed and waited for his powers to regenerate.

And then he'd found Bree.

Logan looked back at the crowd. Not an empty seat at the bar. Not an empty table. And too many vampires for his comfort level. He had accepted the job because Rafe said it would be a good place to lie low—dragons didn't come here.

But they did now. They'd tracked him down.

He suspected Mario lied to him when he told him he was receiving anonymous death threats but he hadn't pressed the issue.

"What's the sitch with Mario?" Logan wanted to know.

"He needed a security guy. He got one."

"He told me he was receiving anonymous death threats but I think he's lying. I think he knows who they're coming from." Logan scanned the crowd as he spoke. "I think it has to do with a vampire."

"Because there are a lot here tonight?" Rafe asked and he nodded. "There does seem to be more than usual. And a few that look like they belong to *Signori Della Notte*." Logan gave him a questioning glance and Rafe leaned closer and dropped his voice so he could be heard. "They're one of the most powerful mafias in the underworld."

A cold tingling sensation crept along Logan's spine. He didn't like the sound of that at all.

Rafe clapped him on the back. "I'm going to do a perimeter check. I'll catch you later."

He melted into the crowd and disappeared from sight.

A commotion near the back caught his attention. Mario and another man were having an animated discussion. Logan drew in a long breath and scented the vampire dressed in impeccable Hugo Boss. He headed over to intervene but before he could get to them, the two of them ducked into Mario's office and shut the door. When Logan got there, he tried the knob but Mario had locked it.

Why would his boss lock his office while fraternizing with a vampire? What could they possibly be talking about? He focused on the muted voices on the other side of the thick door, trying to make out what they said. It was hard to filter out their words over the booming music and the crowd noise but he managed to make out a couple of words—synthetic blood.

It was enough to make Logan think his new boss was in some kind of trouble. He used his shoulder and slammed into the door, breaking the lock and shoving it open. It hit the opposite wall with bang. Mario stood in the center of the room with a bag of blood in one hand and a fist full of bills in the other. Behind him was an open refrigerator. The vampire bared his pointed teeth at his untimely intrusion.

"What's going on here?" Logan demanded.

"This business is not yours, dragon," the vampire said, his voice a raspy hiss.

"It is if my boss is involved." He pinpointed Mario with his gaze.

Mario shoved the blood toward the vampire. "We will finish this discussion later."

He took the blood and strolled past, eyeing Logan as he did. As soon as he was gone, he turned back to Mario whose expression was one of displeasure and annoyance. He grabbed him by the upper arm and turned him back to the door. "This doesn't concern you."

"It does concern me if it's happening in this bar." Logan's voice was a deep growl. "You hired me because—"

"I know why I hired you." Mario shoved him out of the office, swinging the door closed behind him.

But Logan stuck his booted foot between the jamb and the door. "Are you selling synthetic blood to the vamps?"

Mario closed the refrigerator and turned to him, looking less than happy he was there. "It's none of your business."

Logan ignored his brush off. "Why are you doing business with a vampire, Mario?"

He huffed out a breath and raked a hand through his hair. "I can't tell you."

"You mean you won't tell me."

"*No.* I mean I can't." Worry lines creased Mario's forehead. Logan knew there was something eating at him.

"I can't help you if you won't tell me the truth," he said.

Mario sank to the edge of his desk, a thoughtful look on his face. "You're not going to leave until I do, are you?"

"No."

"All right. But you have to swear not to tell Bree any of this."

"Does this have to do with the death threats?"

The look of guilt flashing across his face gave Logan his answer, even though he didn't voice it.

"There's a blood shortage for vamps in the city. I signed an agreement with the *Signori Della Notte* to help distribute the synthetic blood to them and they agreed to pay me ten percent of the profits."

Logan stared at him in mute horror. Did he realize what he was doing? Getting into business with a mafia—any mafia but especially a vampire one—could be deadly. If anything at all went wrong, they'd kill him in a second. Knowing that also explained a lot about the constant flow of vampire traffic in the bar.

"Mario…why?"

"Because it's what I have to do."

It didn't make sense. There had to be more to the story Mario wasn't willing to share. Some reason why he would go into business with the *Signori Della Notte*.

"That doesn't satisfy you?" Before he could answer, Mario continued. "It's going to have to be enough because it's all I'm telling you." He picked up his pen and started scratching a note as if Logan wasn't there.

There were too many questions going through his mind and he hadn't a clue where to start finding answers. How was he getting the blood? Obviously, the *Signori Della Notte* supplied it, but how was it being delivered to the bar?

Getting a camera in Mario's office moved to the top of the priority list. He'd promised not to tell Bree but things had turned deadly and he needed to enlist her help. If he told her Mario was in danger, he was certain she would do whatever it took to keep him safe.

"I'll leave it for now, Mario," Logan said, his words slow and deliberate. "But we'll talk about this later."

Mario looked up at him. "I don't think so."

Logan knew he'd been dismissed. If Mario wouldn't tell him what was going on, he'd have to find out on his own. The only way he knew to do that was to install a security camera in his office and to make sure there were no dark zones outside his office. Since he was here and working, he had to take the job seriously and he'd do the right thing—whether or not Mario wanted a security camera pointed his direction.

It had been a long night. All Bree wanted to do was go home and take off her shoes, strip off her work clothes, and sink into her soft bed and feather pillow. Her feet hurt. Her head throbbed. Avoiding Logan and pretending he didn't exist had been exhausting both mentally and physically. Every time he was near, her body reacted to him in a way she couldn't control.

With all that, the blaring music and the annoying patrons were getting on her nerves. There had been a bachelorette party that had become high maintenance and it was all the staff could do to keep them in food and drinks. It wasn't often she wanted to run from work. Tonight was definitely one of those nights.

She told herself it had nothing to do with Logan or the way he prowled the room keeping her in constant view. Or the way she could feel him looking at her when her back was turned. Or the way she could sense him when he would breeze by her, not bothering to stop and talk.

She had to snap out of it. Acting like a love-sick teenager was no way to behave. She was a grown woman after all.

Closing time was four in the morning and it couldn't get here fast enough. She constantly checked her watch as more and more people drifted out of the bar and into the late-night streets. When the bachelorette party went on to another place to sow their wild oats she was grateful. They didn't bother to tip her wait staff and that was annoying.

The blaring music turned down until it was nothing but white noise in the background. A sure sign closing time was upon them. She was relieved.

A group of four vamps stayed firmly parked in one corner of the bar near the front windows. She found it interesting one had a drink in front of him when she knew for a fact he didn't need it. Bree scanned the room looking for Logan and found him standing under the stairs near her father's office, his arms folded over his chest as he kept his watchful gaze on them.

And her.

Good. At least he was aware of them. It was hard not to be since they were the last few patrons remaining.

She sighed and leaned on the bar as Meg dried a glass. She was going to have to shoo them away. Much as she hated to get rid of paying customers—though what they were buying was a mystery to her—she was exhausted and wanted to get home so she could process everything that had happened that day.

"Looks like they're not leaving anytime soon," Meg said.

"Yeah. I guess I'm going to have to give them a little push toward the door. You can go, Meg. I'll close down tonight."

"You just want to be alone with the hot new security guy," Meg teased.

Bree couldn't help it. She blushed. That might have been part of her diabolical—albeit unconscious—plan. She hadn't considered it until Meg pointed out that she and Logan would be alone. Well, except for her father still holed up in his office.

"I do not." She tried her best to sound offended.

"See you tomorrow," Meg said. "Don't stay up too long."

Bree stuck her tongue out at her as she sauntered away and made her evening exit.

She headed to the vamps, pasting on her best customer service smile and hoped they'd get the hint. "Gentlemen, we'll be closing in about ten minutes."

One of them lifted his glittering dark gaze. "We want to speak with the owner."

She was instantly on guard. She hadn't seen her father all night, though she suspected he was still hiding out in his office, which he did most nights he was at the bar. She hadn't seen him since he'd introduced her to Logan.

"I'm afraid he's indisposed. I'm the general manager, Bree. Can I help?"

The man unfolded from the table to his full height. He topped her by at least six inches and was rather imposing for such a slender man. She couldn't help but notice he was dressed in an impeccable suit—most likely designer.

"You can't. I need to speak with him. Alone."

"I'm afraid my father isn't here at the moment," she said, still pasting on that bright fake smile.

"Your father?" A brief smile played at the corner of his mouth as he looked at his companions. "I did not realize Mario had such a lovely daughter."

Something about that statement made all the hairs on the back of her neck stand at attention. She felt like she'd made a grave error in telling him she was related to Mario. Her mouth went bone dry as she went on high alert, her muscles tensing.

"I will remember that. Thank you for the information," he added.

"What is it you want?" Her patience was wearing thin. All she wanted now was to get away from the guy. She should have known better than to engage a vamp.

"Mario has been here all night. He's in his office. Tell him I wish to speak with him on a rather important matter," he said.

"And you are?" She didn't hide the snooty tone in her voice.

"Niko. He will know me."

There was something chilling about the way he looked at her when he said it. A shudder passed through her, turning her blood frosty.

Before she could step away, a heated presence cascaded over her and she knew Logan was behind her. She exhaled a silent sigh of relief. She didn't want these guys to know they made her nervous.

"Is there a problem here?" Logan asked.

"We meet again, dragon." Niko flashed a smile at Logan.

Dragon? She sucked in a quiet breath and blinked, looking up at Logan's stony expression, his glare so razor sharp, it could cut the vamp to ribbons.

Did that explain what he was? Was he a…dragon-shifter? She had never encountered one before. She'd heard of them, sure, but she had never met one in person. Her heart skipped a silly beat. Dragon-shifters were some of the most badass shifters around. All the furry ones tended to keep their distance.

Bree looked him over with a new appreciation for what he was, if it were true.

"What do you want with Mario?" he asked.

He must have heard their conversation. How long had he been

standing there and she didn't know?

"There are things I need to discuss with him."

"I believe the lady told you he's indisposed. And we're closing." He motioned toward the door as if that would usher them out.

No such luck. Niko waved away the idea, never taking his gaze off Logan. "As if that matters to me. We have unfinished business, Mario and I, and I intend to finish it. Right now."

"I intend to make sure you leave. Right now."

Niko chuckled. The other three got to their feet, forming an imposing force behind the vamp leader. Logan moved to stand in front of her, putting him between her and the vamps. How was this going to play out? She didn't see anything good coming of the situation.

Bree, get Bear.

Her gaze swung to Logan but he never took his gaze off the vamps. He hadn't moved a muscle but she distinctly heard his voice in her head.

"Logan?" Her timid void quivered.

Go now, Bree. Get him and then get to safety.

She moved to stand next to him, glancing up at him. He cut her a look and then gave a jerk of his head toward the door where she knew Bear stood guard.

So, she wasn't insane. She *had* heard his voice in her head. How was that even possible?

She hesitated only a second before she took a step backward and then headed for the door. As soon as she did, all hell broke loose.

Niko threw a punch at Logan who stopped his fist with his hand and then landed his own punch in the guy's gut. Niko doubled over, coughing as the wind was knocked out of him. The other three sprang into action but it was nothing Logan couldn't handle. He moved so blindingly fast, she couldn't make out his form.

Bear ran by her to join the fray. She knew he was a bear shifter—she'd given him the nickname since she'd seen him transform once when she was much younger. He collared two of the vamps with ease and held them still while Logan landed a final punch on the third vamp. He stumbled backward into the table, knocking over glasses. Niko peeled his lanky body off the floor and got back to his feet.

"You want more punishment?" Logan clenched and bloody fists were raised, ready to do damage.

Niko wiped spit and blood off his chin with the back of his hand. His gaze narrowed to slits. "Sylas, show the dragon what we are capable of."

Sylas regained his footing, his face creased with rage. He lifted one hand and turned toward Bear making a pushing motion. Bear released the two vamps he'd been holding and flew backward as if something crashed into him. He collided into several tables and chairs, splintering them. Glasses shattered on the floor. Bear's big body skidded to a halt near the wall under the windows. He was out cold.

She froze, unsure what to do. She pulled her cell phone out of her pocket, intending to call the police but stopped. If she did call the police, would they actually believe they'd been attacked by four vampires? Doubtful. They'd want to lock her up in the loony bin. She pocketed the phone, still unsure what to do.

Sylas turned toward Logan. Before the vampire could act, he lunged and knocked the guy off his feet. They crashed to the floor, fists flying and then Sylas jumped up while Logan remained face down on the floor, unmoving.

Oh, God. Logan. She couldn't see what happened to him. She wanted to go to him to make sure he was all right but there were vamps standing between her and him. And then the worst happened. With all the noise, Mario's office door opened for the first time all evening and he appeared in the doorway gaining all four vamps' attention. She had to warn him.

"Dad, don't—"

She took a step but that was as far as she got when her feet refused to move. Her voice froze in her throat and she couldn't call out even if she wanted to. Sylas focused solely on her, a look of complete and utter concentration on his face.

"Keep her there," Niko said.

He snapped his fingers and the two henchmen followed. Mario looked like a statue framed in the doorway of his office, the fluorescent lighting at his back blotting out his face. From his place on the floor, Logan emitted a groan.

Her heart skittered as she watched Niko and her father, unable to hear what they were saying. She couldn't even see her father's face, so she couldn't get a read on what was happening.

Niko gave Mario a push backward and he stepped into the light of the office. Fear etched the features of his face. He held up his hands as if in surrender and shook his head as he spoke.

She willed Logan to get to his feet.

Niko wrapped a hand around Mario's throat. He shook his head, his eyes wide and round. One of the vamp henchmen moved behind Mario and wrapped his arms around his upper body, holding him in place. The second one grabbed a fistful of hair and jerked his head back, exposing his neck.

Bree wanted to shout, to scream but couldn't. She could think the words, but she couldn't force them out her throat. Sylas remained between her and Logan, his arm outstretched and his hand palm up. She didn't understand but she knew he was somehow responsible for holding her in place.

She glanced at Logan again. *Please get up, Logan. If you can hear me. Please.*

Mario shouted and then Bree saw the flash of Niko's fangs seconds before he sank them into his neck. Her father's eyes widened as a scream of shear agony ripped from his throat. Bree whimpered, watching the horror play out before her eyes and unable to do anything about it.

Sylas licked his lips as he watched Niko and a smile played at the corners of his mouth.

Her addled brain tried to comprehend what was happening but she didn't want to believe it. She didn't want to believe there was true evil in the world that could do such things.

Logan groaned and shoved to his feet and stumbled into Sylas, breaking his hold on her. She was able to move again. Sylas tumbled into a nearby table.

"Logan, my father! You have to help him."

As he focused on her, she could see beads of perspiration on his skin and a moment of indecision as he glanced from her to Sylas as he regained his footing. She was less concerned about herself. All she wanted was her father to be okay. Logan staggered toward the vampires and Mario, leaving her faced with Sylas.

She could take care of herself—she'd had enough self-defense training in her life. She focused on him and allowed the fear to come in. Behind him, she spotted a broken table leg and knew she needed to get that and use it as a weapon. He saw her glance behind him and anticipated her next move when she lunged toward it.

Sylas put his head down and blocked her as though he was a linebacker and she was the quarterback. She barreled through him but she was no match for his fast vampire reflexes. He latched on to her and bared his fangs.

No. She was not going to let him bite her. Her survival instincts kicked in and she stomped on his foot hard enough for him to cry out and loosen his grip on her. She shoved out of his grasp and dove again for the broken table leg. As soon as her hand wrapped around it, he landed on top of her, crushing her against the floor with this weight.

She cried out when his hand wrapped around hers and he dug his long fingernails into her skin. She still gripped the wooden shard, refusing to let go. Bree jabbed her elbow into Sylas's side making him grunt.

He wrapped a hand around her hair and jerked her head to the side, giving him access to her neck. She squirmed doing everything she could to get out from under him, to make things difficult and uncomfortable for him but nothing seemed to thwart him.

She felt the sharp pierce of his fangs as he latched on to her neck but only for a brief second. The next thing she knew his weight was gone. She rolled over, clutching the wooden leg in time to see him fly backward and land against the bar.

Logan loomed over her, his shirt streaked with blood and his face a mask of rage. She should have been terrified of him but she didn't have time to process her emotions when she leapt to her feet and charged Sylas, weapon in hand. But Logan put a hand on her shoulder and gave her a look she couldn't read.

Mario.

A gasp ripped from her when she turned and saw him on the floor, his face and neck and upper torso covered in blood. She dropped the weapon and ran to him, falling to her knees. Tears clouded her eyes. The metallic twang of blood was so strong, she had to force back a gag. Her heart pumped in her throat as her stomach clenched around the icy ball of fright.

His eyes were half-open. She took his hand, held it as she brushed hair from his forehead.

"Dad."

It was clear he couldn't talk as blood continued to spurt from his neck. He blinked once. Twice. Gave her a small smile. It was the last thing he did before he closed his eyes and died.

❧ 6 ☙

The guttural scream Bree emitted was one of absolute anguish. Logan had never heard anything so chilling, so awful in his life. After shoving the wood shard through Sylas, he turned back to Bree who hovered on the floor next to her father's dead body clutching his hand, hoping there might still be a way he would survive.

He wouldn't. He couldn't. The man's throat had been ripped away.

Guilt slashed though him. He had one job—to protect Mario—and he'd failed. His cursed body wasn't strong enough to withstand the beating he took from the vampires. By the time he'd managed to regain his footing and get to Niko, it was too late. He'd grabbed the vamp and jerked him away but it did horrible irreparable damage to Mario.

We are not through yet, dragon.

Then Niko flashed his bloodied fangs before he and his two henchmen used their super speed to get away. Sylas had been so busy with Bree, he hadn't seen them leave. When he saw Sylas on top of Bree, it nearly sent him over the edge. His dragon clawed in his head, determined to get out and fight. He tamped down the urge but put all the rage to good use to rip the guy off her and then use her makeshift weapon to kill him.

Now Logan made his way to her crumpled body as she sobbed into her hands. Pain pierced him when he saw her. He had no one to blame but himself for Mario's death.

He crouched next to her, put a hand on her back. "Bree. Come away."

Without looking at her dead father, she spun into him. Her hands gripped his shirtfront, leaving behind smears of blood as she buried her face in his chest. Since they were so connected, her pain and grief poured into him. It took all he had to erect a wall between them and keep her out of his head. But not without feeling her angst first.

It was a mistake to mindspeak to her but he had to get her out of harm's way. Even though it hadn't worked. What had surprised him, though, was when she mindspoke back to him. She likely didn't know what she was doing, but he could hear her loud and clear. It confirmed what he suspected—Bree was special.

Bree could see the supernaturals as he could. She'd wonder why the vampire called him dragon. She'd have questions. Questions he wasn't prepared to answer. Questions he had to answer to make her understand what he was, why and how they were connected. He had to get her out of here and figure out what to do next. He needed Rafe—but he'd gone home hours ago after his perimeter check, thinking everything was clear.

Logan scooped her into his arms and got to his feet in one fluid motion. She whimpered but it seemed as though the tears had subsided. Her grip on his shirt, however, had not relaxed. He couldn't stay here with her but the only place he could think to take her was where he was staying—Rafe's place.

He glanced down. She was a mess and so was he. They both had blood all over them. Him more so than she did. When he jerked Niko away from Mario, blood had splattered everywhere.

Fuck all.

A groan from the other side of the room caught his attention. He'd forgotten about Bear. The hulking figure got to his feet, his hand on his head as he shook it and focused on the scene around him. Logan charged toward him, still clutching Bree against his chest.

Bear was the only one that could help in this situation—he was a shifter, too. He would understand the severity of what had happened to Mario. He'd be smart enough not to alert the authorities.

"Bear, I need your help."

"What happened here, man?"

"Vampires attacked Mario. Killed him." He jerked his head toward the dead man.

Bear's gaze flickered briefly to him and then back again. His dark skin paled as he turned from the gruesome sight. He swallowed hard, his throat working.

Logan could read the unspoken question in his eyes. "I couldn't get to him in time."

The memory of warm blood splattering on him surged to the forefront of his mind and he swallowed the lump of bile that rose.

"What happened to Bree?" he asked, looking at her cradled in his arms.

"She's fine but in shock. I have to get her out of here."

He nodded. "Go. I got this."

Grateful for the man's help, Logan turned to go as Bree emitted another whimper.

"Hey, dragon. It's not your fault. I'm sure you did what you could," Bear said, trying to make him feel better even though he had no idea what had happened since he'd been out for most of it.

"Oh, yeah? Sure feels like my fault."

Logan stepped into the predawn hours. Even at this time of day, the city was still alive with late night revelers. He shifted her weight in his arms and took off down the sidewalk heading for the building. It would be faster if he walked instead of finding a cab. He didn't want to have to explain their odd situation anyway. Luckily, the building was only a few blocks from the bar and he made it without garnering attention.

The doorman would be another matter altogether. He hadn't decided how he was going to get past the man without him asking a lot of questions or giving him a lot of wary glances. Carrying her against his bloodied shirt looked bad. The last thing he needed was the doorman to contact the police. He waited on the corner in the shadows and peered at the building contemplating his next move.

It occurred to him there was a parking garage for the building. It would be the best way to get in unnoticed by the doorman. He scanned the area, found the entrance and headed to it.

A quick glance down at Bree showed she had passed out. He headed down the ramp to the elevators and juggled her enough to punch the UP button. He was thankful he didn't run into anyone in the elevator or even when he stepped out onto the twenty-third floor.

At the apartment door, indecision flashed through him. The keys were in his pocket, unreachable. He sighed, repositioned Bree by putting her down and then picking her up over his shoulder so he could fumble in his pocket for the key. When he had the door unlocked, he gave it a violent shove. It bounced against the wall. He kicked it closed with a slam then headed to the master bedroom where he lowered her to the bed. She rolled to her side and curled into a ball. His muscles ached from carrying her but it had been worth it. She needed him and he needed her.

Blood caked her hands, under her fingernails. He'd help her wash later. He slipped off her shoes and dropped them on the floor. He pulled the coverlet off one side of the bed and tucked it around her, making sure she was okay before he slipped out of the room and into the kitchen.

Logan's hands shook as he turned on the scalding hot water, pumped soap into his hands and then washed away all the blood. He jerked off his soiled shirt and tossed it to the floor. He'd find another shirt later.

He puffed out a short breath and went to the bar, pouring a drink. He knew he wouldn't sleep, not with Bree in the bed. Logan hated she saw the horrific way Mario died and he knew, from experience, she would never be able to get that image out of her mind for the rest of her days. It would haunt her. It would keep her up at night. It would make her life a living hell for a long time.

Niko's threat was not an empty one. He would be back. For him. For her. Mario was mixed up in something dangerous and the vampires intended to make him pay—with his life. But was it enough? Would they come back for more? Now more than ever he had to stay with her to protect her.

The men who killed Mario weren't to be trifled with. Eventually Logan would have to tell her the truth about them, that they were part of a vampire mob. In the meantime, he would have to figure out how Mario was connected to *Signori Della Notte*.

His cell phone buzzed. It was Rafe.

"We need to talk," Logan answered.

"What happened at the bar?" Rafe countered, as though he knew something was up.

"Not on the phone. In person. And I can't leave the apartment."

Pause. "Why not?"

"Bree is here with me."

Another pause. "I'll be there as soon as I can."

He hung up and poured himself another drink and downed it. He padded to the bedroom, dug through one of the bureau drawers until he found a T-shirt and pulled it on. He rummaged through the closet, finding a stash of guns and ammo. Rifles, handguns, automatic weapons and the like. He made a mental note. They might come in handy later. At the back of the closet was a small floor safe.

Next, he searched the bathroom. For what, he didn't know but he wanted to make sure he knew every inch of the place. He found a first aid kit as well as a small black pouch full of surgical instruments. He had no idea why Rafe would need surgical instruments but then dragons were eccentric.

Back in the living room, he searched for more weapons. If he were an exiled knight, he would have them stashed all over the place. He found a handgun in the front foyer table. There were several assisted opening knives hidden throughout the place.

By the time Rafe had arrived twenty minutes later, he knew the stockpile location of every weapon.

"Tell me everything," Rafe said without a greeting.

Logan gave him the whole sordid tale from when Logan found out Mario was dealing with synthetic blood to the vampires attacking and killing Mario.

"That wasn't the boss that killed Mario," Rafe said. "Likely it was one of his trusted men. And you killed one of them."

"I know," Logan said. "I need to find out what Mario was doing to get himself killed."

"Dealing with mafia—a vampire mafia—is dangerous enough. He could have done any number of things to piss them off. And if the boss didn't get what he was after…" He let the words hang in the air between them.

"Bree is in danger."

Rafe nodded. "And so are you because you interfered. Where's the girl?"

"In there." He nodded toward the bedroom. "Asleep. She's in shock."

"You two might want to lie low for a while," Rafe suggested.

"She won't go for that."

"Convince her," he said and flashed a smile as he headed for the door.

"Where are you going?"

"While you have your hands full with her, I'm going to pay a visit to the boss of *Signori Della Notte*. Name's Dominic. See what information I can get out of him."

"Is that wise?" Logan wanted to know.

"Doubt it." Again, he flashed a smile. "But it's a good place to start."

Bree woke with a raging headache. The kind that started at the base of the skull and radiated forward engulfing her whole head. It took a moment for her to open her eyes and come awake. Late afternoon sunlight pressed against the blinds of the one window in the large room.

Disoriented, she bolted upright, a motion that made her head throb and her stomach clench with the sudden movement. She groaned, put her head in her hands and took a deep breath to ease the sickness coursing through her.

Where the hell was she? She had never been in this room before. How did she get here?

Everything came flooding back with such violence, she couldn't stop the whimper she emitted. The vampires. Logan on the floor. Her father attacked.

Her father dead.

She gagged on the sudden bile that rose to her throat. It took effort to shove the image away. She tried to remember what had happened after she found her father on the floor covered in blood.

She'd screamed.

And then Logan had been there, wrapping her in his warmth, pulling her into his arms and holding her. She'd turned to him and clutched his shirt, comforted by his ancient smell and hulking form.

Bree blinked open her eyes and looked at the neo contemporary furnishings. The furniture was dark wood. Two curtain panels in navy blue covered the window. The comforter matched. There was even a wet bar in one corner with a couple of decanters and glasses. As she glanced around, she noticed there weren't any personal effects. No family photos or pictures of girlfriends. Nothing about it screamed female influence at all. For some strange reason, relief sputtered through her.

She must have passed out in his arms and he must have brought her to his place. She needed answers. She had to get out of the bed and find him. Jerking the coverlet off, she stumbled and landed on the floor with a thump.

As she did, her head exploded with more pain and she pushed up on her hands and knees, keeping her head still while she peered down at the white Berber carpet, trying not to puke. Nausea flickered through her. Her stomach cramped and it took lots of deep breathing to make the dizziness subside.

She heard movement nearby, footsteps and then feet scuffing

on the carpet. She lifted her head ever so slightly to see Logan standing in the doorway, filling the entire space, concern etched on his handsome face.

"You all right?"

She sat back on her heels, squeezing her eyes shut and gripping her head with a groan. Again the last events she'd witnessed played through her mind in a sudden burst of memory and she got that sick feeling in the pit of her stomach all over again. She knew she was recovering from shock and still emotionally drained.

Whiskey. She needed copious amounts of whiskey to get her through it.

"Let me help you up."

His voice was much closer now. He stood next to her, holding his hand out to her in an invitation. She lifted her hand, saw the dried blood. It started to shake. She'd gripped her father's hand, touched him. She bit her bottom lip to keep the emotions at bay.

"I'll help you wash."

Nodding, she placed her fingers in his heated palm. His hand closed over hers and something sizzled through her veins. Something dark and sensual and dangerous and one-hundred-percent need and desire. Even at a time like this, it was impossible to ignore.

Bree climbed to her feet. Standing so close to him, the warmth of his body wrapped around her, cocooning her as though he'd embraced her, keeping her close within his personal space. Reminding her of when he scooped her up off the floor and cradled her against him. Their eyes met—his tawny almost translucent that made that sizzle sing once again through her, an unwilling tightening of her nipples against her cotton bra sending a surge of warmth to her core.

How could one touch, one look, do that to her?

His hands landed on her arms and slid upward, pausing on her biceps.

"You okay?" he asked.

"My head hurts," she said, blinking with the pain.

"Come on."

He took her by the hand and led her into the master bath. His palatial master bathroom was sleek, modern and stark. White marble countertops, a shower with glass enclosure big enough for two, a soaking tub. He had all the bells and whistles. It looked like something out of Architectural Digest.

He turned on the hot water and motioned her closer. His hands on hers, he pushed them under the stream. She cupped them as he pumped soap into her palms. When she'd finished scrubbing away the horror, he handed her a towel and two ibuprofen.

"For your head," he said

Nodding, she downed them.

He took her by the hand again and led her into the kitchen. There was a half empty bottle of whiskey on the counter along with a dirty glass next to it and she wondered if he'd been drinking all night. A quick glance at the clock on the microwave told her it was midmorning. He reached for a clean glass and poured her a drink, shoving it toward her. Then he refilled the empty glass.

She stared down at it wondering if he had somehow heard her thoughts about wanting whiskey, then shrugging it off as mere coincidence.

But then hadn't she heard his voice in her head when the vampires were about to attack? Or had she imagined that?

"Hair of the dog." He handed her the glass.

Bree took it and downed the amber liquid, letting the alcohol burn her innards all the way down to her gut where it churned like acid. She placed it on the counter. He refilled it and shoved it toward her once again. She obliged. Once again downing the drink, hoping it would burn away the horrific thing she'd seen.

It wouldn't.

She knew it wouldn't.

"He's dead."

She croaked the words, her throat raw and burning. There had been so much blood everywhere.

"Yes." He answered as though it were a question, even though it wasn't.

She stood in the white contemporary kitchen staring down at the remnants of the whiskey in the glass, wondering what the hell she was supposed to do now. There was no way they could open the bar that night, not after what happened. Her father was dead. *Dead.* And she was left to pick up the pieces.

And seek revenge for his death. She would find a way to kill those blood-sucking vampires if it was the last thing she did.

And it might be.

"I don't know what to do now," she said, more rhetorically than expecting an answer. She meant about the bar. She had to bury her father next to her mother. She had to find a way to carry on with her life without falling apart.

"We'll figure it out."

We. Did he intend to team up with her and track down the vampire who murdered her father? Did he intend to find out why? Was he prepared to go the distance with her? Because she was. She wasn't going to let it go. She needed answers. She needed to know why those vamps attacked her father.

"You aren't in this thing alone, you know."

Her brows drew together. It was almost as though he had listened in on her thoughts.

"Where is my father now?"

"Bear took care of him."

Bear. She was relieved to know he was all right. But it still didn't answer her question.

"Is he at the morgue?"

"No."

He didn't elaborate.

She huffed out an agitated breath and turned to him. "Then where is he?"

"Bree…" His gaze searched her face as if looking for answers. "I don't know where to start."

"Try starting with answering my fucking question."

Surprise flickered over his face at her use of the expletive. She wasn't one to cuss or use that word but she was tired and scared. She needed Logan even though she didn't want to admit it. He was her lifeline. The only one who seemed to have answers to what had happened in the bar.

"We can't report your father's murder to the authorities because he was killed by a vampire."

She tilted her head in question, trying to use her deductive reasoning. "Because regular humans don't know about them, I'm guessing."

"No." He paused, his gaze hardening. "But you do."

She poured another drink and held the glass, starting down into the liquid. Over the years, she'd managed to up her tolerance for the stuff and drank it like water. She could drink just about anyone under the table. But right now, it was a mere comfort to hold the glass and know it was readily accessible.

"I do."

The admission was hard for her to make. She had spent so much of her life hiding her abilities from anyone and everyone. Logan didn't seem taken aback by her confession. He didn't seem to think she was weird.

"How?"

She shrugged. "I don't know. It's something I've been able to do for a long time."

"And Mario?"

Her mouth went dry. It had never occurred to her that her father would be able to see them. But he must have since he talked to them moments before Niko ripped out his throat.

"I don't know. We never talked about it."

"He could see them," he said as though he had to confirm it for her.

Her father never wanted to talk to her about it when, as a child, she started to notice them. In her class at school. At the grocery store. On the playground. She'd mentioned it to him and he shut her down quickly, telling her no one would understand her and would think she was crazy if she talked about it. He forbade her from telling anyone about what she could do, what she could see. Maybe he was ashamed of the ability or maybe he feared it would bring undue attention to them. She didn't know. Now, she never would.

She looked Logan over, her heart pattering in her chest as she remembered what Niko said to him.

"That vampire called you dragon."

Logan stiffened. An almost imperceptible motion but she definitely sensed it. "Then you know what I am."

Her hand shook as she filled his glass, shoved it to him and faced him. She took a step back, looked him up and down as though seeing him for the first time. He was tall, broad and rather menacing-looking but she wasn't afraid of him. She had never been. Even when she saw him in the park that morning. All she wanted to do was jump his bones and get it on with him. Even at a time like this. It was like her raging hormones had a life of their own and she couldn't control them.

She doubted he felt the same way.

But he was different than any man or supernatural with which she'd come into contact. If he was a dragon-shifter, it must explain why she couldn't get a read on him—why she couldn't see his aura and could only scent him. It must mean the same for Rafe.

And that guy who accosted her at the bar.

He peered back at her, never flinching or shrinking away or refusing to meet her gaze. He let her take him in, all of him. He hadn't even cracked a smile. He hadn't looked as though he were uncomfortable. He looked like he *wanted* her to see him for what he was, know what he was.

She'd heard the talk from other supernaturals in the bar about dragon-shifters. The only regular she knew about was Rafe and even then he was somewhat of an oddity. No one talked to him. No one acknowledged he was even there. He spent his nights at the bar sipping his vodka tonic while waving off the ladies that tried to flirt with him. But the other supernaturals—the other shifters, the vamps, the Fae—they gave him a wide berth.

"Do I? Do I really know what you are?" she asked, her voice laced with disdain.

"Don't play games with me, Bree."

"If you're an all-powerful dragon, then why couldn't you save my father? You were hired to protect him, weren't you?"

She hadn't even realized tears were in her eyes until he reached up and brushed one away with his thumb.

"I was hired to protect him. But he didn't tell me the truth." His rumbling voice was calm, patient. "He said there were anonymous death threats against him. I think he knew where they were coming from and why."

She sniffed, forcing the tears away. "Why wouldn't he tell you that?"

"Because I think he was in over his head and he didn't know how to get out. Those vampires, Bree, are part of a mafia. One of the largest vampire mafias in the city."

A cold sweat broke out along the base of her neck. "How would he get mixed up in that?"

"I'm not sure. Something about synthetic blood. Know anything about that?"

She shook her head. "No. Nothing."

"Then we have to figure it out."

"We can start looking for information in his office at the bar. Maybe we can find something there."

"Not today."

"Why not?"

"I think we should stay here for a while. Keep out of sight."

She folded her arms over her chest. "Why?"

"Because it's dangerous out there, Bree."

"I don't care. I have to find answers. I have to—"

He gripped her upper arms, hard, and gave her a little shake. "You'll do as I tell you or you'll end up like Mario."

The blood drained from her face as anger replaced desperation. She shoved him off. And she knew she was only able to do that because he let her.

"Fine."

She stalked back to the bedroom and slammed the door. When she was alone, she pressed against the wood door, slid down to the floor and allowed the tears to flow.

$$\approx 7 \approx$$

Logan let her walk away, her shoulders rigid with anger. They weren't finished yet. There was more to say, more to figure out.

One thing he'd been right about—she was special. She must have inherited her abilities from Mario. He could only guess he wanted her to hide and suppress them for fear of what would happen to her should humans find out.

But Mario had used his abilities to his advantage. He'd opened Bar Inferno. It was clear to Logan it was a place where supernaturals felt at home and safe. It was also a place where humans could, unknowingly, comingle with supernaturals. It only seemed to reason there were other humans like her and those humans frequented the bar.

Logan clutched the almost empty whiskey bottle, intending to pour another drink and then paused. He'd had most of the bottle and hadn't felt a buzz. This whiskey wasn't as strong as some of the alcohol they had in the Hidden Lands.

It was the first time he'd thought of his homeland since everything had happened. He needed to keep the real reason why he was in the human realm to the forefront of his mind—that he was here to regain his strength, to heal, and then to fight back.

When Bree asked why he couldn't save her father, his chest tightened with guilt as it washed over him. He had been an all-powerful dragon, as she'd put it, before he stepped through the portal. The electromagnetic field weakened him. It hadn't helped he'd been stabbed with the obsidian blade, either. The combination of both those must be why he hadn't regened yet.

A driving need to explain that to Bree pumped through him. He shoved away the bottle, the glass, and stalked to the bedroom door. He lifted his hand, ready to knock but stopped. He could hear soft sobs coming from her on the other side.

It shredded him.

"Bree, open the door."

"Go away," her muffled voice returned.

"We need to talk. Let me in."

"No."

Damn it.

He crouched, placed his hand against the door. He sensed her on the other side and closed his eyes, imagining her sitting with her knees drawn up. He knew he shouldn't, but he couldn't help but tap into her thoughts.

Her mind was a tumble of emotions—everything from fear to grief to anger. In his illicit exploration of her thoughts, he discovered they were not so different. She wanted vengeance for her father's death. He wanted vengeance for his parents' murder. She worried about the bar. He worried about the fate of the Hidden Lands.

She didn't know what to do next and neither did he. There was the matter of the Blood Stone. He hadn't worked out how he was going to find it in the human realm. It could be anywhere.

He also knew he had to bide his time and wait until he was ready to attack. Until he was ready to seek Archer and take him out for good. The timetable for that would likely be accelerated since one of the Drakana found him. Another reason why Rafe wanted him to lie low and stay out of sight. He understood even though he hated it.

A palpable loneliness from her burst through. Her desolation seared him, burning into him, leaving her awash in a sea of grief.

That one hurt him the most.

"Bree. You are not alone."

Silence on the other side. No movement either.

"I'm here for you," he added.

He couldn't leave her. It went beyond *ka daeko*. He wanted so much to explain to her why she had this inherent need, why she thought her hormones had taken on a life of their own. In a way, they had. But if the desire for him had not been a glimmer deep inside her before she touched him, the connection would have never happened.

He'd sensed it, too, that first day in the park when she came to help him. He'd tried to keep her from touching him, from making that connection but she hadn't. As much as he wanted to regret that, he couldn't. He was glad. Glad she had been the one to link with him.

There was movement on the other side of the door. He could hear the swish of her clothes and she stood. He stood, too. And despite his outward calm, his palms broke into a sweat.

The knob turned as though in slow motion until the door swung open. Her cheeks were tear-stained. Her eyes puffy and swollen. She stared up at him, a cross between relief and wariness in her green eyes.

"Are you?" Her voice quivered with the question.

"Yes."

"You'll help me then?"

He knew what she was asking. Knew she wanted him to go after Niko and his men. He had his own agenda with Archer, the Drakana, and the Blood Stone. Killing Niko should be easy but he was mafia and the last thing he needed was a vampire mob after his ass. Still, he couldn't deny her.

"I will."

Because it wasn't about bringing justice to the killers. He knew if he didn't agree, she'd go it alone and he couldn't allow that. He had to protect her. To keep her safe.

Nodding, she didn't hide her relief. "Thank you."

The sudden urge to whisk his hands through her hair pulsed through him. He clenched his fists so tightly, the muscles ached. An awkward silence lapsed between them as she peered up at him, her gaze changed from one of relief to confusion and then questioning. She must have sensed the unexpected surge of emotion through him. She didn't back away. No. She shifted from one foot to the other and then her tongue darted out and wet her bottom lip.

He could stand it no longer. His hands shot out and cupped her face as he stepped toward her. A breath shuddered out of her, fanning his face. His senses worked overtime where Bree was concerned because he had unwittingly attuned them to her. He cupped the back of her head with one hand and rested the other on the fluttering pulse in her neck.

The erratic beat danced under his hand with a quick thump. He pressed his forehead against hers and peered into eyes that reminded him of multi-faceted emeralds. The faint scent of strawberries and brown sugar still lingered on her skin under the saltiness of sweat and the metallic tang of blood still on her shirt.

He didn't know what the hell he was doing. All he knew was he couldn't let her go.

"Logan?" Her voice quivered with uncertainty.

He realized the folly of agreeing to help her. She would be with him at all times. Protecting her was one thing. Having her in his constant presence, quite another. He was an idiot to think he could have her around him all the time and not want to touch her, kiss her, make love to her. Because all he could think about now was carrying her to the bed and taking his time undressing her.

A little mewl escaped her. Bree's hands landed on his waist before slipping around him, pulling him close. She bent her head back as she pressed against him, crushing her lithe body into his, curving into him as though she'd been made for him and only him. He had no choice but to push his hands into her hair, tangling the long locks in his fingers and giving a gentle tug.

They stood like that for a long, heart-pounding, breathless moment. He wanted to kiss her, to feel those full lips against his and taste the recess of her mouth. To connect them in that intimate way that was as sensual and divine as diving his hard length into her soft folds.

Another little moan escaped her.

"Do it, Logan. Kiss me."

She leaned into him, her lips parted and ready. To persuade him more, she ran her tongue over her bottom lip.

The temptation was too much to resist. He couldn't. Wouldn't. His mouth landed on hers in a fiery passionate kiss of frantic longing they'd both felt since that fateful morning in the park. His tongue dove into the honey recess of her mouth, tasting her, forever imprinting that sweet tang on him. Teasing her. Testing her. Wanting her. Needing her.

It was all too much and not enough. It was the beginning of the end. It ripped every shred of resolve he might've had to tatters. She had unhinged him body, mind and soul.

And she didn't even know it.

He broke away from her, releasing her, stepping away even though it sent pain searing through him to do it. Her mouth was red and damp from his onslaught. Her hair a tangled mess around her head. She looked disheveled and oh-so-sexy and he wanted to dive into her again. He shouldn't have given in to his desires and kissed her. He shouldn't even have held her in his arms but she felt *so damn good* there. How could he resist? How could he not hold her or kiss her or want her?

All good intentions fled his brain and he could only want. Desire and need pounded through him with such force at every brush of his fingertips on her face, through her hair, he could no longer think straight.

He didn't want to think straight. He wanted to bed Bree.

That first moment of assaulting her mouth was everything he thought it would be and more. Their mouths fused with such fervor, he knew she had been born to kiss him.

He knew she wanted him, too, by the way she kissed him back. By dragon's blood, the way she kissed tore him asunder. And he realized with some horror he had brought her to this place with nothing but the clothes on her back. He couldn't keep her here without her things—he understood women enough to know they needed their *things* to be comfortable.

"I should take you home to get some of your clothes."

"Oh. I thought you said we couldn't leave."

He couldn't look at her as he moved away. He couldn't be alone with her in this place fighting his craving for her. As it was, it was a valiant effort to ignore the throbbing erection he'd managed to create by looking at her, kissing her, smelling her. Hell, he didn't even have to be near her to get hard.

Yes, Rafe said to stay put, and while he agreed with him, he also knew he would go stark raving mad to hold his actions in check.

"I did but I realize you need your things. Let's go."

He headed away from the bedroom, and a moment later, her footsteps were behind him. He snatched the keys off the kitchen counter where he'd left them earlier and headed for the door only pausing long enough to pull the handgun out of the top drawer in the entryway. Bree gave him a wary look as he checked it, flicked off the safety and then tucked it in the waistband of his pants at the small of his back.

"Just in case," he told her.

Logan whisked open the door, waited for her to exit and then locked the apartment. He would have preferred to carry her to the bedroom and ravish her until dawn.

That wasn't going to happen.

They were silent in the elevator down to the parking garage. He exited the elevator and glanced down at the key fob with the BMW emblem on it. He had no idea where the car was parked. He clicked the lock button and saw the flash of lights nearby and heard the honk. He headed for the black sporty coupe.

"This is yours?" Bree eyed it with some speculation.

"Borrowed."

He clicked the key fob again, this time unlocking the doors. He opened her door and watched as she bent and slid into the leather bucket seat.

He started the car and put it in reverse to ease out of the

parking space. They were silent as he drove out of the garage and into early evening. He could see her clasped hands in her lap and sense her stiffness. He couldn't blame her—he felt the same way. Stiff, nervous, unsure.

He wasn't thinking when he took the turn to her place and a little gasp escaped her.

Bree was about to give him directions to her apartment when he took the turn toward her place located across from Central Park on the Upper East Side. She couldn't stifle the gasp that escaped her. She looked at him, streetlights flashing by and light illuminating his features in slashes. She could see his death grip on the steering wheel and the look of consternation on his face.

"You remember where I live?"

"Yeah," he said, keeping it simple.

A warm gushing feeling went through her at the very idea he had managed to remember where she lived. It wasn't like he had spent a lot of time there. He had only been there once and he had been injured and she had been determined to help him.

She hadn't even kissed him then even though she wanted to.

She'd kissed him now. She'd felt the way his powerful mouth moved over hers. So hot and demanding, yet gentle and slow and giving all at the same time. His tongue had delved deeply into her mouth, tasting her. Tempting her. The heat of his body washed over hers in such a rush, it left her lightheaded, her skin searing, burning, scorching.

Every second of that first kissed was branded in her mind, on her body, in her soul. And when he stepped away from her, she took some delight in hearing the ragged breath seesawing out of him as though it had taken as much out of him as it did her. That cemented the thought in her mind he longed for her as much as she did for him.

Her breath hitched and she gulped in air, telling herself she had to forget in order to function.

"You all right?" he asked, his hands gripping the steering wheel.

"Yes." The word hissed out of her with some force, her cheeks flaming that he'd noticed her breathlessness as she remembered the kiss.

He pulled up to the curb outside her building. She jumped out before he even had the car turned off and headed up the steps to the door. By the time he'd followed her, she was already inside and jogging up the stairs to her third-floor apartment, her muscles throbbing with the quick pace. She hoped it would burn off some of the tension knotting her neck and shoulders and other parts she tried hard not to think about.

At the top of the stairs, the sight of the splintered door jarred her. Her instinct wanted her to step foot inside that door but she knew better. If she entered without Logan, there would be hell to pay. Especially if there was someone in there that could do her harm.

That's where he found her—standing in front of the destroyed door of her apartment, shaking. He put his hand on her shoulder and she moved aside.

"Wait here until I give the all clear," he said.

She nodded.

He pushed open the door and stepped inside the small apartment. She counted to ten, listening to her ragged breathing and wondering what was going on inside. When he didn't reappear those long seconds later, she followed.

A strangled gasp escaped her. The place had been ransacked. Every cupboard had been opened and emptied. Furniture was upended, pillows slashed, bookshelves destroyed. Whoever had been there had come and gone leaving nothing but the mess. What could they have been looking for? She didn't have any jewels stashed anywhere. Her electronics hadn't been stolen, so they weren't in it for that.

"My apartment..."

"Yeah, they busted it up pretty good." He emerged from the

bedroom. "Any idea what they were looking for?"

She shook her head. "No. Who could have done this?"

"My guess? The same people who murdered Mario." He pinpointed her with his steely gaze.

Her stomach dropped into her shoes. She took a step into the apartment but her knees were stiff. Her legs didn't want to work. She shoved aside destroyed books with the toe of her shoe.

"Did he give you anything? Like a gift or anything else?"

"No. Nothing. I have no idea what they would be looking for. I should call the police."

"You should get as much stuff as you can and we should go. It's not safe here."

"You think they'll come back?"

"If they think you came back for whatever they were looking for, yes."

She hesitated, a wave of apprehension sweeping through her as she thought of all the shit that had happened. She wanted it to end. She wanted things back to normal. And she hated the tears that burned her eyes.

"Go get your stuff. I'll wait here until you're done." His tone was soft and gentle.

She hurried to the bedroom and found it in as much disarray as the rest of the place. All Bree wanted to do was crumble to her knees and weep but she couldn't allow her emotions to overcome her. She kicked off her dress shoes and searched for her sneakers. She found a pair of jeans discarded on the floor and took off her soiled ones. Then she found one of her well-worn T-shirts and tugged off her blood-stained shirt, leaving it in the floor. What was one more garment in the pile? She pulled on the shirt and then stuck her feet in the shoes without untying the laces.

It took her several minutes to find her overnight bag—a Vera Bradley in a loud red, white, and blue paisley. It had been so hideous, she had to buy it. She blindly shoved more clothes into the bag. Socks, underwear, shirts. She didn't think about what she was packing. Whatever she left behind she could always buy.

Remembering her cell phone, she fished it out of the pocket of her discarded jeans and dropped it in the bag.

And then she stopped. She could see a corner of some paper sticking out between the mattress and box springs of her destroyed bed. She dropped the bag and fell to her knees, staring at it with confusion and apprehension. She had no idea what it could be as she'd never seen it before.

She tugged the paper corner and pulled out a nine-by-twelve envelope. Her first name was scrawled across the front in her father's handwriting. In some ways, it was like looking at a ghost and her stomach clenched. When had he put that there?

"Bree, we should get going before—" Logan appeared in the doorway of her bedroom and drew up short when he saw her sitting in the middle of the debris holding the envelope. "What is that?"

"It's from my father." Despite her best efforts, her voice shook. She held it up to him. "You open it. I can't."

Logan took it and opened the flap. He stuck his hand inside and pulled out a velvet drawstring bag. They exchanged a curious glance. He opened the bag and peered inside and then stiffened. He swiped debris off the mattress with his forearm and spilled out the contents over her sheets. Precious stones winked back at them except for one in particular. It was out of place amongst the other jewels. Round, flat and dark red.

When she reached for it, he clamped his hand around her wrist. "Don't."

She frowned but didn't complain. "What the hell is that?"

"It's a stone."

"I can see it's a stone, smart ass. What's the significance?"

"It has magical properties."

She started to ask more questions but a noise outside the apartment caught both their attentions. He reached for a discarded sock to pick up the red stone and shoved the jewels into the velvet bag as she shot to her feet and snatched up her bag. Logan pocketed the stones and waved her behind him. He pulled his gun from the small of his back. She scooted into position trying hard not to let fear overtake her as she clutched the handle of the bag in her sweaty palm. He took one step, two, toward the door.

Shots fired and he spun toward her. She stumbled backward as he collided with her motioning toward the window.

"Fire escape?" he asked.

"Yes."

She shoved aside the curtains and thrust the window open. He practically pushed her through it as more shots punctuated the air behind them. He grunted as he followed and they hurried down the fire escape to the street below.

"Get to the car. I'm right behind you," he said through pursed lips.

As she darted down the alley, he turned and fired off several shots. His footsteps behind her was the only confirmation she had he'd followed. As she hurried around the corner, she could see the car. He clicked the unlock button and the lights flashed indicating it was open. But as they approached, there was a sudden flash of light and then the car blew into a million pieces.

She shrieked as he landed on top of her and shoved her to the ground. The only thing that broke her fall was the overnight bag beneath her. She scraped her elbows on the sidewalk but was thankful Logan had covered her, protecting her from the raining shards of metal and glass.

He hadn't fared so well. As he wrapped and arm around her, she could see blood oozing down his forearm and knew he was hurt.

"Fuck," he muttered in her ear.

Logan hauled her to her feet and shoved her down the street in front of him. She didn't argue. She just ran. And as she ran, she realized they were headed straight for Central Park.

Logan didn't expect to be back in Central Park so soon. Nor did he expect to be running from whoever was behind them, with Bree. He didn't know if it was Drakana or vampires after them, and at the moment, it didn't matter.

What did matter was that he'd been shot and tried not to notice. Hard to ignore, though, with blood running down his arm. He'd been lucky the bullet only grazed him.

Also hard to ignore was the weight of the jewels in his pocket. One of them the Blood Stone. How the hell had it ended up in Bree's apartment? She looked as baffled as he felt. How had Mario managed to put it there before he died?

Find the Blood Stone, Logan. It can save the Hidden Lands.

It was the last mindspeak his father sent to him before he blew his Dragon's Breath and died.

Bree panted with exertion next to him. He took her hand and they slowed to a quickened pace along the path at the fence by the reservoir. He glanced behind him but they hadn't been followed. At least, not yet.

"Stop please." She tried to catch her breath as they slowed.

He slowed long enough to allow Bree to lean over, her hands on her knees as she tried to catch her breath. The burning pain in his left arm intensified. He clenched his jaw tightly, fighting his instincts to keep from shifting into dragon form. Even though Bree knew what he was, the rest of New York didn't and he wasn't prepared to advertise it.

"You're hurt." She craned her neck to look up at him.

"I'll be all right. Are you okay?"

"Winded but fine. Logan, they blew up your car." Her voice quivered a little, as though she were in pain over the thought of the car being charred to bits.

"It's fine." Rafe might not think so, though. "We can't stay here long. We have to get back to the apartment."

"I know but I'm so tired." She rubbed her eyes with the back of her hand.

"The longer we stay out, the more of a sitting target we are," he warned. "We have to go, Bree."

"Give me another minute."

He stiffened, his body going rigid as he scented the men coming after them again. He tightened his grip on the handle of his gun.

"Bree, I want you to run as fast as you can to the other side of the park. Get a cab and get back to the apartment. You'll be safe there." He pulled the keys out of his pocket and handed them to her. "Go."

"What about you?"

"I'll be there as soon as I can. Trust me."

"But—"

He gave her a gentle shove. "I need you to do as I tell you."

"You promise you'll follow me?"

"I promise. I won't be far behind."

She hesitated for a moment but then gave him a nod and took off again.

When Bree was safely away, Logan turned back toward the pathway, the gun cocked and ready. He scented them on the wind and knew they followed them, though who *they* were, he didn't know yet. All he knew was there was more than one. He had to get Bree out of the picture and safe before anything happened.

The shimmer of light surrounded him as though he were behind a veil. Two of them stepped out of the shadows. They shot first—they weren't interested in chatting. He fired back and took out first one and then the second. But they both seemed unaffected by his bullets. He dove behind a tree for cover.

Even though he could still see the humans beyond, they seemed unconcerned with what was going on through the veil. It was as though he and the attackers were hidden.

He scented them and knew they were vampires. They were after Bree and maybe even the Blood Stone he had in his pocket, though why they'd want a dragon's ancient relic, he didn't know. He wasn't giving up either so easily.

As he peered around the tree and took aim, there was a flash of silver from someone behind the vampires. Their throats slit, they crumpled to the ground. The veil remained even though the vamps were dead.

"Logan Blake," one of them called.

He stepped out from behind the tree and saw the two dead vampires and the three dragon-shifters standing behind them. Logan could see his face. Recognition was like a punch in the gut. Zak was Archer's nephew. The events of the night when Logan left the clan came flooding back. For Archer, Logan was nothing more than a loose end that had to be tied up.

"Hello, Zak. Archer send you to do his dirty work?" Logan asked.

"He would have come himself, but he's busy running things," Zak said and smirked.

Anger pumped through him. "He's not the rightful clan leader."

"He is now," he said. "You left the clan. And the clan leader didn't like that too much. He sent me to retrieve you. Dead or alive. I prefer dead."

Logan's gaze narrowed. "You had to bring two buddies with you because you couldn't handle it yourself?" He thought he recognized them as Drakana. He could see the starburst on their wrists.

"They're going to drag your dead body back to Archer for me." He said it with ease as if he was talking about the weather.

"Are they? Then go ahead and kill me. Get it over with."

"I don't want to make it too easy. After all, part of the fun is the chase."

Logan wasn't interested in playing cat and mouse. He didn't deem the man worthy of a reply and fired off two quick shots, killing both his henchmen. Zak glanced down at the dead bodies and then back at Logan with a smirk.

"Now you'll have to chase me yourself," Logan taunted.

"Nice shooting. I should have expected that from you."

"But you didn't and now they're dead. That's a message to take back to your boss, your uncle. Tell him I'm not going down without a fight."

"Oh, is that so? And should I also tell him about your girlfriend?"

Panic and fear pumped through him in a surge of heat. Bree may not be his girlfriend but he would die trying to protect her. He'd failed Mario. He'd failed his parents. But would not fail her. No matter if it cost him his life.

"You stay away from her."

"We'll see what Archer has to say about that."

"Will we? I don't think so."

Logan aimed and intended to fire but Zak was faster. He never saw him pull the gun nor did he even realize the man had it on him. He fired off two shots. Logan reacted by trying to dive out of the way, but one bullet lodged in the back of his shoulder. He crumpled to the ground, and before he realized what was happening, Zak was on him.

Logan was an idiot to think Zak wouldn't have similar abilities as he did in the human realm. His dragon blood afforded him great stealth and incredible speed, as did Zak's.

Zak kicked away his gun before stomping on Logan's arm to keep him in place. He pointed his gun in his face.

"I missed on purpose. Next time, I won't. Next time, you'll be dead."

If he were to pull the trigger, he'd be done for.

Logan didn't like to be threatened. His nemesis forgot he had a free hand. He swept it forward in a swift move, punching Zak behind the knees. It jarred him enough to make his foot loosen on Logan's other arm. He pushed it upward making Zak pitch backward, his weapon hand flailing. The gun went off, the bullet straying into the air. Zak tumbled to the ground, the weapon falling from his hand.

Logan wasted no time in pouncing, hauling the guy up by the collar and landing a fist in his face. The pain of the blow shot through his arm right to his wounded shoulder, making him clench his teeth. Zak grabbed a handful of dirt and grass and threw it in Logan's face, playing dirty. Logan lost all his momentum and it gave Zak the window he needed to shove Logan backward, his hand wrapped around his throat.

"You think you're so bad," Zak said. "But you are nothing. Like your father was nothing. Like your whole family was nothing."

Logan gasped for breath, trying to keep his vision clear and ignore the pain in his shoulder. He couldn't get a good grip on Zak who turned out to be stronger than he looked.

"I'm going to enjoy killing you."

As the words spilled out of his mouth, something crashed against the side of his head. In an instant, he released Logan and crumpled to the side. Logan shoved him off and looked up to see Bree with a large tree branch in her hand.

$$\mathref{8}$$

As Bree ran from Logan, her heart rammed in her chest. She was certain running from him was not the right thing to do. She should go back, though she wasn't sure how much help she'd be.

She slowed to a trot as she approached Central Park West. She paused, trying to decide what to do as she shifted from foot to foot. Shots rang out behind her and her heart shoved into her throat.

Logan.

She knew he told her to take cab and get back to his place. That the threat was real and dangerous and she believed him. But she also could not leave Logan if something terrible had happened to him. She had to go to him.

Cursing under her breath, she turned back to the park and launched into a dead run. Her stomach had curled into a knot of dread as she raced back to where she'd left Logan, wondering if she would find him dead in a pool of blood.

She heard voices and slowed, crouching behind a tree and peering around it. There seemed to be a strange veil around them. She glanced around and saw those in the park didn't notice the struggle going on behind that veil. But she could see it and she could sense the men were like him. More dragons, no doubt.

Instead of Logan dead on the ground, there were two others. He faced off with another guy. She couldn't hear what they were saying, only that they spoke to one another before the man pulled the trigger.

She gasped, covering her mouth to keep from screaming as she watched Logan crumple to the ground. Oh, God, he'd been shot and she was frozen in place. The man pounced on Logan, pointing the gun in his face.

Bree dropped her bag and frantically looked around for something—anything—to use as a weapon. She saw a large tree branch and dashed for it. By the time she made it back, a scuffle had ensued. Logan was on his back, guns forgotten, and the guy trying to choke him to death. Now was her chance to act. She hurried to them and swung the branch with both hands, connecting to the side of the guy's head.

He released Logan and toppled off him, unconscious.

"Bree, damn it, I told you to get out of here."

"Gee, you're welcome for me saving your life." She tossed aside the branch as Logan struggled to his feet. She hurried to help him. "I heard shots and…Logan, you're hurt this time."

When she felt the dampness on her fingertips, she pulled her hand away and saw the blood smearing them.

"I'll be all right," he said as he grunted. "Just get me to a cab."

"What about him?" She nodded to the unconscious guy on the ground.

"Leave him. He'll come to soon enough."

"And the dead guys over there?"

Logan looked at them, then back at her. "Leave it, Bree."

"But shouldn't we call the police or someone? And we have to get you to a hospital."

"I said leave it. Take me back to the apartment."

"But your shoulder—"

"No hospitals." There was a hard edge of annoyance to his voice, one she hadn't heard before. It made her shudder. She made a note to never incite that tone of voice from him again.

"All right."

"You still have the keys?"

Seemed like a silly question but she nodded. As they made their way out of the park, she scooped up her bag she'd discarded behind the tree. At the street, she managed to flag down a cab. She helped him into the backseat on the passenger side. He practically poured his tall body into the seat, wincing with his wounded shoulder. She hurried around to the other side and got in.

Logan gave the driver the address and then groaned with his pain as he sat back in the seat, trying not to bleed everywhere. Thankfully it was a short ride back to his place.

"I'll come around and help you," she said.

She hurried out of the car but he was a stubborn man and was out before she could get around to the other side. His face was a mask of pain. Sweat rolled down the side of his face and beaded his forehead.

"Logan—"

"I'm fine. Let's get upstairs. You can help me then."

Bree didn't like the sound of that. The back of his shirt was soaked with blood. Worry gnawed at her as they got in the elevator and she punched the button to his floor. It seemed an eternity before the elevator dinged and they arrived. Thankfully, no one was about so she didn't have any awkward staring moments. She unlocked the door and shoved it open.

"Where's the first aid kit?"

"Bree." He held his arm against his side and grasped her wrist with his free hand. "I need to ask you something first."

Her pulse quivered. "Okay."

"I understand if you don't want to do it, but I need your help. Mostly because I can't reach it."

She blanched and her stomach cramped. "Oh, God. You want me to get the bullet out, don't you?"

He nodded. "I *need* you to get the bullet out. Can you? I'll walk you through it."

She pressed a hand against her roiling stomach. The last thing she ever expected to do was dig a bullet out of Logan. She bit her bottom lip and nodded.

"I can."

The relief was evident on his face as he exhaled. "You're an angel."

"Yeah, well, tell me that *after* I get it out, okay?"

He gave her a faint smile and a nod for her to follow. "Come on. We can do it in the bathroom."

She flushed as she trailed him down the hallway, though she didn't even know why. It wasn't as if he was making a pass at her. It was silly of her to even think it but she couldn't stop the warmth creeping into her cheeks.

Logan flicked on the light and continued into the room but she paused in the doorway. The masculine room was large with floor to ceiling windows along one wall showing off the glittering lights of the city beyond. He pressed a button on a remote and electric shades drew down.

He poured two drinks and handed one to her. "Here. You'll want this."

"Yes, I will." She took it from him and downed it in one gulp. The burning whiskey did nothing to calm the nerves still erupting through her. She eyed the decanter.

"I'll pour you another one afterward." He slid the glass from her hand and placed it on the bar then nodded to the bathroom. "Let's do it in here."

Logan pulled the first aid kit from the cabinet under the bathroom sink and placed it on the counter. Then he reached back inside for a small black pouch which he put next to the first aid kit. When he flipped it open, the light reflected off the steel surgical instruments. Various scalpels, long-handled scissors, and something that looked like a pair of pliers. She blanched and griped the edge of the counter.

"I don't think I can do this." Her voice was a rough whisper.

"You *can* do this, Bree. I believe in you." He gripped her arm and gave it a reassuring squeeze.

If only *she* believed in herself. Her gaze flickered up to meet his and she could see the confidence he had in her. It helped alleviate her fears.

"I need you to help me take off my shirt."

For the love of God, what was he *doing* to her? Her emotions had swung from one end of the spectrum to the other within minutes. Heat flashed over her body and crept back into her cheeks but she would be *damned* if she let him see her blush.

"All right." Even though she wanted her voice to sound strong, it didn't and she hated that.

He used his good arm to pull his shirt up to his shoulders but she could tell it pained him to move his other arm with the injury. With her heart beating at a rapid-fire pace, she reached for him, her fingers brushing against his arm, his hand. She'd come to expect the heating of his skin, so it didn't surprise her this time when she touched him. After a few awkward moments, she pushed his shirt up and over his head and held it out for him while he slid his other arm out, being mindful of his injured shoulder.

Bree tried hard not to look at him shirtless but the more she tried, the more she couldn't *not* look. He was a prime male specimen. Perfect corded washboard abs and a chest that could make any woman melt. His broad shoulders curved into well-defined biceps and perfect forearms ending in his beautiful long-fingered strong hands.

He didn't seem to notice her ogling him as he turned his back to her. She managed to focus on the task at hand and got a good look at the wound. It was caked with blood and starting to clot.

"Oh, God," she whispered.

"You can do this, Bree."

"Yeah, yeah. You keep saying that."

"And I mean it. What does it look like?"

"Um, yucky."

He huffed. "Can you be a little more descriptive?"

"Like I need to clean it. The blood is starting to clot."

He flipped open the first aid kit and pulled out disinfectant and cotton pads, shoving them down the counter toward her.

"Are you sure about this?" Her voice wavered with the words.

"Yes." He lifted his gaze and met hers in the mirror, making her heart flutter. "I'm sure. Do it."

Taking a deep breath, she doused one of the cotton pads in disinfectant. Logan gripped the edge of the counter as she touched the pad against the wound and cleansed it in a sweeping motion. As she cleaned the injury, she realized something odd but wasn't sure if her eyes were deceiving her or not.

Bree got a clean pad, doused it again and went back to cleaning the wound.

"Um, Logan? It appears the wound has closed up around the bullet."

Logan was afraid of that. He knew the bleeding had stopped by the time the cab rounded the corner and drove into the parking garage. He had hoped he could get to the wound before it managed to close but no such luck.

One of the curses—or benefit in some cases—of his dragon's blood was he healed incredibly fast. Even faster in dragon form.

"Is it because you're a…" Her question trailed off.

In the mirror, he could see her swallow hard. "Yes. My rate of healing is different than a human's."

"Now what?" He could hear the nervousness in her voice.

Poor Bree. He would have to find a way to make it up to her. "You have to cut it open."

Her eyes widened with surprise and her face drained of color as he met her reflected gaze. "What? No way. I am not cutting on you."

"You have to. It's the only way to get it out."

"I don't understand. Why can't we go to a hospital? They can take care of it there."

"No, Bree. No hospitals. They won't understand what I am. The last thing I need is to have attention called to me and my kind."

A hospital was the last place he wanted to be. While he looked human to the naked eye, inside was a different story. His organs were generally the same but they were not the same size or shape as a human.

"There are more here besides you and Rafe?"

"Yes. Dragon-shifters are all over the world."

Logan turned to face her, took her by the arms and held her. She refused to look at him. He cupped her chin and tipped her face up so he could meet her gaze.

"Hey. It'll be all right."

"I-I don't know if I can do that, Logan. I don't want to hurt you."

He gave her a reassuring smile. If only she knew, she could never hurt him even when she was cutting him open. "You won't. Besides, I'll heal fast."

"If you're sure…"

"I'm sure." He pulled her to him, kissed her forehead. "You're an angel, you know."

He wasn't sure why he said it or what made him say it. But it was something that bubbled to the front of his brain before he could filter it from his mouth. She had gotten under his skin, buried herself so deeply, she likely would never be able to claw her way out. And since that first kiss, he couldn't get the taste of her out of his mouth nor the scent of her from his nose nor the feel of her out of his mind.

She bit her lip, as though trying to keep from saying something but couldn't. He understood. There were numerous things he wanted to say to her but couldn't.

"Well, then, I guess I better get to it."

"Right."

He turned, facing the mirror. She washed the blood off her hands, then picked up a scalpel.

"It's very sharp. Be careful," he said.

Nodding, she took a deep breath. She placed ginger fingertips on his skin next to the where the bullet had entered. He could hear her inhale another long breath.

"My hand is shaking," she said.

"Bree, look at me."

She lifted her gaze to meet his in the mirror and he was struck by how damned beautiful she was. Standing there holding a scalpel ready to cut into him. She had bags under her eyes and stress lines etched into her face. Stress lines he had managed to put there over the last several hours. He was such a jackass.

"Do it. You have to and you won't hurt me."

Nodding, she focused on the wound again. And took another deep breath. She was killing him. He braced his hands on the edge of the counter when he felt the first prick of the blade. He watched her face in the mirror. She scrunched it as she made the first cut.

"Oh, God, Logan, there's so much blood."

"Keep going," he urged.

"I'm sorry but I have to make another cut."

"Go ahead." He said it through clenched teeth but never took his eyes off her.

He could see the concentration on her face as she sliced through his skin again, the burn of it pulsing through him.

"I need a towel," she said, her voice high-pitched and on the verge of panic.

He nodded to the white hand towel. "There."

"But—"

"It'll wash, Bree. Just use it." He knew what she was going to say before she even said it.

She snatched it off the towel ring. He could feel her mopping up the blood with it. "Shit, shit, shit. I don't like this, Logan."

"I know you don't, princess, but you're doing great. Did you get it open?"

Biting her lip, she nodded.

"Now you have to get the bullet out."

"Shit." She snatched the forceps. "I don't like this."

"You can do it," he coached. Even as he said it, he braced himself for the imminent digging.

Again, she took a deep breath before she started. White hot pain flared through him as she started to probe the wound. Luckily, the bullet hadn't lodged very deeply and she hit it right away.

"Oh! There it is. I got it. I think I got it. Shit, it slipped out. There. Almost. Damn it! Come here, you little piece of shit."

And then she released a string of curses the likes he had never heard before. If he hadn't been in so much excruciating pain, he would have laughed. He broke into a cold sweat as he gripped the edge of the counter.

"Bree, stop fooling around and get it out."

"I'm *trying*, damn it." She sucked in a sharp breath. "Oh! Got it!" She held it up in the light. It was coated with blood. "Tada!"

As she held it up, she got her first good look at it and blanched. Her gaze flickered to his open wound and then she did what any woman would have done. She fainted straightaway.

Thanks to Logan's lightning fast reflexes, he caught her in his arms before she smacked the tile floor. He scooped her up and carried her to the bed. He brushed hair from her face, smiling a little at the way she'd passed out after being so brave. It endeared her to him even more.

After the ordeal of being chased, shot at, and wounded, he needed a shower. But first he needed to offload the velvet pouch of stones. He found a clean shirt in the dresser. Luckily, he and Rafe were about the same size. He pulled the stones from his pocket, holding their weight in his hand for a moment, resisting the urge to open it and look at the Blood Stone again.

If only he could ask his father about the Blood Stone. He knew it would help heal the Hidden Lands. His father must have found some lore or piece of information that led him to believe it was a crucial artifact needed. Now that he had it, he wasn't quite sure what to do with it. For safekeeping, he dropped the velvet pouch in the drawer and closed it with a snap. He headed for the shower, hoping to clear his head and figure out his next move.

⤷ 9 ⤶

Bree awoke to strange surroundings. It took her several minutes to remember she was in Rafe and Logan's apartment and she'd fainted when she held the bloodied bullet. Mortification passed over her and she covered her face with her hands.

How could she have fainted? She wasn't a weakling. She'd managed to stomach the digging out of the bullet in Logan's shoulder without throwing up. Never mind her stomach roiled and clenched the entire time she was doing it.

It was, by far, the most disgusting thing she had ever done and she never wanted to do anything like that again. Remembering how she'd left the open wound, she sat bolt upright in the bed. But Logan was nowhere to be found. She was alone.

Bree slid to the edge and leaned over far enough to look into the bathroom. The light was off. She padded across the room and flipped up the switch to see the mess had been cleaned. The only remnants of the grisly affair were the bloodied cotton pads in the trashcan.

She hurried from the bathroom and burst through the bedroom door looking for Logan. He must have heard the commotion because he came barreling around the corner. She put on the brakes, narrowly avoiding crashing into him.

He'd put on a clean shirt and pants and looked freshly showered. She wished she'd been awake for *that*. To think she'd been unconscious the entire time he was in the bathroom, naked and soapy, and she missed it all.

"Are you all right?"

"Your shoulder. I passed out before I could stitch it."

"You don't need to worry about that. It's already healed."

She blinked her bafflement. "Already? It was a gaping wound."

"You sound like you don't believe me."

Logan had said he healed fast, but…how fast? How could something like that have healed? She lifted a questioning eyebrow.

"You said you healed fast. So how fast is that?"

His reply was to tug off his shirt. Before he turned, she got a glimpse of all that glorious muscle. When he turned his back to her, she could see only a faint line where she'd removed the bullet. The place where he'd been shot was healed as though it had happened a year ago instead of hours ago.

Bree couldn't help it. She had to touch it to make sure her eyes were seeing what they were actually seeing. As her fingertips skimmed the silvery scar with a light touch, he stiffened and sucked in a sharp breath. Gooseflesh erupted on his warm skin. He wasn't as hot as she'd felt before but still warm. She marveled at that and assumed it was his natural body temperature.

It was something of a triumph to illicit such a strong reaction from him. She stepped away, clutching her elbows.

"Satisfied?" he asked.

"It's remarkable. Like it never happened," she said. "I've never seen anything like it."

"If you're convinced, can I put my shirt back on now?"

She wanted to laugh at the way he sounded so annoyed.

"If I had my way, you'd never wear a shirt," she teased.

A moment of hesitation passed through him before he tugged the shirt over his head and started for the dimly lit kitchen where only the pendant lights over the island glowed. She sighed as she watched him walk away and regretted the tease.

"You want a drink?" He threw the words over his shoulder.

It had been early evening when they made it out of the park and back to his place. She had no idea how long she'd been out as she followed him to the kitchen.

"Yes. What time is it?"

"One in the morning." He poured a glass of whiskey and handed it to her. "We'll stay here tonight but I'm not sure it's safe anymore."

"You think they will come after us?"

He shrugged as he poured himself a drink. "Possibly."

Bree knocked back the drink in one gulp, letting the amber liquid burn through to her stomach. "Those men in the park. Who were they?"

He raked a hand through his hair as he turned from her and walked to the windows. He peered through the shades, though she doubted he could see anything at all through the dense material.

"Two of them were vampires. They were likely after you."

A cold sensation crept up her spine at the thought of vampires hunting her. If she hadn't been with Logan, she would be more concerned. But he made her feel safe, secure. Somehow she knew, even in the short amount of time they had been together, he would do whatever it took to protect her.

At some point, she would have to face them, when she took her revenge for her father's death. For now, she would wait until the time was right. Whether or not Logan helped her.

"Does that scare you?"

"A little," she admitted. "But I can't worry about that right now. What about the other man?"

"He was after me."

She poured another drink and held the glass. "He was a hunter?"

"You could say that." He sipped his drink.

The way he evaded questions made her crazy. The guy had something to do with who Logan was underneath that rough exterior and he wasn't willing to share it with her. Was he being hunted because the guy hated dragons? Or was there some other reason he wanted him dead?

Whatever it was, she wished he would tell her the truth. If he only knew he could trust her, tell her anything. She wouldn't judge him. Bree knocked back the drink to keep her nerves at bay and placed the glass on the counter.

"You know who he is, don't you? I can help you. If you'll let me."

"You can't help me."

She moved to stand next to him as he sipped his drink. She admired he could sip whiskey—she never could. She placed her hand on his shoulder.

"Why won't you let me in?" Her voice was low and smooth in the shadowy darkness.

"You got in."

Desire flashed through her when he whispered those three words. Bree could no more stop her hands from moving inside his shirt and over his back than she could stop a subway train. She marveled at the sinew of muscle under her palms. He stiffened again under her touch.

"Why do you do that? Does my touch bother you?"

His hand tightened around the glass, the nail beds turning white. "No, Bree."

"Then what is it?" she demanded.

He sighed and set aside his glass and turned to her. His fingers encircled her wrist as he brought up her hand. He flattened his other palm against hers. Bree shuddered. Her body shook but not from cold. From the intensity burning right through her. The simple touch scorched through her as though she placed her palm on a hot stove. Her cheeks warmed, sending the sensation right to her core. Making the slick heat between her legs burn hot with a desperate need for release.

"I suppose it's time I tell you."

"Tell me what?"

"Why don't you shower first? Then we'll talk," he suggested as though he suggested she have a tomato and basil salad.

"You'll tell me everything?"

He nodded. "As much as I can."

She suspected he would give her the abbreviated version. She complied only because a shower sounded divine. She headed back to the bedroom, pulled clean underwear, shirt and pants from her bag and padded to the bathroom.

She didn't linger long in the shower, though she wanted to. She was more interested in getting the truth out of Logan. After toweling off, she dressed and combed out her hair. When she returned to the living room, her skin scrubbed clean, she found Logan standing at the windows overlooking the city.

It struck her then, how much he seemed to belong in this place even though he wasn't human. She wondered how he ended up here, if the flash of light she'd seen when he appeared was what brought him here or if he had already been here and something else had happened. She'd seen weird things lately. Things she never expected to see in her bar or the city. Things that only just started to make sense to her.

He must have sensed her for he turned from the windows, the faint light flickering over his features and her breath caught in her throat. He looked her over with an appreciative gaze, as though he liked what he saw in her.

She cleared her throat. "I'm ready to talk if you are."

"There are some things you should know about me," he said and paused.

"I'm all ears."

He took a deep breath, blew it out. "A dragon experiences four phases of life. Birth, adolescence, adulthood, elder. When I arrived in the human realm, I recently completed *ka daeko.*"

Her brows drew together. "What is that?"

"Loosely translated it means 'to change' in the common tongue. In your realm, it's akin to a male adolescent going through puberty. While it takes a few years for a human boy to mature, for us it only takes a few months."

Bree's pulse fluttered, the implication sending waves of excitement through her. "And you've...completed adolescence?"

"I have. And entered *ka kladou.*" He paused.

Her eyes widened and she swallowed hard. "And what is that?"

"It means 'to mate.' The third phase of our lifespan in

adulthood."

He brushed the backs of his knuckles across her cheek. Her eyes became heavy-lidded. Warmth rushed through her. Her arousal permeated the air between them.

"When we seek a mate."

His rich voice was like a gentle caress rumbling over her. Her eyes fluttered closed when he placed his hand on her neck. His thumb traced the length in long sensual strokes.

"Bree." His warm breath whispered over her earlobe as he spoke her name.

She hummed a response, lost in the heady ecstasy of his nearness. His lips brushed her skin as he nuzzled her.

"That morning in the park, when you wrapped your hand around my arm. It was the moment you chose me. And I chose you. Whether it was a conscious decision or not. We are connected."

Just like that the spell was broken. Her eyes flew open, her senses on high alert. She tried to push out of his embrace but he held fast.

"Wait a second. Are you saying all these…things…I've been feeling are because I *touched* you? Because I was trying to help a stranger?"

She took a step back trying to move away from him. He laced their fingers, pulled her close to keep her from bolting. He must have sensed it because that was all she wanted to do. She wanted to flee. She wasn't afraid of *him* as much as she was afraid of the feelings burning within her for him. She had not been prepared for that. How could she? She was not like him. She was not of his kind.

"Yes, that's what I'm saying."

"I—"

"Bree, the only way the bonding works is if there is a flicker of desire deep down for the other. You must have had it for me or it would have never happened."

She recalled that morning, remembering the way he had been

hunched on the ground. The way he looked as though he was in so much pain. When he stood and she got a glimpse of his face, her knees had weakened. Yes, it had been instant attraction but she had shrugged it off as nothing but a passing fancy.

Even then, she sensed something different about it. She knew he was not like other supernaturals. Perhaps it was what had drawn her to him in the first place. Why she had the sudden desperate need to help him.

And when she touched him…yes, she definitely recalled the zing of something singing through her veins. Pulsing into her. She thought it odd at the time but dismissed it as her own over-active, sex-starved imagination. Now to find out it meant something…it *was* something…she didn't know how to react. What to think. What to feel.

"B-but I thought you were attracted to me."

"I am." He pulled her into his arms, holding her closely and tightly as his serious gaze bored into her. He wasn't jesting with her. "So are you."

She blinked disbelief and shivered. Her body turned rigid. There was something more he wasn't telling her. Something more he knew between them but she didn't know the question to ask to get the answer she sought.

"It goes beyond mere attraction," he said. "It's on a deeper subconscious level. We are attracted to each other, yes, but because there is that connection, it is…intensified."

"Oh."

She breathed the word as understanding flooded through her. Or at least she thought she understood. He'd picked her as his mate and she unwittingly picked him. At least that explained why she wanted to melt into a puddle of goo every time he was near.

"Do you understand now?"

She nodded. "I think so. So…what do we do about it?"

A smile pulled at the corner of his mouth. "What do humans do when they are attracted to each other?"

Her knees weakened at the suggestive tone of his voice. If he hadn't been holding her, she would have sunk to the ground. Was he insinuating they…yes, of course, he was. Was she prepared for that? She didn't know. And yet a curious swooping pulled at her innards. She could no longer deny the spark between them.

He turned serious then. "Bree, I want you to know you have a choice in this. If you say no, then I release you and walk away."

"And if I say yes?" she asked, testing the waters.

"Then we are bound as mates." He lifted a tendril of hair, wound it around his finger. "Do you approve of that?"

Did she approve of being bound to a hot, sexy dragon for the rest of her life? Hell, yeah. She didn't grasp what that meant, but at the moment, she was driven by the intensity of her emotions. Everything else was details. Even so, the heated flush rose to her cheeks.

"Yes."

Pleased with her response, Logan released her and his shirt came off once again, dropping to the floor. It made her heart race to an incalculable speed. She went with her first instinct. Her palms landed on his chest, curving over his pectorals covered in a smattering of dark hair.

"Go ahead."

She knew it was an invitation to touch and feel every inch of his naked torso. Part of her mind shouted to stop—because she knew the more she touched, the more she would crave. One touch wouldn't be enough. She would need more.

She'd worry about that later.

Bree's nerves were a jumbled mess as her hands moved over the hard planes on his chest, to his shoulders, and down to his forearms. Logan was solid muscle. There was nothing soft and pliable about him. All the while, his intense gaze remained on hers. The heat pulsed from his body and through hers, making her lightheaded.

"There. Was that so hard?" he said when she stopped exploring. His arms wrapped around her waist.

It *was* hard. Every inch of him was hard. Slick heat erupted between her legs and she knew there was only one thing in the world that would make that ache go away.

Her pulse flickered in her throat. Only moments ago, his body heat was nothing more than warmth. Now it had ignited and surged through her. She wasn't sure if that was due to his skin turning hotter or her hormones working overtime or a combination of both.

His arms loosened around her. She tightened her grip. "Don't."

He stilled. She wasn't certain what she meant by don't. Only that she didn't want him to let her go. Not yet. She wanted him to continue to hold her so she could feel the heat of his skin penetrating her. It did all sorts of things to her and if looks could melt the clothes off her body, his would.

Logan skimmed his fingertips along her jaw. The light touch sent her senses reeling. Heated pinpricks erupted all over her skin as her heart sang with delight. His steady gaze bore into her as she tried to decide how to respond. She didn't know if she could accept his caress for what it was or if there was some deeper meaning behind it. She *wanted* there to be deeper meaning.

"Don't what?" He practically purred the words.

A lump of emotion clotted her throat and it was difficult to push out the words but she managed. "Don't let go of me. Not yet."

A sensual flame ignited in his eyes and the beast beneath the cool façade threatened to erupt and claw its way out. The galvanizing look sent a shiver of longing through her and she bit her lip to stifle the cry of delight that wanted to erupt.

"Why do you do that?"

"Do what?"

"Bite your lip like that."

She hadn't realized she did it until he pointed it out. "I don't know. Habit?"

His fist tangled in her hair and pulled her head back. "It drives me crazy."

But before she could respond his mouth landed on hers in a

fiery kiss that was far from gentle.

Their mouths fused together in a demanding sensual kiss that stole her breath and made her want to be with him forever. His mouth left hers but he didn't break contact entirely. He held her quivering body against his, trailing kisses down her throat as he pulled her head back and paused on the pulse in her neck. It beat there at an uncontrollable rate and breath shuddered in and out of her while she gripped him, her fingernails digging into his shoulders.

It unhinged her when the tip of his tongue touched that bright pulse. A shuddering mewl escaped her and for a moment she went limp in his arms. He tightened his grip and kept her upright while he nuzzled her neck under her earlobe, savoring her.

Bree's head spun. She knew what he wanted because she wanted it, too. It was hard to resist his seduction with the way he spoke to her in that deep fluid voice of his. And the way he held her so tightly in his arms and kissed her as if she were the last woman he would ever kiss.

She couldn't resist. She wouldn't.

His hand slid up to tangle in her hair as he cupped the back of her head. He slanted his mouth over hers and took another kiss from her, stealing more and more of her heart with each one. His tongue dipped into her mouth, tasting her again. Even though it wasn't the first time, he kissed her as though it was and it made her heart hammer, threatening to pump out of her chest.

She couldn't explain why it seemed as though each kiss was more intense than the last. She attuned her thoughts only to what was ahead. Being so close to him, to his heat, made her alight with fire. She suspected it also had to do with her own emotional reaction. Her body pulsed with yearning and she didn't deny she was acutely aware heat prickling her skin, making it aflame with a long-harbored need and desire.

He backed her toward the solid wall next to the windows, pushing her against it. She obeyed his silent order as he kissed her, never breaking contact with her mouth.

God, the man could kiss.

It was better than anything she had ever imagined. She was convinced he was born to kiss her and when they did there was something almost divine about it.

When he broke from her it was as though a part of her was missing. Even though his lips had left hers, his body still maintained in contact. He reached for her wrists, taking both in one powerful hand and pushing her arms up and over her head, pinning them against the wall. She could see the intensity of emotion burning deeply within his eyes and, like before, she could see he wrestled with the feral beast within him.

Was it difficult for him to maintain control? She'd seen it once before. She thought she should be intimidated by that but she wasn't. She could never be afraid of Logan.

She shoved all thoughts away when his free hand landed on her thigh and moved at an unhurried pace upward to her hip. The man was going to kill her. All she wanted him to do was take her to bed. Instead he insisted on playing with her.

"I intend to take my time," he said.

It was again as if he could read her thoughts. She would have to figure out a way to keep them closed off and silent. She'd spent her life trying to keep from wearing her emotions on her sleeve, to hide her deepest thoughts and it was as though Logan could read her as easily as flipping open the cover of a book.

"I want to savor you. Cherish you. Honor you."

A whimper escaped through her lips. Oh, God, he *was* going to kill her.

His fingertips fluttered over the button at the waistband of her jeans. She did a quick mental calculation of the state of her underwear. When she'd dressed earlier she had never expected the day would end up with a long slow seduction.

Logan's head dipped and his hot mouth landed at the hollow of her neck. He licked her there once, twice, three times. She couldn't stop the gasp of delight that escaped her. All the while his fingers made progress as he popped open the button and the slid down the zipper. His hand moved into the waistband of her panties and then underneath the cotton.

Bree lost all reason. All coherent though fled her brain. All she could do was feel. Her emotions were raw and ragged. When his fingers slid into her damp curls, her mind seized.

Could this be happening? Was she dreaming? If she was, she didn't want to ever wake because this was the nearest to heaven she would ever get. The nearest to Logan. His fingers stroked her with a gentle touch that made her unravel at the seams. She thought she could hold herself together long enough to know what was happening but she found she was beyond all thinking capacity.

His chest rumbled with what could only be described as a purr. It sounded like liquid heat as it poured over her while his hand did magical things to her. She was pliant in his arms. The only reason she remained on her feet was he held her against the wall. For if he didn't, she knew she would have melted onto the floor.

"You're so soft." When he spoke, his heated breath singed the delicate skin at the base of her throat.

Her nipples turned to rigid peaks, pushing against the material of her bra, chafing her. It didn't seem fair he brushed against her, shirtless, while she had to remain dressed. She wanted to feel his skin against hers. She wanted to skip the foreplay and get to the good stuff.

She'd touch him only he still had her wrists in a vise-like grip over her head.

Likely part of his evil plan.

Bree pushed her hips against his hand and tried to scoot her legs farther apart, but the denim negated that and kept her in place. She whimpered again, wanting to open more to him.

Her clothes had started to irritate her as impatience set in. All she wanted was to be naked.

"I want you naked, too."

Her eyes flew open. There. She'd caught him. He *had* heard her thoughts. "How did you know that?"

"You think too loud, Bree."

She could hear the smile in his voice. He released her wrists but before she could reciprocate any of his affection, he dropped to his knees and pulled her jeans and panties down in one sweeping motion. She complied with his silent request and stepped out of them.

Logan rose to his full height, his hands a sweeping motion up her body as he shoved her T-shirt over her head. He discarded it on the floor. All that remained was her bra.

When she started to reach behind her, he said, "Let me."

She dropped her hands as he moved closer, enveloping her in his heat. He unclasped her bra with one hand in a swift, deft move. She shrugged out of it and dropped it next to the rest of her clothes. Her breasts were dark pink peaks desperate for his touch. He braced his hands on the wall on either side of her head and met her gaze. His gold-brown eyes bored into her, and for a moment, she thought he could see right to her depths.

It seemed she, too, could see to the depths of his soul where the dragon remained. The red scales, fiery breath, *whump* of leathery wings. She should have been frightened, perhaps, but instead she was fascinated.

He blinked then the image was gone. He had never done that before. It was the most intense thing she had ever seen. For a moment, he stiffened, the air tense and blistering between them.

Was it a test to see if she would run screaming from the room? If it was, had she passed?

"I think you're overdressed for the situation," she said, trying to lighten the mood.

Without brushing against her, his mouth took hers in a hot kiss.

"For now." He practically growled the words.

He pushed her against the wall, dropped to his knees and put her leg over his shoulder. The moment his mouth touched her damp center, she lost her head.

❧ 10 ❧

Logan had never experienced anything quite so powerful. He'd looked into her eyes and shown her his true form by projecting the image into her head. She didn't shy away from him or so much as blink. Instead she'd cracked a joke. When he kissed her, he cemented in his mind the way he felt about her.

She was unafraid of who he was and what he could do to her. The gooseflesh that erupted over her was not from horror but anticipation. He could read that about her without even listening to her thoughts. He had attuned himself so well to her, he could hear the whoosh of blood through her veins, the palpitation of her pulse, her ragged breathing. Even if he hadn't touched her, he could smell the arousal emanating off her in passionate waves.

He had never wanted a woman more than he wanted Bree. He dropped to his knees and tasted her. The moment his tongue slipped into her damp core, her hands fisted in his hair and she cried out with sweet delight.

She was nothing like what he expected or imagined, though now that he had her naked and pliant, he was no longer sure of those expectations. They had been exceeded. She was far more beautiful than his fertile imagination had conjured. When he tasted her, her body was like delectable nectar on which he was sure he could get drunk.

Bree cried out with pleasure. He could hear her hammering heart. Her muscles contracted and he knew she was on the edge of coming. He urged her on with more languid strokes, taking his time to savor her as he promised he would do. The orgasm overtook her and her body quivered with release as she cried out again. Her voice reverberated through the room. When he released her, she melted to his level, as though all her bones had turned into water and she no longer possessed the strength to hold her body upright. Her breathing was labored, her upper body coated in a sheen of sweat.

He had time to notice all that before she shoved him to his back and climbed on top of him.

Bree straddled his waist, on her knees as she gazed down at him with those hooded eyes full of desire.

"My turn." Her voice was husky as she said it.

She got busy unbuckling his belt but he could see her fingers shaking. From nerves or lust, he wasn't sure which and it didn't really matter. Logan caught her hands, stilled them, then gave them a gentle nudge out of the way. He finished unbuttoning his pants, his gaze never leaving her lovely face still flushed from her recent climax. He lifted his hips enough to slide down his pants to free his erection.

"Oh." Her eyes widened as the gasp escaped her and her hand immediately wrapped around his length.

"Does that mean you approve?" He was unable to resist the tease.

Bree's lashes fluttered as she met his gaze, her cheeks coloring and then a slow smile curved the corners of her mouth. "I'll let you know."

He would have chuckled had she not bent and taken him in her mouth. His body vibrated when her lips wrapped around him and she took her time with him, doing to him what he did to her. But unlike her, he wouldn't allow release. He wanted to save that for when he was inside her.

Logan swept her long hair out of her face so he could watch the way she slid him in and out of her mouth. Her tongue flicked over his dampened tip, down his length and up again. He couldn't stop his hands from tangling in her hair, fisting the long locks. He had never expected it to be so good with her.

But then, he didn't know what to expect at all.

When he was close to the brink, he pulled her away, cupped her chin and brought her face to his. They kissed, long, slow, and sweet. She braced herself over him, her nipples brushing his chest and driving him mad. Their tongues tangled, each one fighting for control from the other. When they broke, her lips still brushed his.

"Yes, I approve."

Again, he would have chuckled if she hadn't wrapped her hand around his erection and then positioned herself over him. He knew what she meant to do and he was powerless to stop her. He didn't want to stop her. He urged her on by gripping her hips, his fingers digging into her tender flesh. He liked her take charge attitude. Liked it even more when she slid him home inside her.

Bree stilled as she gazed down at him, biting her bottom lip. Her pulse battered the skin in the long column of her throat. Her nipples were hard pink nubs as she remained, motionless, her labored breathing shallow. Her gaze flickered over his naked torso, her hands on his chest, roaming through the sprinkling of dark hair as she outlined the muscles. Was that question in her eyes? Regret? Or something else?

"What is it?" He didn't want to ask, but he had to know.

A heartbeat of silence passed before she said, "Nothing," and then began the slow rocking of her hips.

Bree was not prepared for the way he felt inside her. Nor did she think she would ever get to this point with Logan. She'd had plenty of wild fantasies about bedding him and none played out like this. None ended with them fucking on the floor of his apartment like wild animals.

But wild is what she felt. Wild and free and reckless. She'd lost all reason the moment he went on his knees and slid his tongue against her wet core. She'd tried to keep her orgasm from coming, but her body would no longer obey her mind's request. He'd shattered her control. As her body contracted, needing more than just that release, she knew what she had to do.

Bree didn't want to waste this chance with Logan, so she intended to make the most of it. She slid down the wall, intending to return the favor when suddenly her hands wouldn't stop shaking. As if she was a teenager again and this was her first time.

But it was her first time—her first time with Logan. And she would never get a do over with him. Maybe she should have wanted a magical, perfect evening with him carrying her off to bed. It hadn't worked out like that and she was too impatient to wait.

When he nudged her shaking fingers out of the way—and she tried not to let that embarrass her—she watched with rapt fascination as he removed his pants. The sight of his long, hard length made her mouth go bone dry. And yet at the same time, she couldn't stop from wrapping her hand around him.

If his body was warm to the touch before, he was positively on fire now. Every pore pulsed heat, radiating over her. She was aware of the sweat glistening on her naked skin more than she cared to notice. She was also aware of the dampness on the tip of his erection. And when she slipped him into her mouth, it turned her on even more. Damp heat erupted between her legs and it took all her self-control to keep her hands on him.

Bree hadn't meant to crack jokes. That was not the way she wanted their lovemaking to go. But she found it kept her from being so damn nervous and turning into one of those girls who didn't initiate any kind of sex. She didn't want to be the rigid, unmoving girl who laid still and let him fuck her. She wanted to be the girl who understood how great sex could be with someone you liked.

And she liked Logan a lot.

When he'd stopped her from sucking him, she understood why. But she had never expected him to kiss her like that. As though his mouth made love to hers. Her emotions were raw enough; she didn't need him making this more difficult. That's when she'd made up her mind she wasn't letting him on top of her. She was going to take charge. She was going to be the one in control.

It had taken her off guard when she slipped him inside her. He felt so good, so big, so hot, so perfect. God. So everything. She was with him, sitting naked atop him and touching his rock-hard body while he gazed up at her with adoration in his eyes.

It shook her to the core and rattled all her senses.

When he asked her what was wrong, she almost burst into tears. What was wrong? Nothing. Everything was right. He was perfection and she was with him. She bit her lip harder and lied and told him nothing and then made her first move. It was the only thing she could do to keep from bursting into tears. Tears of joy.

She rocked her hips against his, relishing the jab of his hip bones in her thighs as she pushed him deeper and deeper inside her. His fingers dug into her hips as he held her tightly, helping her move. She didn't argue. She let him move her however he wanted. It only served to turn her on even more. She straightened her spine, arched her back and rode him hard and fast. He groaned his approval, his hands never leaving her hips.

The orgasm took her by surprise and she cried out as it shattered through her. She'd lost her control as her muscles turned to jelly and she fell forward against him. He wrapped his arms around her, held her as he rolled her to her back, readjusted and then pounded into her again.

He hiked one leg, knee bent, to her chest as he plunged deeply inside her. She cried out when the pleasure-pain erupted over her. Her first orgasm had gone but a second one was building. She wasn't sure how much she could take as her nails dug into his back and he merely growled with approval while pounding her against the floor.

And she never wanted it to end.

Their mouths collided with fervor and feral need as they clung to each other while he thrust inside her with such a fury she thought her body might break. Her nails clawed down his back. He bit her bottom lip. She bit his back.

And then the orgasm hit her again. She broke from him and

turned her head, crying out with her pleasure as Logan arched back away from her, groaned and pushed inside her once, twice, three more times. The heat exploded over her, through her, inside her, creating a wild pulsing of light behind her closed eyes as he came inside her.

For a moment, if felt as though she stood inside an inferno, as if the entire building around them was on fire. But she knew that wasn't the case. She cracked an eye open and watched as he came. A vein on the side of his neck bulged. His skin turned red and glistened with perspiration.

Everything stilled. Her heart rammed hard against her chest as he tipped his head down and gazed at her with a look she couldn't read. His eyes had clouded over. His face calmed. He looked sated. Almost drunk. She could no longer see the beast within him, as though it had been calmed or tamed. She had never seen him look like that before.

Logan kissed her forehead before rolling off her, landing on the floor next to her. She couldn't move even if she wanted. Her muscles were weak and she'd swear every bone in her body had melted, fused together into one conglomeration to make her nothing more the one big pile of skin.

Should she say something? Tell him it was the best sex she'd ever had? She dismissed that as sounding cliché. The last thing she wanted to tell him was something ridiculous like that even if it was true. He had likely heard that before from other women.

Logan reached out to her. His hand stroked her abdomen, a hip bone, over her thigh and back up again.

She was still there. It had happened. It was more than anything she could have ever imagined. And she didn't know if she would ever experience it again.

He rose to a sitting position and realized he still wore his pants on the lower half of his body. He kicked off his pants, discarding them with the rest of their clothes before getting to his feet. He padded, naked, into the kitchen. Bree didn't want to look but she couldn't help but steal a peek at his fabulous backside. His ass was as great as the rest of him.

She heard him pouring one drink, two, and then returning to where she had taken up permanent residence on the floor. He sat next to her, still not talking, and handed her the whiskey. As she took it, she watched him down the entire glass in one gulp.

Had she been that bad?

"Bree." Her name rolled of his tongue in a dreamy sort of way.

"Yes?" The word hissed out of her on a whisper. She didn't expect a profession of love but she had no idea what he intended to say next.

He turned his head to look down at her, his appreciative gaze raking over her naked body. "I'm sorry we didn't make it to the bedroom."

"I'm not sorry."

She hadn't intended to say it but her brain-to-mouth filter wasn't quite working. Maybe he had fried some of her synapses during that whole episode. Not that she'd complain.

He turned to face her, leaning on one elbow and brushing hair from her face. "You deserve better than a romp on the floor."

Oh, God. Was he trying to kill her? Her fingers tightened around the glass. She propped up on one elbow and downed the amber liquid. She put the glass on the carpet between them.

"I don't recall complaining."

One corner lifted in a half smile. "No, you didn't." He tucked a lock of hair behind her ear. "Perhaps I could make it up to you."

Heat flashed over her body. When moments ago, she thought she could never be aroused again, here she was ready for him.

She dragged a finger down the center of his chest. "Perhaps you could."

Logan rose and held a hand to help her up. She took his hand and let him pull her up. It was nothing short of a miracle to get back on her feet. Her muscles screamed and she wobbled. He caught her, pulled her into his arms and before she could protest, swept her up and headed for the bedroom.

It wasn't only her muscles that were burning. She had burning questions, too.

"Logan, what happens in the morning?"

"How about we worry about that in the morning," he suggested.

Because she was a woman of absolutes and needed a plan, she worried about it now. She'd always had a plan. She'd never planned for the aftermath. Only the buildup. She had no idea how she would feel afterward, and until the moment arrived, she still wouldn't know.

She was unprepared for getting naked with the man. But she let go of the worry and the questions when he kicked the bedroom door closed and led her to the bed.

As he lowered her to the coverlet, she resolved to forget about tomorrow or the next day or anything else. All she would think about was being in the moment with Logan, being in his arms and letting him love her.

◈ 11 ◈

Bree was aware of the morning light pushing against her closed eyelids, but she was loathed to open them, lest it break the spell she was under. She was still cradled against Logan in his arms as the sun streamed through the windows of the bedroom.

His bedroom.

He was like a portable heater. His body was so warm and comfortable, she didn't even need the coverlet he'd thrown over them sometime during the night. After he'd taken her to the bedroom, he'd made love to her more ways than she could count. Her body was sore in places she didn't know could be sore. They went from wild, reckless, pounding sex to sweet, calm, loving sex. She'd experienced every gamut of the spectrum with him and she had relished in it. She let him mold her in all kinds of positions, making her body bend in ways she didn't think possible.

Now she blinked her eyes open, still listening to his soft snoring, wondering how the morning would play out. Replaying the last events through her mind sent her reeling. Her eyes fluttered closed as she tried to figure out how to feel, what to think. They'd been chased, shot at and almost killed. He'd confessed to her she was part of him now and he was part of her. In a way, she could feel him rustling around there in her mind and it made her remember something.

She'd distinctly heard his voice in her head. He had not explained that little nugget of info in his confessional of all things Logan.

She sighed.

Sooner or later they were going to have to get out of the bed. It may as well be sooner. Bree wiggled free from his arms and slid to the edge, pulling the sheet with her and wrapping it around her. Not that he hadn't seen, touched, or tasted the goods. She still possessed a modicum of modesty. He stirred, rolled to his back and blinked his eyes open.

"Good morning."

She glanced at the clock and saw it was only half past seven. She raked a hand through her tangled hair, trying not to remember the way he'd fisted it the night before, dragged her head back, and ravished her neck, her earlobe, and everywhere in between.

What was going to happen now? How long were they going to stay holed up in this place?

He placed a hand on her back and she flinched though she didn't know why. She slid off the bed, taking the sheet with her and uncovering his long, lean naked form. She tried not to look but couldn't help it. She looked.

There was something sexy and sensual about the way he reclined in the bed, one hand tucked behind his head as he looked her over. His body was all rock-hard lines and sharp angles with velvety flesh in between and a smattering of hair in all the right places. She hated the phrase "rippling abs" but there was no other way to describe what those abs did. He had that V leading down to the place she liked to call the happy place.

He was way too hot for her. She wasn't the kind of girl who attracted the good-looking alpha male. She often thought she was too pudgy, sometimes too brainy, and other times too independent for the guys she dated but none were as full-on sex god as Logan. She had managed to attach herself to him and there didn't seem to be any going back to what she was before.

Was she good enough for him? She was human, not dragon. How did that work? Their species were compatible enough to have hot sexy times but that didn't mean they could actually procreate.

She flushed hot, remembering how she hadn't even thought about using a condom or any other protection. What the hell was she thinking? In any other situation, she would so not be with a guy without some type of contraceptive. Yet Logan made her lose her head.

"You all right?" He was unaware of her internal berating.

"I'm going to take a shower."

She had to get away from him. She had to think because if she ended up pregnant—if she could even get pregnant with him—then she had to figure out what was going to happen next. She'd been an idiot. Worse than a teenage girl on her first time.

With a huff, she padded to the bathroom and shut the door, dropping the sheet in a puddle of cotton on the floor. She started the water, let it get scorching hot until it steamed up the bathroom, and then leaned against the counter.

Lost. She felt lost and alone even though he said she wasn't. Sure, it was nice to be "connected" to Logan but he wasn't the kind of guy she could talk to about how she was feeling. She had responsibilities at the bar. She had to find out where her father's body had been taken. She had to arrange a funeral. What about Bear? And Meg? And the rest of the staff?

The door flew open, startling her. He entered without asking, his big body filling the entire space around them, stealing away what oxygen remained. He looked down at her with those dragon eyes puncturing through her.

She spun to face him. Snatching the sheet fleeted through her mind.

"Don't. I've seen you naked."

His brazen gaze raked right over her from head to toe and everything in between. She stumbled backward toward the shower but he caught her in his arms, pulled her to him.

"I told you before, Bree. You aren't alone."

Anger flared inside her. She shoved him but it did nothing. He held her fast.

"How do you know that's what I was thinking?" Her velvet-edged voice was demanding.

His jaw set with his refusal to answer.

"Tell me, Logan! I heard your voice once before in my head. I thought I had imagined it. Did I?"

She pushed against him, desperate to be free of his vise-like grip around her. He wasn't letting go.

"No." His voice was flat, unfeeling.

She searched his gaze, looking for some hint of information. There was none. "Why? How?"

"I told you why."

"You've told me nothing." She shoved him again. She might've as well as shoved a brick wall for all the good it did.

"I've told you what you needed to know."

"That we share a connection. That we're attracted to each other because of that connection. Blah, blah, blah. That doesn't mean anything! It only means you managed to get my panties off."

God, what was she saying? She wanted him to get her panties off. She'd been thinking of that since the first moment she met him and even more so when he showed up in the bar as their new security officer. She hadn't stopped thinking about him from the moment his big hands landed on her waist when she tried to heal him that first day to their first kiss when his mouth crushed against hers in a passionate fervor.

Everything they did together flared through her mind in a wild rapid flash of naughty memory. The way she tasted—salty and sweet. The way she smelled—like wild strawberries. The way she made him feel as though he had come home when he sank inside her. Pushing into her. Sliding out of her. Pushing into her again. Hands on her breasts. Mouth sucking her nipples.

It wasn't her memory.

It was his.

"Stop it! Stop it! Just stop!"

She shoved at him again. He pushed her backward toward the shower despite her best efforts. It was useless. He was much bigger, much stronger. Her body crushed into him, her breasts nothing but two soft mounds against his sculpted hard chest. And even though she didn't want, she couldn't help but notice his sudden erection.

"You saw that, did you."

Saw it. Felt it. Made the warm slick heat erupt between her legs. An involuntary response she could not stop even if she tried.

It wasn't a question. She knew it wasn't but answered it like it was.

"That was your memory. Not mine." There was a trace of accusation in her tone.

"You're a fast study."

He nuzzled her neck as he pushed her into the spray, against the cold tile wall. She sucked in a sharp breath as he nudged her feet apart. One hand landed between her legs, fingers sliding into her crease and worked over the dampness there. A delighted moan erupted from her and she tried hard to still be mad at him. She forgot why she was mad.

"You unhinge me, Bree." His voice shook as he whispered it.

And that unhinged her.

Her hands fisted in his damp hair as she turned her mouth to his. While water splashed over them, their mouths collided. His tongue dueling with hers for dominance and winning. She was such a weakling when it came to him. She would let him do whatever he wanted to her whenever he wanted and she loved it. She wanted more. She needed more. She craved more.

"Bree."

He groaned her name as he buried his face in her neck and slid two fingers inside her. She bucked against his hand, wanting more and more and more as he pumped in and out of her faster and faster and faster. The orgasm shuddered through her before she could stop it and she cried out, still clutching his hair while he nipped her neck.

His hand stilled, his fingers inside her as he continued to lick and kiss her neck. His thumb flicked over her swollen clit. His warm breath mingled with the warm water on her skin.

"Damn you, Logan. Why are you in my head?"

"Because you want me there." He kissed his way up to her

earlobe, sucked it into his mouth and nipped it. "Because you need me there." Hot breath trickled into her ear.

It was more than that and she knew it but she was so discombobulated she didn't know how to ask the question. The hot water and the hot guy holding onto her made her weak in the knees and dizzy. When he removed his hand, every bone turned to jelly and she went limp. She sagged against him.

Logan reached over and cut the water, then scooped her into his arms and marched from the bathroom. They both dripped all over the carpet. He didn't seem to care one iota.

He lowered her to the bed. Rather than join her, he tucked the comforter around her.

"I'm getting the bed all wet." Her words were muffled by her yawn.

"Doesn't matter. You rest. I'm going to find some food."

Her stomach rumbled in response.

She heard him pad away—still naked—from the bedroom. A moment later the banging of pots and pans came from the kitchen followed by the smell of bacon.

He could cook?

She knew the sex and the cooking was his way of distracting her from her original question. He wasn't going to tell her that easily. She couldn't figure out why.

If he was in her head, was it plausible she could be in his? When the vamps attacked, she remembered shouting to him in her mind to get up off the floor. He had. Had he heard her? Could she repeat that again?

Her eyes fluttered closed and she reached out to him, wondering if she could touch his mind the way he'd touched hers. The sensations she felt when he touched her mind and reminded her of their night together flooded through her, but this time it was her memory not his. How he made her feel sexy and sensual and as though she were the only woman on the planet he wanted to be with. How he kissed his way down her body and licked that swollen nub between her legs. How the hard planes of his body raked against hers when he pumped inside her. And damn if she didn't get aroused again.

A plate crashed to the floor, shattering and startling her. She bolted upright as he appeared in the doorway holding a dish towel and looking at her with fierce surprise on his face. She could read nothing beyond that.

"What did you do?"

"N-nothing."

He flung the towel over his shoulder, standing there in all his naked glory looking at her as though he didn't believe her.

"It was not nothing."

She swallowed and tired hard to keep her eyes on his face. It was difficult when his cock was half mast and ready to go again.

"What do you…think I did?"

He clenched his jaw tightly, the muscles flexing. He did that often when he was angry or agitated. She could sense the latter coming off him now.

"It would be helpful if you put some clothes on because that," she waggled her finger at his naked form, "is distracting."

Logan ignored her request, turned on his heel and went back into the kitchen. He returned a moment later with a plate full of bacon and eggs. He sat on the edge of the bed picked up a piece of bacon and offered it to her.

She took a bite. The strip was cooked to perfection just the way she liked it.

"What are you doing to me?" she asked around a mouthful.

He scooped scrambled eggs onto a fork. "I told you. You chose me."

"That doesn't tell me anything." He extended the fork to her and she took another bite.

She watched with rapt interest as he ate eggs and a few slices of bacon in one or two bites.

"Logan."

"Bree, what I've told you is enough." He held up another piece of bacon for her. She shook her head.

"Why can I hear you in my head?" When he still didn't answer, she clamped her hand around his wrist and pushed away the plate with remnants of breakfast. "Logan, please."

I can mindspeak to you.

She blinked when she heard his voice in her head. "I...don't understand."

Talk to me, Bree. Not with your mouth. With your mind.

She bit her lip and searched his face as if the answer would be there. She couldn't mask her confusion as she frowned.

"I can't do that."

Yes, you can.

She shook her head, about to protest again when he placed two fingers over her lips.

You can.

A fluttering erupted in her stomach as she met his gaze. *All right.*

It was the first time she'd seen his serious face break into a full smile.

There. I knew you could do it.

"How is this possible?" she demanded. "I don't understand how you can hear me and I can hear you in my mind."

He set the plate aside. His hands lifted to her face as he cupped it, kissed her nose. "It's the effects of *ka kladou.*"

Bree's heart skipped in her chest. "What happens now?"

"Now? We enjoy it. Both of us." His lips brushed over hers.

"Logan?"

"Yes?"

"Could you please put on some pants? It's...very distracting."

He chuckled as he rose from the bed. As he rummaged through a bureau drawer she got a glimpse of the velvet pouch of stones they'd found in her apartment. He must have stashed them there for safekeeping. He found a pair of khaki cargo pants. He held them against his frame as if checking the size and then slipped them on. She leaned back in the pillows, a little relieved and disappointed he'd covered up that spectacular backside.

She glanced around the place again and thought how sterile is seemed. She also recalled how he didn't know where the car was parked in the garage. Her brows drew together in question and she thought she understood a little bit more.

"This isn't your apartment, is it?"

He stilled and gave her a cursory glance before going back to digging through the drawer for a shirt. "No."

The confused cobwebs started to clear. "Whose is it, then?"

"Rafe's. I needed a place to crash. He offered it to me."

He had no place to live? Could it be then that morning she found in him the park was when he had just arrived? She started to ask why when there was a thump at the front door made them both take notice. She sat straight, peering toward the open bedroom door and clutching the blanket to her naked chest.

"Get dressed," he said, his voice low.

She flung off the comforter and rummaged through her bag, looking for clean underwear. Logan disappeared into the walk-in closet while she finished dressing. When he emerged, a few minutes later, he had a handgun tucked into the waistband of his pants, a knife stuck in one pocket and carried two rifles.

He was a guy who was well-prepared. Or Rafe was.

"What is it?"

"I don't know. Stay here."

He disappeared out of the bedroom while she pulled on her shoes. She stood in the middle of the room, straining her ears to listen. It sounded like the front door opened and then a man's voice. Logan sounded as though he weren't in any imminent danger so she poked her head out of the room

Logan lowered his weapon and visibly relaxed. "Rafe, you could have warned me you were coming. You could've got your head shot off."

"I've come from a meeting with Dominic," he said. "You need to get the girl and get out."

That sounded serious to her. She stepped into the living area. "What's going on? Who's Dominic?"

"He's the mafia boss your father owes fifty thousand dollars to." Rafe was matter-of-fact with his response.

She stared at him as though he'd grown a second head. "He owes them how much?"

"Fifty grand. He was stealing from them," Rafe said. "Skimming money off the top of their agreed upon ten percent."

She didn't understand. "Ten percent of what? And why would they be paying my father in the first place?"

Logan and Rafe exchanged a look she couldn't read. She tried to touch his mind but was met with forceful resistance. He could read hers whenever he wanted, but she couldn't get into his? That didn't seem fair.

She huffed out a breath. "What?"

Logan turned toward her. "Bree, this may be difficult for you to hear, but I caught your father selling synthetic blood to another vampire. Apparently, he agreed to be a distributor for the mafia boss. They used the bar as a front to sell their black-market blood."

Cold dread trickled over her. She knew something was wrong but she had never expected that. She didn't want to believe him but she knew Logan would have no reason to lie. Her father would never be involved in something like that. Would he?

But then he had been acting strangely for the last several months. He refused to allow her to help with the financial aspect of running the bar, telling her he had everything under control. Telling her not to worry.

"You…caught him?" He detected a faint tremor in her voice.

He nodded. "He admitted it to me."

Her stomach cramped as a wave of nausea passed through her. She clutched her abdomen. "Why?"

"I don't know and it doesn't matter anymore. He may be willing to forgive the debt but he's not willing to forgive Logan taking Mario's life." Rafe glanced between the two of them as he spoke, his tone calm and measured.

Logan raked a hand through his hair, his annoyance evident. "So, he comes after me now?"

"You could say that. Niko had intended to make Mario his blood slave. You robbed him of that. And now he wants someone to take his place."

"You mean he wasn't trying to kill my father?" Her gaze swung to Logan. He didn't hide the look of guilt that washed over his face. "He would have lived?"

"Lived, yes. But Mario would have provided an unlimited blood supply, not the synthetic stuff," Rafe said. "Eventually, he would have killed him."

Bile rose to her throat and she tried hard to swallow it. She couldn't imagine how horrible that would have been for Mario. Perhaps it was better he was dead. Likely Logan knew that, too. Gooseflesh erupted on her arms. If Niko wanted a replacement, then he must be thinking of her.

"Who does he want in his place? He can't have Bree."

"He wants you." Rafe's reply was cool and low.

Bree's eyes widened further as she looked between the two of them. "If I pay back the money will he let him go?"

"Do you have that much cash?" Rafe's deep-timbered voice held a hint of demand.

Instantly, she was deflated. "No."

Rafe turned his pointed stare back at Logan. "He was very clear on the fact that he wants a blood slave and he wants you because you're the one who robbed him of Mario."

"And you know why I can't turn myself over to him," Logan said.

"I do know and it's why you have to get out of the city."

"I'm not leaving. Not until things are…settled. Besides, if I leave they'll hunt me down," he said.

"Not if I have anything to say about it. There's something else. Dominic is dying. Niko will likely be the one to take over once he's gone. And he's not as…forgiving."

"If we can't stay here, then where are we supposed to go?" Bree asked.

"I have a house in East Hampton," Rafe said. "You can go

there."

"You're quite the self-made millionaire, aren't you?" A look of distaste passed over Logan's face. "I won't leave the city."

"Don't be a fool, Logan. You'll be nothing but a sitting duck here."

"For the vampires, sure. But the Drakana—" He clamped his mouth shut, as though he'd said too much.

Bree narrowed her gaze at him, questions rolling through her. There was more he wasn't telling her.

"You can't worry about that right now. Worry about the vampires. Here." He shoved the keys at him. "Just get out of here before it's too late."

Something crashed against the closed apartment door making it crack under the pressure of whatever was on the other side. Logan gave Rafe a straight-face that spoke volumes.

"It's too late."

Another crash against the door and this time it splintered. Fear sputtered through her as she glanced between the two men, each seeming to be rather calm. Logan handed Rafe one of the rifles.

"You have to go," Rafe said. "Both of you. Take the Beemer."

"That reminds me…there's something you should, uh, know about the car," Logan said. "The Drakana destroyed it."

Rafe cursed.

Another crash against the door. Bree kept her eyes trained on it and watched as it splintered again. She lost her patience.

"Can we talk about the car later?" Bree snapped.

"Right. Got another way out of here?" Logan asked.

"Only one way in or out," Rafe said. "I'm not Houdini."

"Then we'll have to fight," Logan said. "Bree, get to the bedroom."

"And do what? Hide out in there? No way. Give me a weapon. I can shoot a gun." She resented being relegated to damsel in distress. She was stronger than that. Even though she may be terrified, she wasn't going to stand by and do nothing. Not after what happened to her father when she had no choice.

"I have more guns," Rafe said just as another crack sounded against the door.

He disappeared down the hallway to the second bedroom and returned minutes later with an assault rifle, ammo and two more handguns.

"Do you have an armory back there?" Logan eyed the guns in his hands.

"I like to be prepared." Rafe handed her a 9mm. "You know how to use that?"

"Yeah," she said with a nod. "Years behind a bar, remember?"

"Fair enough." He turned toward the door. "Bring it on."

He and Logan may have been calm, but she wasn't. Maybe Logan was right and she should have tucked tail and run, hiding out in the bedroom. But would it have been safer there? If they got by Rafe and Logan, she'd be dead anyway.

She cocked the gun.

Another crack of the door and it was destroyed. Three men poured inside. They didn't smell like vampires, either. They smelled like Logan and Rafe which meant they had to be dragons like them. She didn't even get a shot off before the guys killed all three of them.

Silence.

Rafe stalked over and nudged one of the dead man's hands. She could see a starburst tattooed on the inside of his wrist.

"Drakana," Rafe said.

"That was too easy. He wouldn't have only sent three. Would he?" Logan asked.

"He would."

A tall man dressed in Armani stepped into the middle of the empty doorway, a wolfish grin on his face. His hands were jammed in the pockets of his pants making his buttoned suit jacket pucker at the bottom. The man's dark hair had silver at the temples and was long, hanging to his shoulders. He had piercing green eyes and his face was lined with deep-set wrinkles.

She knew he was also a dragon, because he exuded the same

scent as Logan and Rafe. What she didn't know was who he was to them.

"At last, we come face to face. How are you, my boy?" the man asked, the smile never leaving his face.

"I'm not your boy, Archer," Logan said through clenched teeth.

His gaze flickered to her. She clutched the gun tighter in her hand. "And you have a companion, I see."

Logan reached for her and nudged her behind him. She took a step sideways but kept the man in her line of sight.

He chuckled. "We have some catching up to do, you and me. You're a hard man to catch." His piercing gaze landed on Rafe then. "And keeping unsavory company, I see."

"What do you want?" Logan's tone was impatient.

"I want to talk." The oily smile never left his face.

"We have nothing to talk about."

"Oh, I assure you, we do. Zak told me about your lady friend." He removed his hands from his pockets.

A low growl rumbled deep in Logan's throat. His hands tightened around the gun until his knuckles turned white.

"Ah, so I've angered you. My apologies. Call off your dog and put down the guns so we can have a civilized conversation."

"The only thing I have to say is fuck off," Logan said.

He *tsked*. "That's not what I expected from you, my boy. Your father wouldn't approve."

Logan's hands clenched. "You aren't allowed to speak about my father. Ever."

"Of course, I am. We were great friends, your father and me. He was gracious and kind. Right up to the very end when I took his life."

Bree was aware of the beast rattling around inside Logan's head—she could hear it in her head too which frightened her. His hands hadn't relaxed on the gun and now a fine smoke curled upward. Rafe placed a hand on his shoulder and tugged the rifle away. When he'd pried it from Logan's hands, there were imprints where they'd been.

"Calm," Rafe said, his voice soothing.

Bree heard him take a deep breath, his mind a jumble of violent emotions. She got a flash of his dragon that desperately wanted out. All he wanted to do was shift and tear out the man's throat.

"But you know I took his life, don't you?" That wolfish grin was still plastered on Archer's face. "Because you were there."

Her gaze shifted from Archer to Logan and back again as she tried to put the pieces together. She felt like she was a voyeur seeing something very personal about Logan. He had told her nothing of his past or about this man, Archer. But she could tell he was bothered by the man's appearance. No wonder Logan was so upset—the man murdered his father. What did he want with Logan?

"Furthermore, you look as though you're about to burst at the seams. And we can't have that now, can we? There's no sense in scaring your human companion."

"Get to the fucking point." Logan's tone was clipped as he spoke through clenched teeth.

Archer sighed as though defeated. "Very well. I want you to return to the clan. It's time for you to take responsibility for your actions."

He glowered. "Responsibility for what actions?"

"You left the clan without permission. That's punishable by death."

Logan's fingers curled into a fist. "You expect me to return to the clan after what you did to me? To my family?"

Bree watched as the two of them stared at each other, eye to eye. Archer with his cool exterior and grimy smile. She could hear Logan's beast still raging inside his head, pushing at the seams of his skin, desperate to burst free. She wondered what would happen if he shifted here in the middle of the apartment and just what he was willing to do to Archer.

"Go ahead," Archer taunted. "Release your anger and hate. I see it behind your eyes. You want me dead. But know this. If you kill me, there are those who will come after you for vengeance.

Those who will stop at nothing to make sure you pay for my death."

"I would gladly pay for your death to avenge my parents," Logan said, his voice dangerous and low.

"Get out of here, Archer."

Rafe stepped between them, giving the man a shove toward the door. She wondered what had taken him so long to intervene. Archer took a step back out of the apartment, his feet crunching on the splintered wood from the broken door.

"Since I'm on your turf, I'll leave. But we're not finished." He punctuated the last with a glare at Logan.

Archer left, leaving behind the three dead men and a splintered broken door. Only when he was gone did Logan at last relax. She sensed the tension going out of him.

"Sorry about the door," Logan said.

"Don't worry about it. I own the building. I'll have the super come fix it." He flashed a grin. "Will you be going to the Hamptons now?"

"I'm not going anywhere with anyone until I get some answers." When Bree spoke, her voice was shakier than she would have liked.

They turned to her, both looking surprised as though she were still there. She stood ramrod straight, the gun still clamped in her hand. Rafe reached for her, pushed it down so it didn't point at either of them and then pried her hand off it.

"It's time you tell her everything, Logan. But maybe you do that before Niko and his gang show up?" Rafe suggested. "I'll let you two hash that out while I get someone to help me with the door."

He discretely slipped away.

Logan looked her over with an expression she couldn't read. Was he angry she was still there and had overheard everything? He hadn't been forthcoming with any information about his past. He reached for her, took her by the hand and pulled her to him.

"He's right. It's time I tell you everything."

ᨠ 12 ᨠ

Logan couldn't help but notice how Bree's hands shook when Rafe took the gun from her. She hadn't even had a chance to fire it. She didn't need to with both of them there but he admired that she wanted to be able to defend herself. As much as he needed her to understand his past, he wasn't sure she would.

She seemed to understand and even accept their fate, they were bonded to one another. Her body responded to him with a willing need that made it clear she wanted him. But it went beyond the bond they shared. He understood her. The attraction he'd felt for her went deeper much sooner than he was prepared to acknowledge—his feelings weren't just about protecting her.

"I have a car." When she spoke, she couldn't hide her shaky tone. "I could drive us."

He took her by the hand. His thumb caressed her knuckles. "I'll drive."

Not that he didn't trust her but he had to be the one to get them out of the city without any other altercations. They had two factions after them now—Archer wanted him dead and the vampires wanted him or Bree as a blood slave. Even though Rafe hadn't said it aloud, he mindspoke to Logan they would take either of them. They'd have to kill Logan to get to Bree. He would never allow the vamps to get their hands on her.

He'd also mindspoke the location of his house in East Hampton.

"And then you'll tell me everything?" she asked.

"Yes."

"All of it this time, Logan. I want to know everything."

He nodded. "Get your stuff. I'll wait here."

When she was gone, he raked a hand through his hair and blew out a breath. What sort of hell had he gotten himself—and her—into? Bree didn't deserve to be on the run with him but he couldn't leave her behind.

Rafe returned with the maintenance guy, barking orders and instructions on getting the door fixed.

"I thought you'd be gone by now," he said.

"She's getting her things. I'm taking the guns with me," he said.

"I suspected you would."

"I don't want you following us either," Logan added. "If Archer comes after me I intend to face him alone."

Rafe was shaking his head before he even finished. "I can't let you do that."

"You can and you will. This is my fight and mine only."

"What about the girl?"

"She'll be safe with me. There's something else. In your drawer under the T-shirts, there's a pouch of valuable stones." He glanced over his shoulder to make sure she was still in the other room and lowered his voice. "One of them is the Blood Stone."

Rafe stared at him with a mixture of horror and fascination. "Are you certain?"

"Yes. I could smell the blood of our ancients on it when I took it out of the bag."

"You didn't...touch it, did you?"

Rafe knew the lore as he did. Touching the stone without proper protection would attach the stone to the person holding it. In some ways, it acted like a leech in that it would drain the life force and magic from the one holding it. It had been part of their history for a long time but many dragons thought it had been lost. He couldn't figure out how Mario ended up with it or why he'd stashed it in Bree's apartment, but those were mysteries to be solved another day. Today he only worried about getting out of the city safely with Bree.

"No. I need you to keep it safe for me."

"How the hell did you get that?"

"Mario had it," Logan said. "She doesn't know what it is or how valuable it is to us. She'd never seen it before we found it."

"I'll make sure it's safe. What do you plan to do with it?"

"I plan to get it back to the Hidden Lands where it belongs after this whole thing with Archer is settled," Logan said.

Rafe nodded understanding. "All right. I'll lock it in my safe. Make sure no one can find it. Safe travels." This time he put the key in Logan's hand. "There should be plenty of food there for you both. I keep it well stocked."

Logan pocketed the key. "I owe you."

"I'll let you know when things cool down."

Bree entered the living room then carrying her bag. "I'm ready. Though I have to confess I feel sort of weird about leaving town without checking on the bar."

"It's shut down," Rafe said.

"What about the employees? I should tell them where I am."

"No," Logan said. "No one needs to know where you are. It's safer that way."

"But—"

"If it will make you feel better," Rafe said, "I'll check on the bar and let you know what's happening."

"Yes, please. Thank you." Bree smiled, looking relieved.

"You two better go before someone else shows up looking for you," Rafe said. He shooed them toward the door.

Logan nodded agreement and took Bree by the hand. They stepped around the debris and left the apartment behind. Neither spoke as they took the elevator down and then out of the building. It was a short cab ride to her place to pick up her car.

She handed him the keys. "Do you know where you're going?"

"Rafe gave me the address."

Her brow creased with question. "He did?"

Logan tapped the side of his head to indicate he had mindspoke to him. She nodded understanding as they got in the car. As he pulled out of the parking garage, he could hear the questions swirling in her head. He erected the mental wall to keep her thoughts out and to keep her out of his head. He liked her there but he could hear too much angst and worry from her and he had to do something to keep things quiet in his own mind. He had to think. To figure out what and how much to tell her.

Everything?

"When will we talk?" She fidgeted with the seatbelt, needing to do something with her hands.

"When we get there." He sounded gruffer than he intended.

"You expect me to wait that long?"

"Yes."

The finality of his tone must have let her know it wasn't up for debate. She lapsed into silence and stared out the window, her jaw set in a stubborn line. He didn't have to hear her thoughts to know she was agitated.

He'd make it up to her. As soon as they were alone and safe in East Hampton.

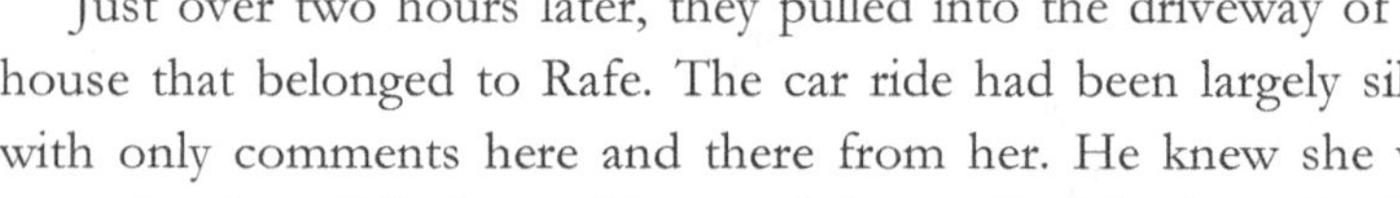

Just over two hours later, they pulled into the driveway of the house that belonged to Rafe. The car ride had been largely silent with only comments here and there from her. He knew she was upset but hopefully he could smooth her ruffled feathers. Both of them stared through the windshield at the house with the gables and wrap-around front porch. It looked like something off the pages of Better Homes & Gardens.

"He owns this?" He almost smiled at the wonder in her voice. "Yeah. Kinda shocked myself. He said it was a cottage."

He pushed open the car door and stepped out. Bree followed as he walked up the front steps. At the side of the house on the wraparound porch were two Adirondack chairs making it seem homey. He unlocked the door and swung it open just as her stomach rumbled loud enough for him to hear.

"Hungry?"

"Yes." When her stomach rumbled again with her reply, she pressed her hand against it.

"Rafe said the place was well stocked. Let's check it out."

He headed to the kitchen with her hot on his heels. She dumped her bag in the middle of the living room and stared at the large windows overlooking the private access to the beach.

"This is a cottage with beach access. Who the hell is this friend of yours?"

Logan glanced out the windows and tried hard not to be impressed. From what he knew about Rafe, he had been in the human realm a long time. Long enough to amass enough money to live comfortably for the rest of his dragon life. He liked nice things and nicer houses.

"What did you say he does for a living?" Bree asked.

She moved closer to the windows as he headed into the kitchen and started looking through the cabinets and then the fridge. He found all the ingredients he needed for Reuben sandwiches. His stomach rumbled at the idea of sinking his teeth into a pile of corned beef.

"I didn't say."

Because he didn't know. He never thought to ask.

Bree huffed out a breath and turned from the windows, her hands on her hips as she watched him in the kitchen. He could feel her glare even across the distance between them.

"Are you going to tell me what's going on or what?"

Logan slathered Russian dressing on bread. "Yes, I am."

He lifted his gaze and looked her over, trying to decide if she was being combative or defensive. She looked mostly annoyed. Maybe because he had dragged her out of her comfort zone. Maybe because she wanted to know what was happening with the bar. Maybe for a lot of reasons.

"I'm waiting."

He put aside the food and reached for a bottle of wine and opened it. "You know what I am but not where I came from."

"Yeah." She nodded agreement to encourage him to keep him going.

"My realm is known as the Hidden Lands. The morning you found me was the morning I escaped through a portal." He paused and gazed at her, waiting for a reaction. Her face was impassive. "That's when you found me."

She was silent for a long moment as she processed what he said. "You came through a portal."

"My father opened it and sent me through." He poured two glasses of wine and slid one her direction, then got back to piling corned beef on the bread.

Her face seemed to blanch of color and her arms relaxed. Her hands dropped to her sides. She picked up the glass of wine, holding it as she watched him add sauerkraut to the sandwich. "You really are a dragon-shifter."

He lifted an eyebrow. "You doubted that? After everything?"

How could she doubt what he told her as anything but the truth? They had been together in the most intimate way. They'd bonded. They'd shared something he would only share with the woman destined to be his mate.

"Well…I thought you told me that just to get in my pants." She grinned as she said it and he knew she teased him.

"I'm not the kind of guy who tells women lies to get them into bed."

She blushed and tried to cover it as she sipped her wine.

But it occurred to him maybe she didn't understand who he was deep down and what they'd become to each other. Thinking of her supple body beneath his hands warmed him. He shoved away the thought as he added two slices of Swiss and then topped the sandwich.

She looked at him over the rim of her glass with genuine awe-inspired curiosity. "You can shift into a dragon?"

"I can. I'm an elemental dragon which means in my true form I can breathe fire." His father was an elemental, too. But as Logan could harness the power of fire, his father could harness the power of air and mastered the Dragon's Breath spell. "What I told you before was all true. Just as what I'm telling you now is all true. Archer murdered my parents when we tried to make our escape through the portal to the human realm. As my father lay dying, he sent me through and then closed the portal with his Dragon's Breath to seal it so Archer couldn't follow."

He put the sandwich on the plate and pushed it toward her, pretending not to see the sorrow that came over her features. She chewed on her bottom lip as she perched on the edge of the barstool, bothered by hearing the news his parents had been murdered. He knew she understood—she equated that to her own father's death. She understood what it felt like to have something precious ripped away. Though she didn't understand what it was like to have a homeland that was dying.

"I'm so sorry, Logan. I didn't know."

"You couldn't know. I never told you. I'm telling you now because...we're together."

She didn't quite understand how together they were. Since their bonding, there was no going back. She was his and he was hers. Period. It was even more binding than a human wedding ceremony. Divorce was not an option. It was literally until death do they part.

"If your father closed the portal, how did Archer follow?"

"Rafe said there are other portals scattered throughout the human realm. I'm glad I'm telling you this now. You have a right to know now that we're together."

"Are we together?"

"I want you for more than mating, Bree."

"Do you?" She breathed out the words as she stared at him.

"Yes."

They looked at each other for a long intense moment so full of electric sparks, he was certain he could hear the air crackle. It was a feeling that went beyond their bonding. It was hard for him to admit the first hint of love tingled through him because he had never expected to find it here in the human realm with a human woman after so short of time. Bree was special, though. And he found himself thinking he would do whatever it took to keep her safe and out of the hands of the vampires and the Drakana.

She cleared her throat and picked up the sandwich, breaking the silence. He got back to building another one.

"So why does this…Archer want you now?" she asked.

"To answer that I have to give you a little bit of history about where I come from. The Hidden Lands is unable to sustain our life force any longer. Most of the dragon clans have moved on already but there were a few under my father's rule that had not. He wanted to migrate to the human realm like the other clans."

"There are more of you?"

"Yes."

"Why is your land dying?" She asked around a mouthful of food.

"No one knows. Maybe because we've been there for millennia and it's time to move on. I don't know."

He paused, wondering if he should tell her about the Blood Stone now. Her mind had gone quiet of questions as she looked down at their hands. He had only felt her try to break through his barricade once or twice and now was not one of those times. She was inquisitive, yes, but she wasn't intrusive. She may understand the unwritten code that going into someone else's mind without permission was rude, even though he had done it to her more than once.

He knew she could read his mind. That was why he had to erect those walls to keep most of his thoughts shielded from her. He was, after all, still a guy.

"Archer didn't like that my father wanted to leave," he explained. "When we tried to go, he attacked us. I was the only one able to get away."

"You said your father's rule." She lifted her gaze again and met his.

"I did. He was Chief Magistrate of the clan, Bree. I was his heir. Upon his death, I inherited the rule of the five clans that were under him. The Council of Five. That makes me a lord."

Bree stared at him in utter shock. Of all the dragon-shifters she had to fall for, it had to be the one who was nobility, didn't it?

Even though he said he wanted her for more than mating, she didn't know what that meant. Was he interested in her as more than just a lover? Did he have feelings for her? She didn't want to think she might have feelings for him because it was far too soon in their relationship. But she understood the difference between lust and love and what they shared was a little—okay a lot—of both. Not only did she want Logan with her in the most intimate way possible, she wanted him with her period. She couldn't stand the thought of going through the rest of her days without him.

He was the one who had pulled her out of hell and protected her and for that she would be forever grateful. But it went beyond that. They had a common goal—stay alive—and they had a common enemy—the vampires. She wasn't sure how that was going to play out, though, while they were on the run.

And she wasn't sure about this Archer person, either. From the moment she laid eyes on him, she knew he was a threat to Logan. She was only just beginning to understand how.

"Does that bother you?"

"No."

On the contrary, she was shocked he was a lord and so nonchalant about it. It gave her many more questions. What did that mean for her? For them? Would he leave her to return to the Hidden Lands to lead, to rule? Where would that leave her? She had the bar, sure, but she had no idea what sort of state that was in since her father died.

"Why does Archer want you to come back to the Hidden Lands?"

Everything about him froze as he stared at her, as though trying to decide how to answer. His jaw clenched and she could see the muscles working along the edge. One vein popped out on the side of his neck. Was he angry? Or something else?

"He wants me dead, Bree." He said it so matter-of-factly she flinched.

"Dead?"

"I'm a threat to him. The only reason he wants me to return to the clan is because I'm the heir and he wants me out of the way so he can take over without opposition."

Her stomach cramped into a knot, turning the food into a lump. "You're not going back, are you?"

"I will have to, eventually." He picked up his sandwich and took a bite as if telling her he would eventually abandon her was the most natural thing in the world.

Her appetite was gone. All she could do was stare at the half-eaten sandwich and wish she didn't feel like she was going to die.

"But you said he wanted you dead." Even to her own ears, she sounded as though she were in a tunnel.

"I did and he does but that doesn't mean it's going to happen. I intend to fight him on my terms when I'm recovered."

"When you're recovered?"

"Before I left the Hidden Lands," he said around a mouthful of sandwich, "Archer stabbed me with an obsidian blade. It's like poison to my system. When you found me, I was suffering from the wound."

She peered at his shoulder where she distinctly remembered cleansing the injury. A memory of them naked together flashed through her mind and she recalled the silvery scar. She hadn't bothered to notice when they were sweaty and getting busy.

"It's why I had to find Rafe," he continued, unaware of her internal memory flash. "He's the only one I knew in this realm that would have the healing skills to help me."

"Oh. My rudimentary healing skills didn't help?" She meant it as a joke since she knew she was no Florence Nightingale but he answered anyway.

"They did." He met her gaze, his face serious. "Because of you,

I was able to find Rafe and get his help. If it hadn't been for you, I would have died." He reached for her hand and squeezed. "You have to know that, Bree."

Well, even if she didn't before, she did now. She was glad to know she had a hand in making sure Logan lived long enough to get the help he needed. She, however, had no idea Rafe was such a healer. Rafe had been a fixture in the bar for a long while and she couldn't help but wonder how long he'd been in the human realm.

"He's been in the human realm longer than most of us. He was exiled here."

She tried not to scowl at the way he was able to mine that thought from her head.

"Why?" She had a genuine curiosity about the man.

Logan shrugged as he released her hand and got back to his sandwich. "Don't know. He was once a knight. That's about all I know."

She picked up a piece of corned beef that fell off her sandwich and munched on it as she contemplated her next question. There were so many. She started in the safest place she could think of. "What is your plan?"

"The poison from the obsidian blade is still in my system. I haven't quite healed. The gun shot didn't help either," he said. "As soon as I'm recovered I plan to take him on. One on one."

"Are you sure that's wise?"

"It's the way such things are settled."

"In your world, maybe. But this isn't your Hidden Lands. This is the real world."

"Right and I intend to fight him here if I have to. I can't go back to the Hidden Lands. At least, not yet."

"Because it's dying."

He nodded. "It's toxic to us."

"Then why does Archer stay?" she wanted to know.

"He thinks it's not as bad as my father thought. He thinks by killing me and taking over the clans, he'll have what he always wanted."

"Which is?"

"To rule. There has been a long-standing blood feud between my father and Archer," Logan said.

"And it's all about to come to a head, isn't it?"

And she was caught in the middle. She wasn't sure she wanted to be around when those two fought each other. She didn't want to voice the question but she had to know the truth. "And so…what does that mean for me?"

"If you don't come with me, he'll come after you and use you as leverage against me."

She couldn't stop the pulse of anger going through her. "So, what, you think I can't take care of myself?"

"I think you're very capable of taking care of yourself," he said. "It has nothing to do with that and everything to do with you staying alive. Archer won't hesitate to kill you if he thought it would get him once step closer to killing me."

"I see your point. You think he won't find you in the Hamptons?"

"Oh, I'm hoping he will. In fact, I'm counting on it."

His broad smile scared her more than his calm demeanor. He intended to kill Archer, no matter how or where or when. And she knew, she would likely be an unwilling participant.

But that was the least of her worries. Her primary concern was finding and killing the man responsible for her own father's death. She wanted her own form of vengeance, vampire or no vampire, dying or not.

"Thank you for telling me," she said.

"I know what you're thinking."

She stiffened, her internal walls going up on instinct. Had he heard her thoughts? "You do?"

"You're worried you've been caught in the middle of my blood feud," he said.

"Partly." She shoved away the plate, unable to eat any more. "There is something else I want to tell you."

She gathered her thoughts, trying to decide how to tell him.

"And that is?"

"I intend to get my own justice for my father."

13

Logan waited for her to laugh it off as a joke. She hadn't even cracked a smile. When she didn't, he realized she was serious.

"Bree, no."

"Yes. I told you before I wanted justice."

"You asked me to help you and I agreed but I never agreed to help you wipe out a vampire mafia."

"Oh, I'm sorry if I wasn't clear. Let me be clear now. I intend to go after Niko."

He moved around the end of the counter to stand next to her. "Those are vampires. You realize that, right?"

"I'm aware of what and who they are, Logan. They were still responsible for my father's death and I intend to make sure they pay for it."

He couldn't deny he was somewhat relieved she didn't blame him for her father's death—he certainly blamed himself enough. But he also couldn't allow her to go after them.

"The only way they'll release the debt your father owes is by taking your life," he said.

"They can try." She lifted her head in defiance.

He admired that about Bree. That she was so willing to go after dangerous criminals who stole her family from her. Admired it even though he thought it was crazy.

"Bree—"

"Don't try to talk me out of it, Logan. My mind is made up."

"I won't let you do it."

Fire flashed in her eyes as they narrowed. "Who the hell do you think you are? You don't get to tell me what to do." She poked him in the chest, hard. "I may not be a bad ass shifter like you are, but I'm a big girl and I can take care of myself."

"Taking on a vampire mafia is not something I recommended. It's dangerous, Bree. And you're…"

He bit off his words, unsure he should tell her she was under his protection. He'd taken on that role as soon as Mario died. He knew what she was up against. She may think she knew what she was doing but she wasn't the vengeful type. She was nothing like him.

"And I'm what?"

"You're playing with fire."

Amusement flickered over her features before she got it under control. "Isn't that what you are, Logan? Fire? I feel it coming off you in waves." She blushed as soon as she said it and turned away.

He was fire. Deep down, there was an inferno boiling inside him waiting to burst out. He knew it was from the dragon inside that wanted out as soon as he saw Archer. Eventually, he would have to shift to calm that side of him.

Or have sex wither her. Sex with his bonded mate would tame and cool the beast.

For now.

She pushed away the plate and jumped off the stool. In one fluid motion, she snatched her bag off the floor and started for the bedroom. He caught her arm and pulled her to him before she could get away.

"Where do you think you're going, princess?"

"To clean up. I'm allowed to shower, aren't I?"

A vision of her naked body soaped from head to toe burst through his mind. His walls must have been down because she sucked in a sharp breath and shoved him away.

"You are not showering with me."

"What's the matter? Too intimate?" Before she could get away, he reached for her, pulled her into his arms. "We've done it before."

She pushed against his chest, trying to break free. He could hear the questions about their relationship filter through her mind. She wondered how things would work between them since she was human and he wasn't.

"Stop that." Her whisper was calm and control.

"Stop what?" He pulled her closer, his lips brushing hers.

"Get out of my head, Logan."

"I like being in your head. I like knowing what you're thinking. Feeling."

"Well, I don't like you knowing what I'm thinking and feeling." She gave him another half-hearted shrug. Like she wanted him to let go.

"Why not, princess?"

"It's private."

"It's part of being bonded," he said.

She bit her bottom lip. "If that's true then why can't I get in your head?"

"You can."

"Ha. You shut me out, Logan."

He couldn't deny she was right about that. There were things he didn't want her to know. Still were. Like his plan to get back to the Hidden Lands and heal the realm. He wasn't sure how to break it to her that she would be coming with him. He'd have to bury those thoughts deeper while letting her in a little.

"You're right. I did and that was wrong. I shouldn't have," he said. "Go on."

She blinked surprise. "Now?"

He nodded. "Now."

He felt the first tentative touch of her mind to his and he pulled her in. Her breath seesawed in and out of her as he held her and showed her things they had done in the past. Their night together. Fleeing the city. He could hear her question about their future.

"We can be together, Bree. It doesn't matter that you're human and I'm not."

She swallowed so hard, he could see her throat working. "We

can?"

"Yes. We have the same physiological makeup."

Her gaze moved to his lips and lingered there. "What about…" Her question trailed off.

"We can have children together if that's what you mean."

Again, she swallowed. He resisted the urge to touch her mind, to hear what else she was thinking. She was right—it was a private place and he shouldn't be so free with it. It was wrong and he knew it but it was hard for him to resist.

"Is that important to you, Bree?"

"I don't know. I guess, I thought I would have children someday but never planned it."

He didn't want to tell her it was important to him to sire an heir. If he survived the fight with Archer, that is. He would need someone to inherit the title of Chief Magistrate and carry on once he was gone.

She lifted her gaze back to his. "Is it important to you?"

Logan hadn't been careful with his thoughts and must have heard them. "Someday, yes." He pulled her closer to him, one hand fisting in her hair. "Let's not discuss that right now, though."

Before she could reply he covered her mouth with his, tasting her. All the questions went out of her head as she focused solely on him and that kiss. When he broke form her, he took her by the hand and led her toward the master suite.

"Let's get you to that shower," he said.

And he made a valiant effort not to envision her naked.

There were still questions Bree wanted answered about their future together. Questions he didn't want her to ask—either in his mind or otherwise. She could read that about him without even poking her way around his head. Though, he had shared a lot of information with her about his past and how he ended up here, he didn't tell her what he had planned once Archer was out of the picture.

Their bonding had connected her to him in a way she had never expected nor anticipated. She'd let him pull her into him so deeply she wasn't sure she could claw her way out. She'd survive, sure, but she would never forget him and he would always be a part of her even if he wasn't with her.

Bree shoved all those negative thoughts away. If he left her, there wasn't anything she could do about it. She sure as hell wasn't going to beg him to take her with him. She wasn't that kind of girl. She was made of stronger stuff. She had the bar, after all. When all of this was over, it would be nothing but a distant memory. She would get back to work running the bar and the more time that expanded between them, the more she would forget him.

She hoped.

For now, she would give herself over to the moment. She was a grown woman, after all, and she could handle whatever consequences there were that came out of their relationship. Like any woman, she thought marriage and kids were in her future but she had never been in a hurry to get there. She wanted to wait for the right man to come along. She didn't know if Logan was that right man. All she knew was he felt like the right man.

He led her through the master suite to the bathroom where he released her hand and turned to go.

"Enjoy your shower."

She wrapped a hand around his upper arm to stop him. "Logan, stay with me."

As soon as the words were out of her mouth, the heat erupted from his skin. It radiated from him and enveloped her. Her body responded to the sudden pulse of heat. She dropped her bag and waited for him to reply.

He looked at her over his shoulder. "You sure about that, princess?"

Nodding, she pulled her shirt up and over her head, dropping it on the floor, and then toed off her shoes. "I'm sure." Then she unbuttoned her jeans and shoved them down, stepping out of them. "Come with me."

Logan turned toward her and she could see the heat rippling off him in waves, reminding her of the way pavement looked on a scorching summer day. She knew his dragon threatened to come out. She could see it in the depths of golden-brown eyes, too.

It should have terrified her but it didn't.

It turned her on.

His eyes clouded over with desire and need as he stripped off his shirt and tossed it to the floor with hers. She turned on the water in the shower. As she reached behind her to unclasp her bra, he was in front of her in a second, shoving her hands away and then taking control. He unhooked it and pulled the material away from her body.

Her breasts were pink peaks. He bent to take one in his mouth, his tongue swiping over the taut nub. Her hands tangled in his hair as she arched her back and a breath shuddered out of her. He did magical things to her with his mouth.

Bree shimmied out of his embrace and moved away, stepping back toward the shower. She slipped one hand inside the front of her cotton panties and let him watch as she slid a finger into her damp crease. With her free hand, she palmed her breast and squeezed, her heart pounding so hard, she could hear it throbbing in her ears.

He groaned as he watched her and continued to undress. He kicked off his shoes and shoved his pants and underwear to the floor, freeing his hardened length. He took a step toward her but she shook her head.

"No. Wait. I want you to watch."

"Bree." Her name came out as a strangled gasp and she knew she was killing him.

Good. Because if he left her, it would kill her. She wanted to see his face while she touched herself. She wanted to watch his hooded expression full of desire and need while she moved her finger in and out of her wet center. She wanted to brand that image of his face in her mind so she could recall it when she was alone and had to do this very thing to relieve her pent-up need for him. Because she knew, deep down, she would always want him.

Her climax came much too soon but she couldn't prolong it even if she wanted to. She cried out with her orgasm, her body shuddering from the pleasure pain of it all.

He was on her in a second, pushing her into the hot spray and then against the cold tiles. The two sensations crashed through her with such a force, she was unprepared for either. His mouth was on hers, his hands on her, pushing her against the wall and his hard length seeking her damp core. She was faintly aware of the ripping of material before he hiked up her leg and shoved deeply inside her.

All she could do was dig her nails into his shoulders and hold on while he pounded her against the wall. Thrusting deeply inside her. Pulling out and then thrusting in again and again. Over and over. Between the heat of his body and the hot spray on her, it was enough to make her lightheaded.

The orgasm exploded through her in a flash and she couldn't help the cry of pleasure. His own climax followed shortly. He groaned and pushed inside her one last time. Her bones had all turned to jelly. The only reason she was upright was because he pinned her against the wall.

He nuzzled her neck, his breath hot and heavy. Mingling with the water. She didn't want him to move. She didn't want it to end. Even though she knew it would. She realized she still gripped his shoulders and relaxed her fingers. She left crescent indentions in his skin. He didn't seem to notice or care.

"You're a tease, princess."

Bree wasn't sure what had come over her. She had never done that for anyone before. She was a sex-with-the-lights-off-under-the-covers kind of girl. Nothing about what they'd done together had been normal for her. All she knew was she wanted him to see how he affected her. How he made her feel. Proving she had lost her mind where he was concerned.

"Am I?"

"You know you are." He placed feather-light kisses along her jaw. "And a dirty girl."

"Then you better do something about that, too."

He reached for the bar of soap. "Turn around and I will."

"I don't think I can."

"Why not?"

"Because all my bones have fused together and I can't move."

He chuckled. "Then I better keep holding you up."

She nodded. "Yes, I think so."

With their bodies still connected, he placed the bar of soap between her breasts, then flattened his palm over it and began a slow jaunt back and forth and up and down. He left a soapy trail behind. She dropped her arms to her side, limp. He outlined the rest of her upper body, shoulders and arms and hands.

Logan put the soap aside and tangled his hands in her hair, pulling her to him. They kissed, long, slow, sensual. His upper body pressed against hers and it was only in her haze of ecstasy she realized he was transferring the soap from her body to his.

It was erotic and sexy and one of the hottest things that had ever happened to her.

He started to move inside her, pulling back and then pushing inside. She had no idea how she could even want to do it again. His hands slipped down to cup her ass and pull her against him. Instinct took over and she wrapped her legs around his waist as he continued his slow thrusts.

As she shattered once again, she knew she had utterly come undone in his arms.

He pressed against her one last time with his release.

And then everything stopped. The only sound was that of the shower and her ragged breathing.

"I think I'm clean now."

He cocked a grin. "If you're sure."

She let her feet down as he released her, then reached over and turned off the water. She leaned against the wall, feeling like nothing more than a wet noodle tossed against the tile to see if she would stick. She was pretty sure she was stuck.

"You may have to carry me out," she said.

Without replying, he scooped her up and stepped out of the shower. He placed her on the edge of the counter as he reached for a towel. She watched him, admiring the strength of his muscles as they worked under the golden skin. He wrapped the towel around her, drying her with up and down motions that made her feel like she was a princess. His princess.

He even made that sexy.

"What's going to happen now?" she asked.

"Now? I'm still hungry. You made me work up an appetite." He grinned at her.

"That's not what I mean," she snapped.

"Then what do you mean?"

She huffed out a breath, exasperated. He seemed to have forgotten about the vampires, Archer, and everyone else. It was as though none of that mattered at the moment. She had a suspicion he knew what she was getting at but he was once again trying to avoid it.

"You know what I mean." She was scared to ask the question but dying to know the answer. "What's going to happen…with us."

"Everything between us is fine, Bree." When he was satisfied how dry she was, he tucked the towel around her, then wrapped another around his waist.

She was partially glad he'd covered up because his body was completely distracting. But she knew he was avoiding her real question. She would have to be more direct.

"And when Archer shows up?"

He stilled and leveled his gaze with hers. "We don't have to worry about that right now."

It shocked her he seemed unconcerned. Bree needed a plan.

"What are we going to do? Sit around and fuck until he shows up?"

"We might as well. You seem to enjoy it." He stalked from the bathroom, unflustered. He left a trail of drips along the floor because he hadn't bothered to dry off. Just wrapped the towel around his waist as though that were enough.

Her anger flared deeply inside her, burning hot, as she hopped off the counter, clutching the towel around her shoulders and stomping after him.

"Is that all I am to you? A good fuck?"

He reeled on her, his big body closing in on her personal space and taking all the oxygen in the room. He had done that once before. Perhaps as an intimidation tactic but she was far from intimidated. He had never been able to do that to her. Even the first day they met when she found him in the park. She was close enough to realize his skin seemed to sizzle and she couldn't help but notice he was dry.

The heat was back and radiating from him and around her like a current ready to tow her under. She started to understand when he was aroused or pissed off, the heat returned. She'd managed to do both in the last few minutes.

"Get off your high horse, Bree. You can't pretend like you don't want it after your performance in there." He jerked his chin toward the bathroom, reminding her of her little sexcapade.

There was no way she could stop the burning blush that crept up her neck, into her cheeks and then stopped at her hairline. Her face was on fire. She clutched her hand into a fist. Her first instinct was to hit him but that wouldn't be ladylike and she had been raised better than that.

"You have an explanation for that?" he asked.

She didn't. All she knew was she was overcome with need and lust. That and she wanted to remember how he looked at her in that moment. And as she started to understand what his reactions meant, she also started to understand more and more about how he affected her.

She knew it had something to do with how deeply they were connected but that was as far as her deductive reasoning went. As far as her rational mind would allow her to go when she was in the throes of trying to seduce him. And she wanted to seduce him a lot.

"It's because we're bonded." She clenched her jaw so tightly, her back teeth ached.

He straightened his shoulders, still peering at her. His expression was impassive and gave nothing away so she reached out to him with her mind to probe his thoughts. Giving his mind a tentative knock. He seemed to be waiting for her and opened the door, allowing her to step inside.

He folded his arms over his massive chest. It was hard to ignore the sinew of muscle beneath those powerful forearms.

"Go ahead. You want to know." He said it as though it were an invitation.

His dragon side was there, ready and waiting. Ready to pounce and take him over. But Logan's inner control kept him from shifting into full dragon. She could see it as a silvery thread—the human side vying for dominance over the dragon side. For a brief moment, she got a spark of what he would look like in that form. Powerful. Regal. With a mighty wingspan reaching twenty feet. A breath of fire and scales the color of a ruby reflecting orange and red and yellow.

Like the center of a blistering flame.

And the only thing that was the same about him was that golden-brown color of his eyes.

She heard the gasp escape her before she could stop it.

"Still want to fuck?" he asked.

God, yes. She was wet and ready again with a pounding need her fingers itched to touch. But she was not going to be derailed again. Instead, she pressed her cold fingertips against her temples and rubbed, trying to maintain her focus.

"What does it meant to be bonded, Logan?"

"It means what you think it means."

Frustration curled low in her gut. Why could he never answer a direct question? Or, more specifically, that direct question? "Tell me what it means," she said between clenched teeth. "I want to hear you say it. I need to hear you say it."

"It means the first time you touched me, we were instantly connected. It means, Bree, we are bonded for eternity." He paused, took a step toward her, moving close enough for her to smell that sexy otherworldly scent unique to him. "In my realm, it is the same as marriage in yours."

∽ 14 ∾

Bree stared at him a long, silent moment chewing her lower lip. She waited for him to touch her mind with his but he didn't. He waited for her to respond, but the truth of the matter was, she had no idea what to say.

Her idea of marriage had never been something like this. There was no kneeling. No proposing. No romance and wooing. No nothing. She had merely stopped to help a stranger. To offer kindness.

Did he not understand what marriage meant to her? No, of course not. They had never discussed it. They had never talked about a future because she never thought there would be a future with him. She had fallen into his arms with an ease and comfort she had never experienced with another man. Even so, she had never expected it to be forever. Men like Logan were nothing but a fantasy. Certainly not a reality.

She thought back to that first day in the park when saw him, when she touched him. And he had snapped at her to stop touching him. From that very first moment, they had become part of each other. He wanted her to go away, but she couldn't because she had an overwhelming need to help him, to be with him, to stay with him.

The attraction to him had been instant and intense—even before she managed to touch him. He had once told her it wouldn't have happened if she didn't desire him even a little. But then she didn't even realize how much she desired him. How much she wanted him.

"Well?" he asked.

She looked him over. The big hulking man standing in front of her waiting for her to respond to his sudden declaration they were forever joined.

"What happens if we…aren't together?" she asked.

"Dragons mate for life, Bree."

Her mouth went dry. He hadn't answered her question, did he? She didn't know what his statement that dragons mated for life meant. She had a lot more questions. Was she supposed to accept that she was stuck with him forever? And how long was forever? Was his lifespan longer than hers? Where would they live? What about kids?

"Get some rest. It's been a long day." He stalked out.

When she was alone, she sank to the edge of the bed. It had been a long day and her life was in upheaval. She glanced at the bag still in the middle of the room. She hadn't packed a lot, but hopefully, it was enough to keep her clothed until the ordeal was over.

She rummaged through it, found underwear, a pair of jeans and a T-shirt. Her cell phone was buried in the bottom of the bag—she haphazardly tossed it in there at some point, though she couldn't remember doing it. After she dressed, she glanced at the open bedroom door and strained her ears to listen. She couldn't hear any movement outside the room and wondered where he'd gone.

Clutching the phone, she tiptoed to the doorway and peered out. Logan sat on one of the sofas, slumped over with his arm over his face. He still wore the towel and she tried hard not to notice his muscular chest. She pushed the door closed, leaving only a small crack so she could hear movement outside the room and then dialed the number for the bar.

There was no answer. She hoped someone had answered but perhaps it was still closed.

She tried Meg. On the second ring, she picked it up.

"Bree! Where are you? Are you okay? What the hell is going on?"

Her hand tightened around the phone at the sound of panic in Meg's voice. She hadn't meant to cause her alarm. It must have made her crazy when she disappeared without a trace. "I'm fine. What's happening there?"

"Bree…Mario is…he's…"

She could hear the emotion in Meg's voice. Bree's eyes fluttered closed as the sick feeling went through her.

"I know," Bree said. "I was there."

"God, what happened? Bear said you, Logan, and Mario were all attacked."

"We were. It's a long story and I don't have time to explain everything right now. I called the bar but there was no answer. I need to know what's going on." Even though Rafe said he would check on things and let her know, she couldn't wait for him to get back to her. She had to know what was happening now.

"We've been shut down," she said. "Indefinitely. Or at least until the investigation is over. The police have been there several times trying to find out what happened and find you. I thought you'd been kidnapped but Bear said Logan was taking care of you."

Bree tried to recall what had happened that terrible night, but she had been in shock and out of it. All she recalled was Logan carrying her out, away from the grisly sight.

"He is," she said. "I'll get back there as soon as I can."

"Good because all sorts of weirdoes have turned up in the last twenty-four hours."

Bree drew her brows together with concern. Meg wasn't like Bree. She wasn't able to see all the supernaturals that frequented the bar. "What do you mean?"

"A woman cop. Said her name was Shi'Ann Jones. She came looking for Mario and was real twitchy when she found out he was dead. She wanted to know where you were."

"What did she want?"

"Something about a pouch of stones. She said Mario had it and was supposed to turn it over to her along with some woman named Raelee. Except Raelee is dead, too."

A cold feeling of dread went over Bree. She'd found that pouch of stones in her apartment when it had been ransacked. She had wondered then how her father had managed to get it to her place and hide it without her knowing.

"Also," Meg continued, "Korbin brought me a key to your place."

"What?"

Korbin was one of their security officers. How in the world did he get a key to her place?

"Yeah. Weird, huh? He said Mario asked him to deliver something to your apartment the night he died. He wouldn't tell me what though."

So that's how he did it. He must have sent Korbin because he knew the pouch of stones was hot and he didn't want to keep them on his person. Had he stolen them? And if so, why hide them in her apartment? It didn't make sense. Nor did Bree understand what sort of shady business dealings were going on. That added to the mystery. Who was Raelee and why was a cop looking for her father? Unless he was suspected of murder, too.

She immediately pushed that thought out of her head. There was no way that was true. Her father was a lot of things, but he wasn't a killer.

"It's doesn't matter," Bree said. "I think I know. I'll take care of it."

"And one more thing," Meg said.

Bree pinched the bridge of her nose between her thumb and forefinger. She wasn't sure if she could take more bad news. She heaved a sigh.

"Did your dad have a gambling problem?"

"No."

"Well, that's not what this loan shark says."

Oh, God. "What loan shark?"

"The one wanting ten thousand bucks."

Holy shit.

She stared at the wall across from her, numb and

dumbfounded. That was why her father was stealing from the vampires. He wanted to pay back his gambling debt. As more pieces fell into place about her father and what he'd done, she realized she didn't know him at all. He was a stranger to her.

It was her fault. She hadn't been as close to him after high school when she went off to college to sow her wild oats and become a young woman. Things had been different when she returned. That's when she noticed the supernaturals hanging around the place more and more.

For the first time, she connected the dots. Her father could see them, too, and welcomed them into his place of business. He also had side dealings with them all so he could fuel his own bad habits. Somewhere along the line, his bad habits turned into something shadier and more dangerous.

"You still there, Bree?"

"I'm here. Thanks for the update. I have to go."

"You aren't even going to tell me where you are?" There was a hint of desperation in her voice.

Bree considered telling her for a moment but something niggled at her. "I can't tell you. All you need to know is I'm safe."

"With Logan?"

Was that a hint of jealousy she heard? "Yes."

"Lucky girl."

They hung up. Bree tossed the phone on the nightstand next to the bed. She moved to the bag still in the middle of the floor and knelt beside it. With her heart in her throat, she reached into the pocket on the side and pulled out the pouch of stones. She pulled open the drawstring and poured them out on the carpet, looking them over. The one red, in particular, caught her attention. She picked it up, held it and examined it.

Had these stones gotten her father killed?

It was the size of a walnut. Not perfectly round. For a stone, it was heavy and dark red. Blood red. There was something odd and different about it. She swiped her thumb over the smooth surface and for a brief moment it was as though stone had attached to her.

Like some sort of strange suction. When she removed her thumb, her skin was stained red.

Strange, she thought the stone smelled of blood.

She scooped them all back in the pouch and pulled it closed. For safekeeping, she shoved the stones into the bottom of her bag. She curled up on the bed and let fatigue overtake her.

Bree had spent twenty-four hours with Logan alone in the house in East Hampton. After their little episode in the shower and the subsequent discussion, they hadn't talked much except when it came to necessity and pleasantries. He brooded a lot and kept a vigil in the living room while she stayed in the back bedroom most of the time trying to come to terms with the idea she might be married to Logan.

And she was bored.

She suspected he was, too.

The following afternoon was a rainy one. Not that he would let her outside. He kept her under house arrest. If things were different, they might have had sex more but as it was she kept her distance while she worked through her own feelings.

He appeared in the doorway that afternoon, leaning on the jamb with his arms crossed as he looked her over.

"Hungry?"

Her stomach growled. Breakfast had been earlier that day. "A little."

"Let's get out of here."

"We're leaving?"

"I need a change of scenery. So do you."

"You think it's safe?"

"Safe enough. No one knows where we are. Besides, I'm tired of cooking. Come on." He gave a jerk of his head indicating she should follow him.

She stuck her feet in her shoes. She would have offered to cook but she wasn't Suzy Homemaker. The best she could do was boil water and sometimes she even burned that. Coffee was about the extent of her culinary skills.

"Where are we going?" she asked as she slid into the car.

"There's a diner not far from here. Supposed to be pretty good."

It was a short drive up the coast.

Inside the diner, elevator music played from the aging ceiling speakers, the vinyl booths had seen better days and the tabletops were scarred and well-worn. Bree followed Logan inside who didn't wait to be seated since they were the only customers. He picked the booth in the middle next to the windows to keep an eye on the entrance as well as the car.

A woman dressed in a pink and blue waitress uniform walked up. She gave Bree a snooty once over before looking back at Logan. Her brown hair was pulled up in a ponytail, making her look younger than her actual age. There was a hint of crow's feet around her eyes and smile lines on either side of her mouth. A mouth that wasn't smiling now. She plopped two mugs on the table in front of them and then poured coffee. Her nametag read Vera.

When she paused at the edge of the table, Bree was aware of the scent coming from her. Now that she recognized it, she knew the woman was a dragon. She glanced at Logan to see if he had an inkling of a reaction but his face remained passive.

"Hadn't seen you here before." She practically grunted the words at them.

"We're new in town." He tried to warm up to her with a smile but she wasn't interested.

"Want menus?"

"Sure," he said.

She huffed and stalked away.

"Nice place." Bree scowled as she put her paper napkin in her lap. She pulled out her hand sanitizer, squirted it along the table then wiped it down with a spare napkin. Then she used another dollop of hand sanitizer on her hands.

"It's not that bad," he said looking over the table. He lifted his elbow off the table and something sticky left behind a residue.

One corner of her lip curled in disgust. "Hold out your hands."

When he obliged, she squirted the clear gel into his palms. He used the excess to clean the sticky off his arm while she got busy with the spot on the table.

Vera returned a moment later and dropped off menus before sauntering away again. Bree leaned across the table and dropped her voice.

"Are you sure about this place?"

"It's fine." He picked up the menu and looked it over, feigning interest.

Bree folded her arms over her chest and sat back into the booth, the vinyl squeaking with her movement.

"It got five stars on Yelp," he said, sounding miffed.

She couldn't help it. She giggled. "Do you even know what Yelp is?"

"Just because I'm not from here doesn't mean I'm not in touch with technology." He never lifted his gaze as he continued to peruse the menu. "We have been studying the human realm for a long time."

"Have you?" It was intriguing to hear him talk about it. "How long?"

Now he lifted his eyes. "A long time."

"The waitress is a—" Bree began.

"I know."

She glanced to where she'd retreated. "You do? Did you know before we came?"

"No. Just act casual and we'll be fine."

But Vera had to know what Logan was. Bree knew Rafe and Logan could sense each other so it stood to reason the waitress would be able to do the same. She flipped open her menu and tried to find something that wasn't a heart attack on a plate.

Most everything was deep fried and covered in gravy. She

wrinkled her nose.

"When all of this is over, I promise to take you someplace nice," he said.

"Like a real date?"

"Is that what you want?"

"Yes."

"Then a real date it is."

Bree realized what was bothering her about the whole situation. They had done everything backward, it seemed. From the bonding/marriage to the sex. The attraction between them might be like throwing fuel on a fire, but that was no excuse for them to jump into bed together.

Oh, who was she kidding? She'd wanted to jump into bed with him from the moment she laid eyes on him. She watched him through her lashes as he looked over the menu and it hit her. Like a punch in the gut. She was with him until death whether she liked it or not. And luckily, she liked it. She wanted to be with him. She couldn't stand the thought of not being with him. Something deep inside her had been ignited and Logan was the only one who could keep the flame alive.

Dare she think she was in love with him?

Did he love her? Or was he trying to do right by her simply because they were bonded?

"Logan, I've been thinking about what you told me yesterday." The words spilled out of her before she could stop them.

He dropped the menu and gave her his full attention. "Have you?"

"About the bonding thing."

He folded his hands over his menu. "And?"

"I think it was hard for me to accept at first but I understand who and what you are."

One eyebrow lifted. "You have my attention."

She huffed out a breath. "What I'm trying to say is I like you a lot, Logan."

A corner of his mouth twitched into almost a smile. "I like you a lot, too, Bree."

Her heart fluttered. "You do?"

He reached across the table for her hand. She placed it inside his palm and he squeezed. "I do."

Two cars pulled into the parking lot outside the diner that caught Logan's attention. Two men stepped out of each car. One of them was Archer. He released her hand and shot from the booth.

"Come on."

She looked to the front of the building and saw men exiting both vehicles. They were dressed in suits and carried guns as they started for the building. Logan grabbed her by the hand and turned from the dining room toward the kitchen. Vera came out, blocking their path.

"Sorry, bucko. You're staying right here," she said.

"You gave me up." He sounded genuinely surprised.

"Sorry to break up such a sweet moment, but I had to."

Bree sensed the anger flickering through him. He scowled. "Are you loyal to Archer?"

"I'm loyal to Vera." She thumbed at her chest.

As the men entered the building, she turned and disappeared into the dining room. Logan pushed Bree behind him and faced off with the men. But it was six against one. There was no way he could take them. The man in front she recognized as Archer.

"Well, well. We meet again and such a short time later. How fortunate for me, Logan."

Logan had no reply as he stared the man down.

"My nephew tells me," he waved to the man standing next to him, "that you two got acquainted in Central Park. He thought he shot you."

"I did shoot him," the nephew said.

Logan nodded. "He did. But you forget how fast dragons heal, Archer."

"Do I? I didn't forget I stabbed you with that obsidian blade. You should be dead by now. But you're not. And I understand a certain exiled knight saved your life." Archer glanced over his fingernails as though he were talking about the weather.

Logan tensed next to her. "He has nothing to do with our fight."

"No, but he was quite willing to give me information on your intended destination." Archer smiled that oily smile and Bree shivered.

Heat poured off Logan and she knew he was close to losing his temper. She could sense the heated anger boiling under the surface. She could also sense the dragon wanting to get out. To calm him, she placed her hand in the crook of his arm. He didn't glance at her but she did feel him relax.

"What did you do to him?"

"He's alive, if that's what you're wondering," Archer said. "I let him go when I realized he was no longer useful. Though, I should have killed him. What's more blood on my hands?"

Logan jerked and pitched forward, his hands gripping his head as a cry of pain ripped from him. He landed on his knees.

"Logan!"

"There's nothing you can do for him, my dear, so don't even try," Archer said.

Fear clutched her gut as her hands tightened into balls. "What did you do to him?"

"Oh, nothing but used a little dragon magic on him. As for you…"

"You stay away from me." She crouched next to Logan, wrapping her arms around his shoulders and whispered to him. "Logan, you can fight him. You can beat him."

"Oh, I'm afraid he can't fight me. You see, he's still ill from the effects of the blade. Even though the wound may be healed, the poison remains in his system and I've used a bit of magic to remind him it's still there." Archer snapped his fingers. "Bind her. Put her in the car."

Rough hands grabbed her and pulled her away from Logan. She kicked and flailed trying to get the men to release her but it was no use. They were bigger and stronger than she. One grabbed her by the wrists, held them together while a second one wound duct tape around them. They dragged her away.

Logan's body writhing on the floor was the last thing she saw before they shoved her out the door.

↞ 15 ↠

When Logan came to, his wrists were bound and he had a raging headache. A thick rope was around his torso, tying him to a chair. Each ankle was bound to a chair leg with more rope cutting into him. His senses flashed to high alert as he took in his surroundings. Night had descended. He was at a beach house—but not just any house. It was a palatial estate and he wondered who Archer had to kill to make use of it. He could hear the faint crash of the surf in the distance. One lone lamp bathed the living area in a warm yellow glow.

He knew Archer and his men were nearby. He could scent them.

He appeared to be alone and his first thought was of Bree. Where was she? Had they harmed her? He saw her carried away. He'd failed to protect her. He'd been lured into a false sense of security by thinking they would both be safe at the diner. Vera must have contacted Archer and told him they were there. He had been careless and now he and Bree would pay the price.

Vera would eventually pay for what she did to him. If he lived and he planned to.

Archer got to Rafe, too, and likely tortured the information about of him, heaping more guilt on Logan. He hoped the man was all right. With a tentative thought, he reached out to Rafe to see if he could mindspeak to him. He asked if he was all right. For a long moment, there was silence. Then, at last, a gruff response.

I'm alive. That's about all I can report. Sorry, Logan.

Relief sputtered through him as he blew out a breath. Don't

worry about it. Archer has Bree and me but I think I have a way out of this. I need your help.

A long silent pause persisted before he replied. No promises.

The Blood Stone. Still have it?

It wasn't in the drawer where you left it.

Fuck all. Had Bree found it and taken it? He should have handed it to Rafe directly.

Sorry, man, Rafe said.

Logan told him not to worry about it and then erected his mental walls to keep any more mindspeak from interfering in his thoughts. He stiffened and watched as Archer and Zak entered the room and made their way toward him.

"Hello, Logan." Archer's oily greeting wafted over all of them. "I apologize for the way we had to treat you, but I can't risk you not wanting to cooperate with me."

"Where's Bree?"

"Oh, yes. She's quite a beauty, isn't she? And a feisty little thing. We had to cover her mouth with duct tape because she kept trying to bite my men."

If Logan hadn't been so worried about her, he might have smiled.

"And she's a kicker. She nailed one of the men right in the crotch before we could get her under control," Archer continued.

"Leave her out of this. It has nothing to do with her," Logan said.

"On the contrary. It has a lot to do with her." He gave a jerking nod to Zak who walked into the next room. "She's going to persuade you to do what I want."

Logan pinpointed him with his best glare. "You think using her is going to get to me?"

"I know it is."

Zak returned, dragging Bree along beside him. Her wrists were bound together by duct tape in front of her. Her mouth was still taped shut. Archer grabbed another chair and set it front of Logan. Zak pushed her down into the chair. Then he ripped off the duct tape from her mouth. To her credit, she didn't scream or even cry out. She merely glared at the men.

"You know what I want, Logan. If you don't agree, your girlfriend suffers." Archer thumbed in her direction. "I'll leave you two to talk things over. We'll be back shortly."

Logan waited until they were gone before speaking. "Are you all right?"

"Yes. No. I don't know." Her voice quaked with emotion. Her chin quivered but she was doing her best to keep it together. "I'm scared."

"I know you are, princess, but everything is going to be all right. I promise."

She shook her head. "You don't know that. You can't know that." She craned her neck to see if Archer and Zak were still behind her. "He wants me to tell you to return with him, Logan. To the Hidden Lands. I…I think he's going to kill you there."

"I know what he intends to do."

"What are you going to do? Why can't you just turn into a dragon and burn him to a crisp?"

It was a valid question but things were not that easy. "I can't do that here."

Which meant he shouldn't do that here in the human realm. Fighting Archer in his dragon form would be so easy. He knew he was bigger and could likely take him out. But he couldn't risk humans other than Bree seeing his true form. She knew what he was—others didn't.

"You're going to fight him, aren't you?" Her voice held a hint of desperation and fear. He could tell by the look on her face she wanted to talk him out of it.

No one was going to talk him out of killing Archer.

"Yes," he said.

She bit her lip and looked away and he knew she was trying not to cry. He'd done that to her. He put the fear into her. Because he couldn't protect her like he should have.

"I don't want to lose you, too." She lowered her voice as her words shuddered out of her.

Hearing her admit that was like a knife in the gut. "You won't."

When she looked back at him, worry lines creased her face. "I hope not."

He understood then what she had been trying to tell him back in the diner. What she couldn't say—not yet—because she thought it was too soon for them to be confessing true feelings for each other. Maybe she had been right to keep it to herself. God knew he couldn't tell her what he felt even though he wanted to. All he could come up with was that he liked her, too.

"What are we going to do now?"

"I'll think of something." He gave her a half smile.

The truth was he was totally out of his element here. While he didn't feel sick, he suspected the poison from the obsidian blade was still in his system. It didn't seem as though his powers had fully regened. If only he could have stayed under the radar a little longer to heal and recuperate to be at full strength. He wasn't ready to face Archer, not yet. But he didn't know how much more time he could buy.

His dragon banged against the inside of his skull, letting him know he was still there and still agitated enough to want to come out to play. He glanced at Bree who was looking at him with a mixture of hope and worry. He was their only shot at getting out of there.

Then he noticed she was busy fidgeting. She was trying to pull her wrists apart.

"Bree, what are you doing?" He kept his voice low so it wouldn't alert Archer or Zak.

"Giving you a chance."

She jerked her hands upward and broke through the tape with a grimace. Again, to her credit, she didn't cry out with the pain. They hadn't tied her to the chair as they did him. She rushed to his side and started tugging on the knots.

"Leave it. It's me he wants anyway."

"No." A stubborn edge laced her tone. "We're getting out

together."

"He'll be back any minute. It's too late for me."

"I'm not leaving you, Logan. I love you, damn it." Her hands stilled on the ropes as she looked up at him. "I hope that's okay."

His stomached bottomed out. "It's more than okay."

He wanted to reach for her, to brush his hand over her upturned face but he was still tied to the damn chair. Logan scented Archer then.

"He's coming."

She gave another tug on the knot but it wouldn't come free. "My fingers aren't working. I can't get it undone."

"Bree—"

"Well, isn't this cozy. I hope she's doing her best to convince you to do what I ask," Archer said as he entered the room.

"You can go to hell."

Archer's eyes narrowed. "Get her away from him."

Two of Archer's Drakana charged her. But she never stopped trying to undo the rope even when they grabbed her by the arms and dragged her toward the open door.

"Let her go, Archer. She has nothing to do with this."

"Wait." Archer held up a hand to stop them. "Perhaps I was too hasty. Hold her here." Then he looked back at Logan, cutting him a sharp look he didn't like. "I will release her on one condition only. If you agree to return to the clan with me."

"So you can kill me?" Logan shook his head. "No."

One jerk of his head toward the Drakana was all the signal they needed. One of them landed a punch in Bree's stomach. She doubled over, coughing and gasping for breath. The moment the guy's fist landed on her, the blinding red rage surged through Logan. The dragon inside him exploded against his head, fighting to get out, to make him change, to burn the guy to bits.

"How about now?" Archer asked. "Have you changed your mind yet?"

"Don't do it, Logan." She gasped for air and lifted her head so he could see the stern look on her face. She meant it.

But he couldn't let them hurt her.

"Tell me you'll return to the Hidden Lands and I'll let her go," Archer said.

She met his gaze and shook her head with one jerk to the side. He knew what she meant. He dropped his mental walls. *I won't let him hurt you.*

And I won't let him kill you, she replied.

"It's that simple," Archer said.

Indecision went through Logan as he watched her catch her breath, her face red. She was serious about not wanting them to kill him but he couldn't stand the thought of them torturing her.

"Release her," Logan demanded.

"Only if you give your word to return through the portal."

"Don't do it, Logan."

"Shut her up," Archer snapped.

One of the Drakana punched her again. This time in the face. The force of it was too much and she crumpled to the ground. The dragon inside him shrieked with rage. The anger and hate boiled through him as he surged forward. Bree had loosened the knots enough to give some slack to the rope. It was all he needed.

He didn't recognize the feral growl he emitted, nor did he realize his dragon started to push through his control. Smoke rose from the singed ropes and he shoved them off, released from his bonds. He reached for the unfortunate Drakana who punched Bree and wrapped his hand around his throat. And crushed it without a thought. He threw the man's limp body aside as though he were nothing but a ragdoll.

He turned his attention to the second man who held Bree. He released her and backed away, hands up as though he surrendered. He wasn't quick enough, though, as Logan snatched him by the shirt and yanked him forward. Archer shouted something but Logan had no idea what it was because he was so focused. Bree uncurled her body from the floor and stumbled to her feet, staggering toward him. He pulled back a fist intending to pummel the guy.

"Logan."

Somehow her voice got through his haze and he stopped with his fist midair. He blinked, the red haze dissipating as he focused on his surroundings once again. There were more Drakana in the room, this time armed.

"Let him go. I'm all right."

His hand uncurled from the man's shirt as he released him. The guy scurried away. Bree stepped in front of him and put her hands on his chest, looking up at him. When he saw her, that wild part of him that wanted nothing but blood and death calmed.

Logan focused on her face. She had a red spot on her jaw where the guy hit her. The corner of her mouth had a drop of blood.

There's too many of them to fight, she said, her gaze on his.

He glanced around the room and saw she was right. There was no way he was getting out of this alive. And if he did, he'd only be dragged back to the Hidden Lands to be killed there. He wrapped his arms around her, pulled her to him and hugged her hard.

"Isn't that nice. Two lovers embrace." Disdain dripped from Archer's words. "I knew she was a weakness for you but I had no idea how much."

"Call off your Drakana, Archer," Logan said.

"Ah, so you've come to your senses. You intend to come back with me?"

"No. This fight is between you and me. It comes down to that. I have a proposition for you."

"Intriguing." An eyebrow lifted in amusement. "Do tell."

"Let Bree go and I will fight you for the clan," Logan suggested. "A fight to the death."

She stiffened in his arms and knew she'd have something to say about that so he erected those mental walls to keep her out. He didn't want her trying to talk him out of it. His mind was made up. He had to take care of Archer once and for all and get back the clan. Get back to the Hidden Lands and save his realm with the Blood Stone, though how he was going to do that, he still had no idea.

"A fight to the death?" Archer repeated and then laughed. "My boy, do you know what you're getting yourself into?"

"Yes." The word hissed out on a heated breath. His inner beast pounded against his skull, wanting out with a fervent desperation. He could have shifted, any moment, into his true form and taken Archer and Zak out with one fiery breath. But that was something he didn't want Bree to witness, ever.

Besides, he wanted to fight Archer face to face, man to man. He wanted this to be over.

"I should have fought you before I left the Hidden Lands instead of running. You have no right to my clan. The clan belongs to me as heir," Logan said. "Not you. Never you."

A darkness came over his face as he looked at Logan. His brow creased with his distaste, his disgust, his disdain. Full of menace. He must have truly hated his father, Eli, for him to want to wipe out his entire line. Archer had transferred that hate toward Logan and wouldn't stop coming after him until he was dead.

"You are no longer a lord." Archer was all too happy to point that out. "You gave that up when you left to come here. You abandoned your realm like the coward you are. You expect me to give it back to you?"

The dragon flame flared bright and hot deeply inside him. Bree sucked in a quiet sharp breath. She must have felt it too.

"And that was a mistake. One I plan to rectify now." Logan's voice was surprisingly calm despite the rage bubbling through his veins.

"Ah, then you plan to give up her? She is a human after all." He spat as though the word human was something revolting.

Indeed, some dragons didn't believe in procreating with humans or even fraternizing with them. They were a lesser race. And dragons were far superior. But his father had never thought so. His father respected them, studied them for ages, and learned as much about them and their realm as he could. Perhaps that was why his father thought it would be best if they migrated to the human realm to live out their remaining days.

Logan squeezed her tighter in his arms. He knew what he had to do even though it pained him to verbalize the words.

"Even her." The lie seared through him when he heard her gasp again.

"You don't mean that," Bree whispered, her voice wavering.

Her upturned face had drained of color. Her body shook from what he could only suppose was a combination of fury and heartbreak. She pushed against his mind, trying to probe him to see if he was telling the truth of not. He pushed her back, away, not wanting even her to know his plans.

Of course, he didn't mean it. He could never give up Bree. She should know that no matter what he said aloud. Even so, he didn't want her to know the truth on the off chance her facial expressions would give it away.

Logan squeezed her again, hoping that would be enough to reassure her.

"Do you wish to duel to the death for clan leadership as our forefathers did in ancient days?" Archer asked.

"I do. Do you accept the challenge?"

Bree stiffened in his arms again. But he had to accept. It was the only way to be rid of the man.

Or it could be the end of him.

"What are you rules with this challenge?" Archer folded his arms over his chest.

"Hand to hand combat. Weapons optional. No shifting," Logan said.

Even though Logan's dragon was bigger than Archer's, he was more powerful magic-wise. That would give him an edge when Logan wasn't sure his power had returned to full strength. He didn't want to give him an advantage.

"Very well. I accept." A smile spread on Archer's face. "And where shall we have this duel?"

"Right here. Right now."

"Logan, no. You don't have to do this." He could hear the panic in her voice.

"Oh, but he does. Once the terms have been accepted, there is no going back. Zak, escort the lady away from here. Have one of the men take her back to the city."

She shoved out of Logan's arms and turned to face Archer. "I'm staying."

"Bree, you should go back to the city," Logan said.

She spoke to him over her shoulder. "Are you saying you're okay with having some lunatic drive me back? Who's to say they won't kill me as soon as we're away from here? I'm staying. Don't try to talk me out of it."

Archer chuckled. "She's a clever girl and high spirited. No wonder you like her."

As much as he hated the idea, he knew her mind was made up and how stubborn she could be.

"We will face off in four hours," Archer said.

"Why four hours?" Logan wanted to know.

"To give you time to think about how you're going to die. Use your time wisely to mentally prepare." Archer made a motion to Zak to take Bree away.

"Where are you taking her?"

"I can't have you two together, now can I? We'll be taking care of the lady until show time."

Logan's hands clenched into a fist. "If you harm her—"

"I assure you, she will be well cared for. You have my word."

His word wasn't good for much but he had no choice. He met Bree's blazing gaze one last time before she was shoved out the door. He kept his gaze on her for as long as he could before she disappeared from view, down the steps, and into the night.

"You realize you can't win," Archer taunted. "I know the poison is still in your veins."

And to prove it, he used his dragon magic on Logan. The pain sliced into him as it had in the diner and he crumpled to his knees. The burning poison seared him from the inside out. A cold sweat popped out on his brow as he huddled on the floor, trying to catch his breath.

Archer preyed on his weakness to make him more vulnerable to attack. Logan knew, then, what he'd have to do to survive and keep Archer from winning. He'd have to shift into dragon form. He hated knowing Bree would see him that way. He had hoped to keep that part of him from her.

"I am going to enjoy killing you. In four hours."

Two of his Drakana lifted him off the floor and put him in the chair. They tied him up again, leaving him to think about everything.

And nothing.

❧ 16 ❧

Four hours later, Logan was untied from the chair. His whole body was numb as he was hoisted up by the Drakana sent to get him. Pinpricks punctured his fingers and toes as feeling rushed back into them as well as his arms and legs.

Every hour on the hour, Archer had returned to inflict more of his dragon magic on Logan to stress the effects of the poison. By the time the four hours were up, Logan was in such a weakened state, he wasn't sure if he could fight.

He knew that was Archer's plan all along.

Fuck all.

And it wasn't like he could fight Archer in his weakened state. His own magic had yet to make an appearance.

"Time to die," one of the Drakana said and chuckled.

His head hung between his shoulders as the two Drakana dragged him from the beach house. It took all his energy to make each step.

Logan had lost track of time but he suspected it was nearing dawn by the way the sky began to lighten from black to indigo. Archer had set up a large perimeter of torches on the beach giving it the feel of the Grand Arena back home. The place where such combats would have happened many years ago.

Archer must have called on a few friends because the crowd had grown. Not only were the Drakana there, but also others he recognized from the Hidden Lands. They must have come to watch them fight. He recognized a few as supporters of Archer from the Hidden Lands. He also recognized a few of his father's supporters.

He spotted Bree standing between two Drakana guards, her hands bound with rope. Despite the fierce look of defiance on her face, she appeared to be unharmed. In his haze when Archer continued to attack him, he had felt her try to probe his mind and resisted her. He didn't want her in his head.

Even now, he felt the tentative push of her mind against his. He opened it a little.

Please don't do this, she said.

He looked away. There was no way he would reconsider after everything Archer had taken from him. He needed vengeance for his parents. She had to understand that since she wanted her own vengeance for Mario's death.

His only regret was not telling her he loved her, too. He should have said it. At the time, he had been taken aback by her sudden admission. But as he was being tortured by Archer, the only thing he could think of was Bree. How much she had come to mean to him in the short time they had been together. And it went beyond their bonding. His feelings went much deeper. He loved her and he wanted to spend the rest of his days with her.

Coming to terms with his feelings for her was all the determination he needed to stay alive.

Logan knew she shot him a dark glare of frustration, anger, and fear. He didn't want her to see him like this nor did he want her to see him change into his dragon form but he knew it was the only way to defeat the man. He knew it was the only way he would survive.

Even though he had agreed to no shifting, he would be willing to break that agreement to save himself, his clan, and the Hidden Lands.

He paused in the center of the perimeter. Archer moved forward and waved one of the Drakana with him. The man carried what looked like a silver tray supporting two swords. Another Drakana carried a shield and a whip. This was why Archer wanted four hours to prepare. He wanted to make a spectacle of their duel.

He must be confident that he was going to win. But that was Archer. Always the showman. Always the one who wanted the most attention. Proving that he was more powerful than anyone. That he should be followed no matter what.

Logan intended to take him down a notch.

It had been a while since Logan fought with swords, but it was something his father taught him years ago when he was still a young man.

"I hope you don't mind I invited a few friends to witness the duel." Archer waved toward the gathering.

Logan scanned the crowd, the firelight flickering over the faces. He paused when he noticed, Jaxson, his friend since childhood. The friend he had left behind in the Hidden Lands when he went through the portal. He hadn't even thought about him or what fallout might have happened after his abrupt departure. When Logan's gaze landed on him, Jaxson gave him a slight nod. As if to say he was on his side. Then he indicated the man standing next to him.

Rafe.

Rafe had a black eye and his face had seen better days. But he was standing on two feet, ready to do battle if necessary.

Hope swelled. Even though he had been prepared to face Archer alone, he wasn't. Rafe had said from the beginning he would be there when he decided to go after him. He kept true to that even though Logan didn't want him there. Even though Logan knew Rafe was as weak as he was.

Rafe gave him a nod, too.

We stand together. His voice pulsed through Logan's mind.

"You said weapons were optional. I have provided these in case you choose to have a weapon." Archer motioned toward the Drakana guards standing next to him.

"I did say that." Logan nodded agreement. "If we're to fight as our ancients, then I choose to fight with a sword."

A smile broke out on Archer's face. "I'm so glad you decided that."

Archer picked up the sword and the whip. That left the other sword and the shield for Logan. He took them and then waited as the Drakana exited the perimeter. Again, Logan felt Bree's tentative push against his mind. She was desperate to get to him but he pushed her back. He didn't need her in his head right now. He needed to focus.

The two of them faced off. The only sounds were the crashing waves against the beach and the flicking of the flames of the torches.

"Shall we begin?" Archer asked.

They circled each other, closing the distance between them. Logan gripped the hilt of the sword tightly in his hand, the weight of it almost more than he could hold in his weakened state. He could see the glittering excitement in Archer's eyes as though he were about to get everything his heart desired.

Logan would make sure to crush that dream.

Archer charged with his sword hand raised as he dragged the whip behind him. Logan lifted his shield and widened his stance to brace for impact. It came a moment later, the blade striking the wooden shield and sending a vibration through his arm. It rattled his back teeth.

He recovered and went on the attack. Their swords clashed, metal singing against metal in a high-pitched ting. Archer's face was close to Logan's. He could see beads of sweat popping out on the older man's brow.

"You won't win," the man taunted. "Give yourself up now and save your humiliation."

Logan thought of his parents, his clan, Bree. "Never."

They parried and clashed swords again. Logan found a surge of energy, slamming his short sword over and over against Archer's. He'd been so intent on what he was doing, he'd forgotten about the whip until the metal claws dug into his back and ripped. He arched, a shout of pain erupting from him before he could stop it.

Archer jerked the whip away and the little metal points ripped his shirt and flesh.

The crowd surrounding the perimeter of torches shouted with a mixture of cheers and boos, but Logan couldn't tell who was rooting for whom. Nor did it matter. All that mattered was Archer falling dead.

"You are no match for me, boy," Archer said. "Everyone knows it. Even the other clan leaders."

Archer hadn't been prepared for his next move as Logan pushed him back and back and back. He swung wide, slashing across the man's chest. He ripped his shirt and thought he'd missed until he saw the drops of blood welling along the cut. That gave Logan satisfaction.

But Archer bared his teeth in a silent, feral growl. Losing patience with his sword, Archer dropped it and opted for the use of the whip. He lashed out at Logan. He managed to block most of his shots with the wooden shield but after several moments of being pummeled, the wood splintered and cracked.

He wasn't sure how much longer he could keep from getting lashed with the spiky whip. He had no way to counterattack even if he wanted to since Archer came at him over and over and over. When he continued to miss, Archer paused long enough to emit a shout of frustration.

That was Logan's moment of opportunity. He lunged at Archer, his blade connecting with his shoulder. The surprise was evident on the man's face when he realized Logan had injured him. Blood dripped from his wounded shoulder.

Archer stumbled backward, still holding the whip and trying to regroup. Logan paused to watch him, seeing him get his bearings and knew he would have to parry the next attack but he wasted too much time trying to decide when and how that next attack was going to come.

Then something strange happened. A shout erupted from the gathering crowd catching both of their attentions. Logan and Archer turned toward the sound. Logan could see men moving in the shadows just out of the circle of light. He couldn't quite make out who they were.

Until Niko stepped into the circle, his fangs bared and blood on his chin.

Logan glanced toward Bree. Her face paled as several vamps surrounded her. The Drakana guarding her were dead, their throats ripped out in the most horrible fashion.

"Dragon," Niko greeted.

"Who the hell is this?" Archer demanded. "This isn't your fight."

"It is where he is concerned." Niko pointed to Logan. "I've come to claim my blood slave."

Even though he hadn't been tuned to Bree, he heard her intake of breath. His gaze swung to her on the other side. She shook her head.

"You'll stay away from her," Logan said.

"Then you offer yourself?"

"No," Logan said.

"What is this about? What are these...things doing here?" Archer scrunched up his face with a look of distaste at the vampire.

Which was the wrong thing to do. A dark look came over Niko's features as he hissed and bared his fangs at Archer.

"You will be dealt with later," Niko said then swung his gaze back to Logan. "Your decision has been made. The girl belongs to me."

Niko spotted her and started for her. Logan moved to block his path.

"Get the filthy intruder!" Archer shouted.

Drakana swarmed into the make-shift arena. A second later, Niko's soldiers followed and attacked the Drakana who were trying to apprehend Niko. A fight broke out between them. It gave Archer the distraction he needed to attack Logan. He lashed out with his whip, the leather coiling around Logan's sword arm, the metal spikes digging into his forearm. With a wicked grin, Archer jerked back on the whip, making Logan stumble forward since the metal teeth from the whip still had hold of his skin. Pain shot through his arm to his fingers, turning them numb.

Logan lost sight of Niko and immediately called out to Rafe to protect her. He got no reply as he then shut off his mind to the agony and tried to concentrate. Sweat beaded his forehead and rolled down his back. Archer had rendered his sword arm useless. His fingers opened and the blade hit the earth in a silent thud.

Archer pulled him closer, that same feral smile on his face. "You are defeated. Give up and I will show you mercy."

"And if I don't?" Logan's eyes narrowed, his head cocked to one side, as he looked at his enemy.

"Then you will die a slow, painful death. I assure you I have more weapons at my disposal."

Logan didn't doubt that for a second. But he also had no interest in seeing what those other weapons were. He focused on the man in front of him and got a resurgence of adrenaline. He swung his free hand balled into a fist. It connected with the man's nose with a sickening crack. His head snapped back and he'd given enough slack on the whip that Logan could wrap his hand around it and jerk it away from him.

He spun, kicked up, and landed a foot on Archer's chest, knocking him to the ground. He placed a booted foot on his chest and pushed him down.

"How about now? Still think I'm going to lose?"

Archer gazed at him with a cross between amusement and annoyance. He grabbed his foot and wrenched his ankle, making him topple to the ground. Damn it, he should have seen that coming. Archer reached for the handle of his whip and gave it a wild jerk. It released from Logan's arm, taking with it more flesh. Blood seeped from the fresh wounds. But even so, Logan refused to cry out with the pain. He clamped his jaw so tightly, the muscles ached as he ground his back teeth and hustled to regain his footing.

Archer was on his feet again, using the whip. This time Logan ducked, narrowly missing the wicked tines. He'd lost sight of his sword so now he'd have to rely on his fists and wits. Most of all, he needed to get that damn whip out of Archer's hand.

Chaos reigned around them. He tuned his thoughts to Bree and found her with Rafe and Jaxson as they fought off the vampires. How the hell did they even find them?

Logan ducked again from another crack of the whip, this time going all the way to the ground. He fisted a handful of sand and tossed it into Archer's face. The rules never said they had to fight fair. He coughed and sputtered and was disoriented enough for Logan to kick the hated whip from his hand.

Logan threw a punch but Archer anticipated and returned the favor. His fist landed on the side of Logan's jaw making his head snap back. Before he could recover, Archer hit him again, this time connecting with his nose. He heard it crack and knew immediately it had broken. The next hit knocked him off his feet. He landed in the dirt on his ass. Archer kicked him hard in the ribs.

Logan was losing. Somehow, he had to find that inner strength. He had to dig deep and deeper.

While Logan reeled, Archer found his sword and put the point to his throat.

Logan focused on the cold steel at this throat, the evil grin on Archer's face, the throb of his pulse in his ears. The beast within him had gone eerily quiet and he searched for it, calling to it. He conjured a vision of Bree getting punched because of him, of Mario dying because of him.

"You can't beat me," he taunted. "I will destroy you like I destroyed your father."

Archer reared back and flung the sword away. Logan knew what was coming next—he could sense the change before Archer's body contorted and a minute later he had transformed into his dragon self—a large black dragon.

The lying sack of shit cheated.

Logan should have known he wouldn't keep his word. It would force him to do the same. He knew it was now or never. He had to shift into dragon form.

The rage wavering through him surged forward. His body shifted ever so slightly and the first twinge of change rippled through him. He morphed from man to dragon.

Logan's giant, red-scaled body surged upward, shoving back a surprised Archer. His wings flapped against the night sky as he went upward, as though to escape, but then he turned and headed straight down for the large black dragon.

Logan pulled back, flapping his wings hard to stabilize his body as he met Archer head on. They both hovered in the air in a silent standoff before colliding into each other.

Below them everything stilled as all eyes—even the vamps— focused on the two massive creatures above them. He heard the flutter of Bree's mind against his—now that he was in dragon form she would be harder to keep out. But it was to Rafe he sent the message.

Take care of Bree.

Take care of her yourself, damn you, his terse reply.

And then he heard Bree's voice. *Logan, if you die on me, so help me I will kill you.*

Now was the time to tell her. *I love you, too, Bree.*

Her mind went silent in his. He re-focused on Archer and what he had to do. As soon as he shifted into dragon form, he could feel his wounds heal, the effects of the poison were gone. And his magic had once again made an appearance. He was bigger than Archer. Stronger. Faster. He had a chance to win.

He *would* win.

He lunged and clamped his massive jaws onto Archer's neck, his teeth breaking through the thick scales with a sickening crunch. Archer emitted a howl. Logan dove toward the ground, releasing the black dragon only a few feet above it. Archer's body slammed against the sand with a reverberation that shook the beach and flickered the torch flames.

Blood seeped across his scales as he tried to lift his head. But Logan had pulled back up into the night sky. He'd had enough of Archer. The steam built up in the back of his throat, the heat hovering at boiling point until he was ready to release it.

Archer's elongated head turned upward and their eyes met one last time.

"Logan!"

Her panicked voice squelched the fire building inside him, making a bit of his rational human mind return to him. He didn't want to incinerate Archer in front of Bree or the clansmen. He had to show mercy, to show he was the better leader. He'd broken the no-shifting rule of their duel. Would he now murder the man in front of them, too?

He landed on the ground next to Archer and belched his sulfuric steam at him. Then turned away, making eye contact with Bree. She stood with her hands fisted at her side. Behind her, Rafe and Jaxson held off the vampires.

The clan is mine. You will step down, he said to Archer.

So you say, was his snippy reply.

"Look out!"

Bree's sharp yell made him turn in time to see Archer rise up and release his own blue-white flame. Logan ducked, narrowly missing the stream. But others were caught in the flames. The scent of charred flesh and scorched earth surrounded them.

Logan lowered his head and charged, emitting a feral growl. His hard-scaled head landed in Archer's throat. The black dragon emitted a screech, his front claws scratching at Logan. Logan sank his claws into his throat and ripped. A gurgle erupted from Archer before he fell to the ground. Blood seeped from the open wound into the sand.

Their long-standing feud was over.

Knowing Logan was a dragon and seeing it were two different things entirely. Bree was in awe as she watched the man she loved transform from human to dragon in a matter of seconds. His long, lean body was covered in iridescent red scales that reflected the firelight in an ominous way.

He still had those same tawny eyes, sharp and alert. His powerful limbs with splayed digits ended in sharp claws that cut his target to ribbons. Graceful, closed-set leathery wings ran from his shoulders to his lower back and hosted a twenty-foot astonishing wingspan. A ragged membranous crest ran from the base of his skull to the tip of his spiked tail. And when he turned his elongated head and opened his wide mouth showing off huge teeth, he belched a ball of fire that destroyed everything in the nearby vicinity.

She was momentarily awestruck by the beauty of him as he glided through the night sky following Archer who had also shifted into his dragon form. Archer had unreflecting black scales which would have given him somewhat of an advantage had the duel been in the dead of night. As it was, the sun peeked over the horizon and the torches' firelight illuminated him as a black hole with eyes and large protruding teeth. Not a beautiful, graceful dragon. Sharp horns protruded from his head, glistening in the half-light.

Rather disconcerting.

Everything had happened so fast, and yet at the same time, it seemed like time stood still. She had been on edge from the first moment Logan picked up that sword. Even more so when it appeared Archer would win the match and kill him.

And then the vamps showed up.

Watching Logan and Archer fight one another in their dragon form had been terrifying and beautiful at the same time.

Logan had moved to keep Niko from her but Archer had struck again, giving Niko another opportunity to head toward her. But Rafe was there and another man she didn't know standing in front of her like a shield.

Niko and his band of mafia soldiers charging to attack her struck terror through her. Rafe and the other man moved to intercept them, shoving them off and trying to keep them at bay while overhead Logan fought for his life.

"Stand aside, dragon," Niko said. "She's mine."

"Not if I have anything to say about it. She isn't," Rafe said.

Behind them, the black dragon landed on the ground with such force, it was like a small earthquake had hit the area. It jostled everyone on their feet and Bree reached out to steady herself on Rafe's shoulder.

Bree could see Logan was about to burn the black dragon alive and shoved past Rafe and Niko.

"Logan!"

She wasn't sure what made her call his name other than the sudden impulse to stop him. It didn't seem right for Logan to kill the man that way in front of his clansmen.

He hesitated then landed next to the half-dead dragon. When his gaze met hers, she shivered. The feral beast he was peered at her but she saw it fade, and for a moment, she got a hint of the man behind the dragon. The man she loved. Movement behind him caught her attention.

"Look out!"

The next thing she knew someone grabbed her from behind, wrapping powerful arms around her. Someone else snatched her by the hair and yanked her head back. There was a commotion out of her line of vision. A burst of blue-white flame and then a sickening smell of charred earth and flesh. She saw the glistening fangs of Niko then.

"I am going to enjoy this." His breath fanned her exposed neck.

She wanted to cry out but couldn't. Niko's head dipped toward her neck. Where the hell was Rafe?

She got her answer a second later when Niko flew backward out of her line of vision. The arms around her went slack and she was free.

"Your vampire magic doesn't work on me," Rafe said. "And she's not going to be your blood slave."

Niko hissed and then moved so quickly he was nothing but a blur. He was on Rafe in a second. The man who had come with Rafe moved to stand in front of her.

"Who the hell are you?" she asked.

"Jaxson. I'm a friend of Logan's. I should get you to safety."

"I'm not leaving."

She watched as Niko made a valiant effort to sink his teeth in the side of Rafe's neck but he was having none of it. He landed a punch on the cheek of the vamp, which made him release his hold on him. Niko stumbled backward in the sand, his feet tangling on the mini sand dunes until he stumbled and fell.

The crowd went quiet. Archer supporters hurried away. Others stood outside the ring of fire and waited to see what was going to happen next.

Logan landed in the circle, his big body hovering over the vampire. And something about his stance reminded her of the T-Rex in *Jurassic Park*, even more so when he threw his head back and roared so loud, she had to cover he ears.

"He's pissed now," Jaxson muttered.

Logan's elongated head tipped downward and he was nose to nose with Niko.

Niko's eyes widened and even as he tried to move out of the way, he couldn't. The dragon had pinned him to the ground, his front legs on either side of the vamp's body. He puffed out a gust of white steam, ruffling the vamp's clothes and hair.

She reached out to him with her mind but he was in such a rage she couldn't get through. She glanced behind him and saw why. Archer's black dragon body lay lifeless on the beach, bleeding, coloring the pale sand crimson.

"Logan," Bree called.

He lifted his head and those glittery golden-brown eyes met hers. She moved out from behind Jaxson, next to Rafe and stood close to him. He huffed out a breath. Warm steam surrounded her. But she didn't flinch. She refused to flinch.

Bree couldn't help it. She reached a hand toward him, to touch him. She had to find out if his dragon form was as hot to the touch as his human form. Her hand landed on his snout as he dipped his head toward her, reminding her of a big cat as she petted him.

His scales were indeed warm to the touch, but nothing like the man inside. The only thing she recognized about the creature in front of her was those eyes she knew so well, fierce and intelligent and determined.

"Don't kill him," she whispered.

He will never stop hunting you. There was something primitive and feral about the voice in her head. It sent a shiver through her. She had never heard that from the man behind the beast.

What if I could make a deal with him? she suggested, thinking fast.

He blinked but didn't answer. She took that to mean he was considering.

I will offer his life in exchange for him leaving me alone and forgiving my father's debt. If he refuses, you can fry him.

A deep chuckle went through her mind. *Deal.*

"I do not need you to bargain for my life, *human*," Niko said.

"Shut up." She pinned him with her best glare as he clamped his mouth shut. "My father owed you money. If I bargain with the dragon here for your life, will you release me from that debt?"

Consideration flickered over his face as he paused for a long moment. "I will."

She met Logan's gaze again. "Release him, Logan."

The dragon didn't respond for a long moment. He lowered his head as if to acquiesce and then backed away. Niko scrambled to his feet, brushing sand from his expensive designer suit, a look of disdain crossing his pale features.

"How did you find me?"

"I tapped your phone." He grinned, proud of his resourcefulness as he glanced toward the dragon with a wary eye. "You called your friend, Meg, and talked to her just long enough for me to locate you. It was easy to follow you here to the beach. Dragons are not very stealthy creatures."

The dragon emitted a deep rumbling growl and she could hear him in her head chastising her for her stupidity. She shoved him away. She'd deal with that later, even though she knew he was right. Calling Meg had been a risk. She knew it at the time she did it, but she had to know how things fared at the bar.

Niko clamped a hand on her wrist then and brought it up to his face, sniffing her as though she were a juicy piece of meat. Logan didn't like that. Neither did Rafe or Jaxson. The two men closed in around her. The dragon head-butted Niko hard enough to make him release her.

"Don't touch her again," Rafe warned.

"I still need a blood slave," Niko said. "As payment for the one taken from me."

Steam spurted from Logan's snout, surrounding the vamp.

"Do you want to live?" she asked.

"My life does not matter as much as Dominic's. I want him to live. If I could, I would give my life to save his. But as it is, I still need a blood slave."

"That's what I asked," she said through clenched teeth.

And Logan growled again.

"The dragon behind you wants to fry you. How do vampires react to dragon fire, I wonder?" she said. "All I have to do is give him the word. I will not be your blood slave and neither will anyone else. Is that clear?"

Niko clenched his jaw. "Very."

"Good. Now take your henchmen and go."

She had to admit, bargaining with the man made her feel powerful. He may walk away alive today, but she still had vengeance on her mind. She would make sure Dominic, the leader of the vampire mafia, and Niko would pay for what they did to her father. They had taken so much from her. It was time for her to repay the favor.

In time. Whether Logan liked it or not.

She hadn't planned out when that would be, but it would happen sooner rather than later.

"Very well. I release you from your father's debt and will no longer hunt you as a blood slave."

"He's lying," Jaxson said.

Bree's heart tripped as she looked at the man who stood rigid next to Rafe. His intense gaze was focused solely on Niko who glanced back at the dragon still hovering behind him. He made a signal to his vampire soldiers. They started to move toward them.

"How do you know that?" Even as she asked it, she knew he had to be right.

"I just do," he replied.

Logan snorted, ruffling the vampire's perfect coif. The dragon reared back on his haunches and blew out a heated breath. He swiped the vampire into his front claw and took flight into the pre-dawn sky, leaving her standing on the beach with Rafe and Jaxson, mouth agape.

Logan had kidnapped the vampire.

❧ 17 ❧

Logan could have killed the vampire with one mighty squeeze of his claw. But he didn't. He resisted the urge as he flew through the early morning air toward the beach house. He could smell it from the air.

He hadn't meant to destroy the house by crashing through the roof, hind legs first, but he had to get that Blood Stone. He left a path of destruction behind him as he made his way to the bedroom where the scent of it was strong inside Bree's bag and even the velvet pouch.

He released the vampire. Niko stumbled to regain his footing and then watched with curiosity as Logan tried like hell to get to the Blood Stone. He had no dexterity with his oversized claws and ended up shredding the material of her bag to get to the small pouch. He puffed out an annoyed breath, frustrated he couldn't shift yet. He eyed the vamp but there was no way he'd trust him with the Blood Stone.

"Do you wish for help, dragon?" Niko didn't bother to hide his snide tone as he folded his arms over his chest.

A deep rumble sounded in Logan's chest.

"Oh, you want that?" He bent and reached for the pouch.

Logan puffed scorching air across his face and snarled. It fluttered the man's hair and he didn't like that much. His jaw clenched tightly, the muscles flexing along the edge as he stepped back, holding his hands up in surrender.

"Then get it yourself."

Oh, he would as soon as he could shift again. He lowered his head, closed his eyes and concentrated on the metamorphosis. Logan's body arched upward then fell forward, allowing the change to overcome him. When he was a man again, he crouched on the floor, naked as the day he was born.

He looked up at the vampire, who watched his transformation with astonishment in his black eyes.

"I have never seen the likes of that," Niko said.

"And you likely never will again." His voice was raspy and raw from puffing the sulfuric dragon flame everywhere.

Logan snatched the velvet pouch, then got to his feet and prowled the room, stepping over debris as he looked for clothes. He searched through a drawer and found black cargo pants and a shirt. He pocketed the velvet bag. It was sheer luck he and Rafe were close to the same size. Even when it came to shoes. In the closet, Logan found a pair of black combat boots and pulled them on. When he exited the closet, he had a gun in his hand pointed at the vamp.

Niko lifted one eyebrow as he eyed the gun. "You think I'm a threat?"

"Jaxson said you lied about letting Bree go. You still intend to take her as your blood slave, don't you?"

"A debt must be paid," Niko said coolly. "Someone has to pay it."

"It won't be Bree. Never Bree."

"Ah, I see. You're in love with the human woman." He snorted which seemed rather uncharacteristic for a vampire.

"That's between me and her. Now, you're taking me to Dominic."

"I will not."

"You will if you want him to live."

He scoffed. "You intend to save him, then?"

"I have a hunch, and if I'm right, what's in this bag," he patted his pocket, "could be Dominic's salvation. Let's go."

He waved him out of the destroyed house with the gun. Bree's car was still outside. He planned to drive it back to the city to

Dominic. He crouched and grabbed her keys from her destroyed bag. All he needed was the car key and removed it.

"And if you're wrong?" Niko asked.

"Then Dominic dies anyway."

"Fine. I will take you to him. But I want something in return if you're wrong."

Logan narrowed his gaze. "What?"

"Your life. If Dominic dies anyway you become my blood slave."

The damn vamp was determined to get a blood slave out of the deal no matter what, wasn't he? Logan knew it was a gamble. He wasn't certain the Blood Stone would be able to heal Dominic, but he suspected it would. If the lore was right, all he had to do was place the stone on the vamp's wound for a few minutes and allow it to heal.

It was a gamble he had to take.

"Fine."

"Then we leave at nightfall."

"No, we leave now," Logan insisted.

"The sun is coming up. I cannot be in direct sunlight, as you know."

"Then we best hurry, eh?"

Logan wasn't taking no for an answer. He led him to the car, hoping he hadn't made the worst mistake of his life.

"Logan!"

Bree shouted to the departing dragon form and shook her fist but it was too late. Logan was out of sight. Frustration and anger pierced her. Damn him! He took her father's murderer away from her. Did he know she had decided she would track him down and kill him after letting him go? Had he read that in her mind? She clenched her jaw until it ached, hating he bonded to her in such a way he could read all her thoughts. She'd hoped she had guarded those closely but that wasn't the case.

And when Jaxson announced Niko was lying, that seemed to anger Logan all the more.

He was going to kill the vampire. She knew it. He was going to steal her revenge out from under her.

"Damn fool," Rafe muttered.

"It's for the best," Jaxson said. "Niko was planning on taking you as a blood slave, anyway."

She reeled on him. "How do you know?"

He flashed a grin. "Dragon magic."

"Some of us have special abilities, Bree," Rafe explained. "Jax's…superpower is the ability to tell if someone is lying."

Bree turned toward the mafia soldiers still hovering in the vicinity. She glared at each and every one of them. "Get out of here, all of you. And don't show your faces in my bar ever again."

They hesitated for only a moment.

"Unless you want to end up like your boss." She flung her hand upward to the sky to press her point.

They headed away from the beach in a hurry.

"Nice work." There was true admiration in Jaxson's voice. "Rafe, what are we going to do about that?" He indicated the dead dragon.

The remaining crowd had moved inside the ring of torches, surrounding him. Rafe and Jaxson joined them. Bree stayed where she was, looking over their shoulders. They watched as Archer transformed from his dragon into a human. There was a gaping wound on the back of his neck where Logan had bitten him. Bree couldn't help but think how broken and sad the man's body looked.

"Take him back to the Hidden Lands and bury him there," Rafe said.

"But Archer was—"

Rafe cut him off. "It's our way. He deserves a final resting place in our homeland like any of us. No matter what he was. It's the honorable thing to do."

Bree wondered if that was sadness she heard in his voice or something else. Rafe was an exiled knight. He wouldn't be able to return to the Hidden Lands, even in death. She couldn't help but feel a little sad for him. What would it be like to never be able to go home again?

It struck her then. Would she face that, too? Would she have to leave the human realm to live in the Hidden Lands with Logan? Now that he had defeated his enemy, she knew Logan would claim his rightful place as Chief Magistrate.

But he'd betrayed her when he kidnapped Niko. She didn't know if she wanted to go with him anywhere. She didn't know if she could forgive him for taking away what was rightfully hers. He had his justice. She wanted hers. Now she may not get it.

"All right," Jaxson said. "I'll make sure he gets back and receives last rites."

"Good," Rafe said.

One of the onlookers took off his cloak and laid it over Archer's body like a funeral shroud. Jaxson gave him a nod of farewell. He and a few others picked up Archer and started down the beach.

"Where are they going?" She kept her gaze on them as they walked away.

"Back to the portal, most likely. To get back to the Hidden Lands."

"There's another portal?"

"There are portals everywhere. Come on. I'll take you back to the city."

"What about Logan?"

"Logan can take care of himself."

"But…he's in his dragon form. And he has that vampire."

"The vampire shouldn't have lied," Rafe said, matter-of-factly.

"He's going to kill him, isn't he?" Her voice quivered, not from fear or sadness but from anger. Anger that Logan had taken away Niko.

He shrugged. "Maybe. Come on. Let's go." He waved down the

beach in the opposite direction of the others.

"I want to go by the beach house and get my bag first."

She was thinking of that velvet bag with the precious stones. She didn't want to leave it behind since it belonged to her father. And there was something very odd about the large red stone.

"All right. It's a short walk from here."

He wasn't kidding when he said it was a short walk. She was amazed at how close the beach area Archer claimed and Rafe's house were to each other. But when they arrived in the first light of day, they could see something was horribly, horribly wrong with the house. The roof was caved in or ripped off. It was hard to tell which but it was clear there was a gaping hole in it where something—someone—had torn through it. Luckily it hadn't attracted the attention of any of the neighbors.

She gasped. "What happened?"

"Son of a bitch. Does destruction follow that man everywhere?" Rafe sighed and headed for the door.

"Logan did that?" She stared up at the destroyed roof with awe as she followed him inside.

It was a disaster area inside, too. It looked as though a cyclone had been through the house. Or a giant dragon. Either way, there was a path of destruction along the way. Her heart launched into her throat as she realized where that path led. She hurried past Rafe, following the trail of debris to the master bedroom.

Her bag remained in the middle of the floor but it was ripped to shreds. The velvet pouch with the stones was gone.

Rafe moved to stand behind her. He puffed out an exasperated sigh. "Guess, I'll have to get this place fixed, too."

"He took the stones," she said absently.

"What stones?"

"My father had a velvet pouch full of precious stones. And one that was different from the others."

She sensed him stiffen behind her. "Different how?"

"About this big." She made a motion with her fingers showing him the size of the red stone. "It was dark red. Blood red. And when I touched it—"

"You touched it?"

She blinked, surprised at his terse tone. "Yes. It was the strangest sensation, too."

"How do you mean?" he wanted to know.

"It was as if the stone…latched onto my thumb for a brief moment. You know, like a leech or something. And when I pulled my thumb away, my skin was smeared with blood." She looked at her thumb now, remembering the odd sensation and the way the stone smelled of blood.

"Bree…Did Logan tell you what that stone is?"

"No."

He clenched his jaw. "It's called the Blood Stone. It's an ancient dragon relic."

She stared at him in shocked silence, trying hard not to let her mouth gape open. How the hell did her father acquire an ancient dragon relic along with all those other precious stones? And why stash it in her apartment for safekeeping? Did he know what he had? Was he trying to get rid of it?

"So why did he make a stop here to pick it up?"

A look of disgust passed over his face. "I think I know why and you're not going to like it."

She folded her arms. "Try me."

"The Blood Stone is said to have magical healing properties. He kidnapped Niko to force him to take him to the mafia boss, Dominic. If I were Logan, I'd use the Blood Stone as a bargaining chip to heal Dominic and release you from your father's debt."

A cold sensation pierced through her. Logan was going to heal the very man who ordered her father's death. She'd had plenty of time to think about it over the last few days and she'd concocted the idea the mob boss wanted her father dead because he owed him money. Dominic allowed Niko to decide how and when Mario died—so Niko decided he'd turn him into his blood slave while he tortured him.

Dominic and Niko were both her enemy and she wanted them

dead.

If Logan took that from her, she would never forgive him.

"You mean, he heals Dominic with the Blood Stone and because Logan gave him his life back, he says we're square," she said.

"Something like that." He nodded.

"Take me to him."

"Bree—"

"Don't give me an excuse." She wagged a finger in front of his face. "You spoke with this mob boss, didn't you?"

"Well…yes."

"Then you know where he is. Take me to him."

"But…why?"

"Because I'm going to stop Logan."

"And if you can't?" he asked.

"Then I'm going to kill Dominic myself."

The sun was up and burning brightly as they arrived in Manhattan. Niko found an old jacket of Bree's in the backset and covered up as much of his exposed skin as he could. He was not happy about the situation, but Logan didn't care much about what made him happy. Only that he was going to get to Dominic and put this thing with the mob to rest once and for all.

For Bree.

Likely by now, she had figured out what he intended to do and he would have to deal with the fallout. He knew she was going to be angry. He had prepared for that. He was also well aware of the way she had tried to barge into his mind to tell him off. He'd shut her down.

It wasn't so easy for her to get inside his thoughts now that he had shifted into his human form. He hated doing it to her but it was for the best. He didn't want her talking him out of doing anything and he didn't want her taking on the mafia by herself. It was too dangerous. She didn't understand that now, but in time, she would realize he was doing this for her, keeping her safe.

"Where is Dominic's nest?" Logan asked as they navigated through town.

"The Meatpacking District." Niko gave him the address. "There's a parking garage you can use. Park in there."

Logan complied, knowing he wanted to stay out of the sun as much as possible. He knew the only reason Niko continued to do what he said was because he feared the dragon inside him. He should. Logan was prepared to shift into dragon form and reduce the mafia's nest to ashes if he made one wrong move.

When they were parked, they got out of the car. Logan, still armed with the gun, followed Niko through the garage to a bank of elevators. He punched the level three once they were inside. A moment later, the elevator opened to a private residence.

The apartment was richly decorated with antiques and furnishings that reminded Logan of a bygone era. But he didn't let that distract him. He stayed focused as they made their way through the apartment to a back bedroom. Niko paused at the door.

"You should prepare yourself," he said. "Dominic is not in good condition at all."

Logan nodded.

But when Niko opened the door, he could have never been prepared for the smell that wafted out of the room and accosted his senses. He tried hard not to gag. He put his hand to his nose to block out the horrible scent but it wasn't much of a barrier.

Niko led him to the bed where the mob boss was propped up on pillows. He had a sickly pallor that rivaled that of the healthiest vampire. His sunken eyes were closed as he rested his head against the fluffy pillow. The coverlet was tucked around his thin frame.

Dominic, the once powerful mob leader, was wasting away.

"Why have you brought another dragon to me?" Dominic's voice was quiet and weak. He was hard to hear.

"He's come to help you." Niko moved to stand on the opposite side of the bed.

"He cannot help me. No one can."

Logan stuck the gun in the waistband of his pants at the small of his back. He pulled out the pouch of stones and held them in his hand, feeling the weight. Even though the Blood Stone was inside the pouch, he could scent it.

Dominic rolled his head toward him, his eyes blinking open. "I smell blood."

So, he could scent the stone, too. "I've brought something I believe can heal you."

The man's gaze flickered to the velvet pouch in Logan's hand before his eyes closed again.

"He's too weak," Niko said. "It may be too late."

"Come, help me," Logan ordered. "Show me the wound."

Niko moved to stand next to Logan. He reached for the sleeve of Dominic's old-fashioned gown and shoved it upward, revealing the festering gash. It reeked of sickness and death. Bile rose to the back of Logan's throat. He swallowed it back, trying hard not to be ill.

Logan spilled out the contents of the pouch onto the bed next to Dominic. The Blood Stone was the biggest and glittered back up at them. Niko stared down at it, eyes wide.

"What is it? It smells like blood...blood of more than one person." He looked back at Logan. "Where did you get that?"

"It's an ancient dragon relic. It's been part of my realm for centuries. I believe it will help him, but I can't touch it."

"Why not?" he asked.

"Because it's not meant for me. I need a piece of cloth. Anything."

Niko looked around and found a discarded handkerchief on the bedside table. He handed it to Logan who used it to pick up the Blood Stone.

"Hold his arm. I'm going to place this on him," Logan said.

Niko placed one hand on Dominic's wrist and the other above the wound at the crook of his elbow. Taking a deep breath, Logan placed the stone directly on the wound and then released it. When nothing happened, Niko turned his glare on Logan.

"You see. It doesn't work."

"Wait." Logan help up his hand to silence him.

The stone began to glow faint red. Dominic's brows drew together as he emitted a quiet groan.

"What's happening?" Fear tinged Niko's voice.

"It's working. Watch."

Logan couldn't take his gaze off the stone as it began a faint pulse and then grew brighter and brighter, faster and faster. Dominic twitched, his head jerked to one side.

"Hold him tighter," Logan bit out through gritted teeth.

Niko pressed his arm against the mattress. Dominic's face contorted as though he were in pain, his brows drew together. A whimper escaped him.

"It's hurting him."

Niko reached for the Blood Stone but Logan batted his hand away. "Just wait."

The stone glowed bright now. A flash of red light bathed the entire room before it faded away and the stone was dark once again. Niko released Dominic's arm and stepped back from the bed.

"Get it off him."

Logan used the cloth to remove the Blood Stone, though it wasn't easy. As he knew it would, it had attached itself to the vamp. There was only one thing he knew to do. He placed the cloth in one hand and with his bare fingers, plucked the stone from Dominic. It came off the healed flesh but tried to fuse to him. He dropped it in the cloth but not without leaving behind a smudge of blood.

When the stone was removed, nothing of the wound remained but a faint blue-tinted scar.

Niko moved toward the bed and leaned over him, listening to see if he still breathed.

"I'm still alive, you idiot."

Dominic's voice was stronger as Niko snapped back to an upright position. The mob boss's gaze landed on Logan. His color started to come back and he looked better.

"That was a most strange experience," Dominic said. "It was as though I could sense everyone that stone had touched from the moment of its inception until today."

"What did you see?" Logan wanted to know.

"I saw men, women, conquerors, dragons, a human..." He paused. "Your human?"

Logan suspected then Bree had touched the Blood Stone. He didn't know much about the Blood Stone. No one did except for maybe his father but the secrets died with him. The only hope he had was to get back to the Hidden Lands and find his father's notes on how to heal the realm with the stone.

"Would you care to explain what you did to save me, dragon?" Dominic asked.

"My name is Logan Blake. You can call me that instead of dragon." Logan held up the stone. "I used this. You're welcome."

"Only one other dragon has dared use an insolent tone with me. His name was Rafe. I let him live. Since you saved my life, I owe you a debt," Dominic said.

"That's what he wanted, too." Niko crossed his arms over his expensive suit and glared at Logan. "A debt owed. Letting him live is payment enough."

"I confess it is," Logan said.

Dominic shoved upward, trying to sit up more in the bed. He waved to Niko for his help as he sat forward. Niko fluffed the pillows behind him and helped ease him back into them.

"Tell me what it is you want, dragon. I will see if I can accommodate your request."

"Mario Anderson owed you money—" he began.

Dominic interrupted. "Mario Anderson stole from me and had to pay with his life. He did. But his heir still owes me money. I do not forget a debt."

Logan lifted an eyebrow at the mafia leader. A smile lifted the corners of the vampire's mouth.

"Ah, yes. I see what you're after now. How foolish of me not to realize. His daughter…what's her name?"

"Bree," Logan supplied.

"Yes, Bree. You wish me to forgive the debt her father owed me?"

"I do." Logan gave a nod.

"Master Dominic, I don't think—"

Dominic held up a hand to silence Niko. "I would have surely died this day had you not come with that magic stone of yours. If Bree agrees to continue to sell my synthetic blood—"

"No," Logan said, his tone terse. "She will not. And you and your kind will stay out of the bar."

"You go too far, dragon."

"My name is Logan. Use it."

"I will call you dragon or shithead if it suits me," Dominic replied. "Just because you saved my life does not mean you dictate to me how and where I conduct business."

"It does where Bree is concerned."

He wasn't backing down. He didn't care if he had to kill the mob boss and every vampire in the city. He wasn't going to fail Bree again. When she leaned he saved the life of her nemesis, she likely would never speak to him. Making sure she and the bar were safe from now on was the least he could do.

Niko leaned over and whispered something to Dominic who smiled and nodded.

"Of course. I understand now," Dominic said. "A dragon in love with a human."

Logan's dragon banged against his skull, tired of the vampires. He wanted out and he wanted to belch fire at the two of them and watch them burn.

But he refrained. He clenched his fists and kept his dragon in check, despite the overwhelming urge to shift.

Dominic sighed. "Very well. I will find another distributor for my synthetic blood. I will also release Bree from her father's debt."

"Thank you." Logan relaxed his hands, uncurling his stiff fingers.

"There is still the matter of the blood slave," Niko said.

"No, there isn't." Logan pinpointed him with his dark look as his dragon rattled his head again.

"What blood slave?" Dominic glanced between the two of them.

"You agreed to release me and Bree if Dominic lived." Logan gave a nod toward the vampire leader, ignoring his question. "He lives."

Niko looked as though he had his new toy taken away. "Be gone then, dragon."

Logan dropped the Blood Stone into the velvet pouch then scooped up the remaining stones. He gave him a nod and a jaunty wave as he cinched up the bag and strolled out of the vampire's lair. He hoped that would be the last time he would ever have to see a vampire again.

He exited the building and stepped out onto the busy street. Archer was dead. Bree was safe from the vampires.

He only had one more thing left to do.

$$\approx 18 \approx$$

Bree and Rafe arrived in the Meatpacking District in the early afternoon. Logan, that bastard, had taken her car. He'd removed the ignition key from her key ring and left the rest. It took some time for Rafe to get a ride back to Manhattan. When she asked him how he ended up at the beach, he shrugged, not wanting to answer.

"You mean you didn't come via car?" She pressed the issue.

"I'm sure you knew other dragons were there," he had explained. "Jaxson found me and helped me get to the beach via a portal."

Frustration clawed through her as they waited for an Uber to arrive. Even more frustration went through her when there was a five-car pile-up on the 495. Over four hours later, they arrived in the Meatpacking District. He took her to the three-story building where he said Dominic would be.

"Are you sure about this, Bree?"

"I'm sure." She started for the entrance.

He grabbed her arm, stopped her. "You might not like what you find in there."

"Which is?"

"Dominic healed," he said.

"Because of Logan?" she asked.

He nodded.

It was something she hadn't yet faced. Something she didn't want to face because she didn't want to believe Logan would do that to her. She jerked her arm free.

"I have to see for myself."

"Bree, wait. You don't have to do this."

Her stubbornness reared. "Yes, I do."

"Logan did what he did because he cares about you and he doesn't want these vamps bothering you again," Rafe said. "Can't you see he did it because he loves you?"

Her heart twisted in her chest. Yes, deep down she knew that. But that didn't change anything. "He stole my revenge, Rafe."

"Revenge is cold. Unfeeling. Empty. Even if you got your revenge for your father's death, would you feel like you had justice?" There was something about Rafe's tone that said he knew what he was talking about.

She didn't like how much sense he made. She folded her arms over her chest and refused to look at him. She focused on the door in front of her. "Yes. Logan got his revenge. Why can't I?"

"Because you're not a dragon. You have to understand when a usurper rises and takes over the clan from the rightful leader, the only true way to settle the score is to duel. Archer almost wiped out Logan's entire family. He *had* to do it."

Maybe she didn't understand all the dynamics of the dragon world. Maybe she was being far too hardheaded for her own good. All she knew was that she wanted the men who took her father away to suffer. When her mother died, the only thing she could blame was a faceless villain—cancer. She couldn't get her revenge on the taking her mother's life. Now she had a chance to right the wrong with her father's death.

"Can't you see that?"

She wanted to ignore him. To push him away. To tell him to shut up. But she couldn't. Deep down, she knew he was right. That Logan did what he did to save her from the vampires. It didn't mean she wasn't any less mad. She wasn't. She couldn't stop the anger from boiling inside her. The very least he could have done was talk to her about it, tell her what he planned. Instead, he'd kidnapped the mafia's number two guy.

Was Niko dead? She didn't know. Should she care? Probably

not. She had to get her priorities straight. She had to let it go. She had to bury her father and get back to the bar.

She turned away from Rafe and started down the street.

"Bree, where are you going?" he called after her.

"Home. I'm going home."

She never looked back.

She walked all the way to her apartment. Eighty-plus blocks through the Garment District, past Hell's Kitchen, and Times Square until she made it to Central Park West. She'd managed to salvage her belongings from the beach house and had her keys with her but she knew her apartment was still in a state of disarray.

At this point, she didn't care. She wanted to be home with some semblance of normalcy returned to her life. Ever since she met Logan, things had spun out of control. Nothing had been normal. Her father was dead. Her apartment was in shambles. Her bar was closed down. She needed to figure out what to do and how to get things back to the way they were.

Things would never be the way they were.

When she arrived at her place, tears burning her eyes, her feet throbbing with blisters and her muscles aching, she almost broke down in relief when she saw her apartment door. She shoved the key in the lock and pushed open the door, happy to be home.

Of course, things were still messy. She made her way to the bedroom. Icy pinpricks pierced her followed by a wash of heat.

Furniture had been righted. Her clothes had been picked up and folded neatly or placed in the nearby hamper. The bed had been cleared off and made. Pillows were stacked neatly at the headboard. The comforter smoothed across fresh sheets. There in the center was the garnet velvet pouch and her car key.

Logan had been there. Logan had come to her apartment. He must have been the one responsible for returning her bedroom to order. She couldn't help it. She choked on a sob as she rushed toward the bed and picked up the velvet pouch. There was a hand scrawled note under it that read, *I'm sorry. I had to. Forgive me.* She dumped out the glittering stones on the white comforter and counted them.

The only one missing was the Blood Stone.

He still had it. Rafe was right—Logan had used it on Dominic. Her enemy still lived. The only consolation was she had the remaining stones. Perhaps she could sell them and turn a profit to help get things restarted at the bar. That was her livelihood. She needed it.

She scooped the stones back into the pouch, closed it, and placed it on the bedside table. She would worry about all that later. She climbed in the bed, allowing exhaustion to overtake her.

But try as she might, she couldn't fall asleep. She stared at the ceiling, remembering everything she and Logan had been through together. He'd told her he loved her in her mind. Where had he gone? Why didn't he stick around and wait for her? Why didn't he come back for her?

She huffed out a breath and sat up. She couldn't deal with the mess in the living room, so she turned on the small television in her bedroom and flipped through stations. All the local channels had breaking news about a large fire in East Hampton. A diner had been incinerated burned to the ground. As she watched the foundation smolder—the only thing left—realization smacked into her. The location of the diner was the one where Archer had captured them. The one Vera owned.

"Oh, God, Logan. What did you do?"

One of the reporters on the scene interviewed an eyewitness who said they saw something flying overhead that shot out flames to set the place on fire. They thought it was some new secret technology the government had developed. But Bree knew better. A lump formed in her throat.

She knew what he'd done. The woman at the diner betrayed him, gave him up to Archer. And he was getting back at her. The reporter said there were no casualties but she wondered if that was true. She was surprised Logan was willing to risk shifting into dragon form in broad daylight which made her wonder if he was ever coming back.

Unable to watch anymore, Bree clicked off the television and curled up on the bed. Tomorrow, she had her own demons to face. Tomorrow, she had to make the arrangements to bury her father.

A couple of days later, Bree buried her father in a cemetery on the Upper West Side. When he died, Bear managed to get his body to a supernatural morgue and not the county morgue. To avoid any police entanglements, he'd said. She found it strange and a little beyond her comprehension there was a whole underground of supernaturals that lived and worked and partied under humans' noses. At least she was able to put him to rest.

The days since her father's death had blended together. She couldn't remember the exact sequence of events. Maybe because she hadn't allowed herself to dwell on the fact Logan left her without even saying goodbye. It was over between the two of them, bond or no bond. She hadn't even been able to poke into his mind. It was as though he was gone. Or had erected some serious mental walls to keep her out.

There had been a large turnout for the funeral. The graveside was no exception. Even Rafe showed up along with Meg, Bear, and a mix of supernaturals she recognized as regulars from the bar. Now that she knew who and what they were, she could easily pick them out of a crowd. Thankfully, there were no vampires.

After the graveside service, when her father's casket was lowered into the ground and all the condolences had been offered, she remained seated in the front row. Now she had closure. The warm late summer breeze ruffled her hair. She didn't have the heart to leave. Not yet. She remained a while longer after everyone else filed away.

She smelled him standing behind her. That exotic mystical scent wafted on the breeze. Her eyes fluttered closed as she visualized him. His tall, lean form standing with his arms folded across his broad chest as he kept an eye on her from behind black sunglasses. He was dressed in khakis, black boots, and a three-button Henley with the sleeves pushed to the elbows.

Then she realized that wasn't her visualization of him. He projected his presence into her mind. She sensed the reason he stuck around was his need to protect her. From what, she had no idea. Hadn't he neutralized those threats?

Perhaps it was his way of making up for past deeds. Of leaving her. Of taking away her desire to kill Domenic and Niko.

"You don't have to hang around, you know. I'm a big girl. I'll be okay."

"I'm not leaving you."

Her heart skipped. She didn't want him to leave her but at the same time she wasn't ready to see him.

She sighed. She should ready because there was no avoiding him. At last, she stood and turned away from the fresh grave next to her mother. They stood several feet apart, but it may as well have been miles. She sensed his reluctance to leave.

She couldn't see his expression behind the dark sunglasses. His face was chiseled control that gave away nothing. She stared at him, trying to decide what to say. How to say it.

"You decided to make an appearance, did you?" She pressed her lips together in a thin line.

"I've been busy."

"I saw that on the news." She stuck her small handbag under her arm.

He visibly swallowed, his throat working. "Did you?"

"Did you do it?" She knew he'd know what she meant.

"I had to. She betrayed me."

And he betrayed her but she wasn't going to point that out yet. "Did you kill her, too?" she asked, referring to Vera.

"No. I got even."

She shook her head. "By burning down her place?"

"Dragons take betrayals personally," he said.

Bree pressed her lips together in a thin line. Rafe was right in that she would regret killing but she didn't get to decide. Logan decided for her without first trying to convince her going after Dominic was a bad idea.

"It was a bad idea," he said.

She scowled. "Stop listening to my thoughts."

"Then stop thinking so loudly."

The only way out of the cemetery was around him. He knew it. She knew it. But she couldn't stand there much longer. She had to get past him to get away from him. He refused to step aside. He blocked her path like he had done other times. Taking up all the space. All the air.

She huffed. "Get out of my way, Logan."

"Not until we talk."

"We are talking."

"No. *Talk*. About what happened."

She clenched her jaw. She didn't want to talk about what happened here. Or anywhere else. "There's nothing to talk about."

"There's a lot to talk about and you know it."

"Damn you, Logan." She shoved against his solid body. He didn't even flinch. She may as well shove a brick wall. "Move out of the way."

He gripped her arms. Her instincts took over and she struggled against him, knowing it was a fruitless effort. He held fast, his hands gripping her in their steely grasp firm enough to make her understand he wasn't giving up.

"You reopened the bar," he said.

How did he know that? "I did. Two days ago. Are you following me?"

"I've been keeping watch over you since you made it back to your apartment."

The fine hairs on the back of her neck stood at full attention. Had he been there when she arrived back home and discovered the pouch of stones? Why had he waited so long to approach her? It had been days since she'd been back in the city. Days she had to navigate without him or anyone else to help her make funeral arrangements for her father.

"I know you're angry," he said, again as though reading her thoughts.

"You're right. Maybe we do have a lot to talk about. But not here. Take me back to the bar."

"As you wish." He dropped his hands and turned to leave.

She could have made a break for it then. She could have kicked off her heels and run to her car but he would have caught her. And what was the point of running? It was time to face him and listen to what he had to say. Could she forgive him? She didn't know yet.

She took the lead, heading for her car. He fell in step beside her as though it were the most natural thing. But for her, she couldn't help but feel a little on edge.

"I see you found your car key," he said.

"I did."

She didn't elaborate or comment further as they got in and she drove them the short distance to the bar. It was early afternoon still. They wouldn't officially open for the night for a few more hours, so she and Logan could duke it out and get it over with.

"You think we're going to fight?" he asked as they exited the car.

She glared at him over hood. "Would you please stop doing that?"

"I can't help it," he said. "Since I shifted, your thoughts have become even clearer in my mind."

"Well, since you shifted, I can't hear you at all."

He remained motionless and she could only assume he stared at her from behind the shades. She sighed.

"Would you please take off the glasses so I can see your eyes?"

"Why?"

"Because I want to see your eyes, damn it."

His movement was slow as he reached up and slid the glasses from his nose. Those sexy eyes peered at her, making her shiver with delight. Damn, but he always had that effect on her.

"Better?"

"Yes, thanks."

"You can't mindspeak to me?"

Bree shook her head. She had tried a couple of times since he did his disappearing act but was unsuccessful. She hadn't been able to get through to him. It was like they were on a different frequency or something. Before, though, when he was in his dragon form, his mind was loud and clear inside hers. She had wondered more than once if the shifting had done something to their bond. Fractured it, somehow.

Logan motioned toward the door. "Let's go inside."

She wasn't sure why that sounded like a sexy invitation but it did. And it made her pulse race. Her palms broke into a hot sweat. It wasn't as though they were about to get hot and heavy in her office. They weren't. They were just going to talk and she was going to wrangle an apology and maybe some groveling out of him if it killed her.

Logan held the door open for her. As soon as she stepped across the threshold, Meg spotted her and came around the bar with a too-wide smile.

"There you are. I'm glad you're here." She intercepted them before they could make it very far into the bar. Meg gave Logan a good once-over, her nervous smile softening a bit.

"What's wrong?" Bree asked. She sensed something was off about Meg but she didn't know what.

"There's a woman here to see you." Meg leaned forward and whispered, "Shi'Ann Jones."

Aw, crap. "What is she doing here?" Bree scanned the large room for her but didn't see here. "And where is she?"

"She's in your father's…your office." Meg nodded toward the stairs where her father had once occupied the office.

Bree hadn't been prepared for that and a short stabbing pain lanced her heart.

"I told her to wait in there," Meg added. "I hope that was all right."

"It's fine."

"Who's Shi'Ann Jones?" Logan's gaze cut over to the closed office door.

"A cop," Meg replied.

"What does a cop want with you?"

"I'm sure it's more of my father's unfinished business." Bree started toward the office and Logan followed, falling into step beside her with ease. She spun toward him. "Hold on, mister. What do you think you're doing?"

"I'm coming with you."

"No. You aren't."

"I don't plan to let you out of my sight again, so I am. I'm coming with you whether you like it or not." His tone held a finality that told her it wasn't up for discussion.

It reminded her much of the night on the beach when she refused to leave his side. She refused to return to the city without him.

She huffed and spun on her heel and stomped toward the closed door, her heels clicking on the floor with her agitation. When she opened the door, she had not prepared herself for the sight of her father's office with all his belongings still intact. She froze, her breath catching in her throat.

Logan's hand landed on her shoulder. "You all right?"

The low comfort of his voice rippled through her and she nodded.

The woman, Shi'Ann Jones, had made herself at home by sitting in one of the guest chairs and propping her feet on the edge of the desk. She was dressed in skin-tight black pants with shiny knee-high boots. Her black tunic had gold buttons down the front. The lapels and pockets were trimmed in gold braiding. All that was missing were epaulettes on the shoulders to make her look as military as possible.

"Please remove your feet." Bree's terse tone sliced through the air with such animosity, the woman dropped her feet and stood.

"Sorry." She stuck out her hand then. "I'm—"

"I know who you are." Bree folded her arms across her chest. "What do you want?"

"I don't know who she is." Logan stood behind her, looking over her shoulder at the woman. Bree hoped he was giving her his best glare.

She reached for her ID and flipped open the leather case, showing off her name and badge. "Shi'Ann Jones, 135th Precinct, Supernatural PD." She put it away and her gaze focused on Bree. "I'd like to offer my condolences on the death of your father, Ms. Anderson."

It took all Bree's strength not to roll her eyes. She didn't know why she instantly didn't like this woman, but she didn't. Logan moved to stand next to her and slipped an arm around her shoulders.

"What can we do for you, Officer?" Logan's polite tone irked Bree.

"I'd like to ask a few questions about some business dealings of your late father," she said.

"I know nothing about them." Bree didn't bother to hide her hostility.

"Nothing?" She lifted a brow as if to say Bree might be lying.

"Ms. Jones, today I buried my father after a harrowing ordeal of being chased down, shot at, kidnapped and threatened to be taken as a vampire mafia's blood slave. This is not my idea of a swell time. When I say I knew nothing about my father's business dealings, I meant it. He kept those things from me. All I did was manage the bar."

"You were threatened by a vampire mafia?" Shi'Ann's wide-eye stare went from her to Logan. "Where do you fit into all this, dragon?"

"You leave him out of this." Bree's body stiffened as though she were ready to do battle.

"Bree...I think you should answer her questions."

"Don't tell me what to do."

"She's still upset," Shi'Ann said. "Perhaps I'll come back another time."

"No, you'll do this now and get it over with and then you'll never come back." Even Bree was surprised at her hostile tone. But she was tired of all these little surprises about her father. It cemented the fact she knew nothing about him. She had lost touch with him. Her family was all gone. She had no one.

Logan squeezed her tightly. "You still have me."

A perplexed look came over the cop's face.

Bree rubbed her forehead, trying to make the throbbing headache go away. "I'm sorry."

"You've been through an ordeal. So perhaps I should come back another time."

"What do you wish to know?" Bree asked.

She hesitated a moment, glancing between the two of them before proceeding.

"There was a woman who came to see Mario. A Fae smuggler. Her name was Raelee. She was murdered on the edge of town. The person who killed her was looking for something: a red velvet pouch full of precious gemstones," Shi'Ann said.

Bree stiffened. She had been carrying those damn stones around with her since Logan returned them. She didn't want to leave them in her apartment because she didn't feel like they would be safe there.

"This person came here looking for them but discovered Mario was dead. He then tracked them to your apartment," Shi'Ann said.

"He didn't find them there," Bree said.

"No, but he messed up the place pretty good, didn't he?" she asked.

Cold dread went over her. Maybe that was why Logan was sticking so close to her. He knew something she didn't. Bree nodded.

"He was interrupted in his search," the cop continued. "He didn't find what he was looking for but someone came along and he had to leave in a hurry. Perhaps this vampire mafia looking for you. Either way, he wasn't able to get his hands on the stones."

"Who is this person?" Logan asked.

"I don't have a name, only a race. I've identified him as a kobold tracker."

Bree had no idea what a kobold tracker was but it didn't sound like something she wanted to get to know.

"I can only guess he scented the stones on the Fae and knew she had them. He followed her here hoping to get his hands on them. Have you seen the stones?"

Bree bit her lip. "Yes."

"Do you know where they are now?"

"Perhaps."

"If you do know where they are," Shi'Ann said, "then perhaps you could turn them over to me. They were stolen from the king and queen of Andonia, a small kingdom in Europe. All they want are the stones back."

The flush crawled up Bree's neck and settled into her cheeks. "Is that all? There will be no charges or arrests?"

"None. As long as you hand over the stones," she said.

Bree opened her handbag and pulled out the garnet velvet pouch. She handed them over to Shi'Ann.

She smiled. "Thank you. Their royal majesties will be very happy to have them back."

"Is that all then?"

She nodded. Bree and Logan stepped aside. She headed for the door but paused and turned back, pinpointing Logan with her sharp assessing gaze. "Oh, there is one more thing. You wouldn't happen to know anything about a dragon flying over parts of East Hampton a few days ago, would you? Appears it burned down a couple of buildings."

Logan shook his head. "No, ma'am, I don't."

She stared at him a long moment, as though considering if he was telling her the truth or not. Bree clamped her jaw shut as she shifted from one foot to the other, hoping her fidgeting didn't give her away. She knew the truth. She knew Logan was in the skies that day, breathing fire and burning buildings.

"Very well, then." She looked back at Bree. "Thank you for your help, Ms. Anderson."

As soon as she was gone, Bree blew out a heated breath.

"Why'd you give her the stones?"

"Because it was the right thing to do," she said.

"You know she'll be back, don't you?"

"Because you have the Blood Stone," she said.

Logan nodded. "I need to find out who these royals of Andonia are."

"You think it belonged to them?"

"Don't know. If it did, then it makes me think they must be dragon-shifters, too. And if they had possession of the Blood Stone, then maybe they know how it will be able to heal the Hidden Lands."

Bree moved toward the door, uncomfortable in the office. "Could we talk upstairs?"

"After you."

Logan followed Bree up the stairs reminding him of the day he had been introduced to her as the new security guy. They, of course, had already been acquainted when she helped save him from the effects of the poison running through his veins. She had been irresistible then as she was now.

More now as she was dressed in a straight black skirt, black shirt, and sensible black heels accentuated the muscles in her calves. Calves he'd had the supreme pleasure of running his hands over.

He loved that woman.

At the top of the stairs he reached for her, took her by the arm and spun her around. Just like that day, he fisted her hair in his hand and pulled her head back. She whimpered with a soft little mewl when his lips landed on her throat. And just like that first day, her pulse quivered under his touch.

She gave him a shove. "Logan, no. I'm still mad at you."

Even though he could have held fast, he didn't. He released her. Let her turn to the door and push it open. It took a lot of willpower to keep from grabbing her by the hand and dragging her into the private office, shutting the door, and ravishing her from head to toe.

He understood why she was mad. Didn't she realize he did what he did for her own good? To save her from the vampire mafia?

He tried to erect those mental walls between them again but he could hear her racing thoughts with lots of questions and a jumble of emotions. It bothered her to be in her father's office so fresh after the funeral and not having been back since that fateful day. She idly wondered when she would have the nerve to go through his things. And thinking of her father's death made her think of the day he died, which flared the anger inside her once again.

"Being in your father's office was hard for you," he said.

She fidgeted, distracting herself by arrangement the remotes to the security televisions on the desk like little soldiers. When she didn't like the order, she rearranged them again.

"It was," she agreed.

"Bree, I'm sorry. I never meant to make you unhappy."

Her hands halted as she looked at him with an unreadable expression. "You saved my enemy."

"I made a bargain with your enemy," he said. "Those men will never bother you again because I gave Dominic his life back."

"But that doesn't make it okay. Aside from the fact that he killed my father, Logan, he's a criminal."

"He is. He's also looking for a new distributor for his synthetic blood which he will never be able to produce again."

She tilted her head to the side, her brows drawn together in question. "Why is that?"

"Because I burned the plant to the ground."

When he made his jaunt over East Hampton to do away with Vera's greasy diner, he made a stopover at the place in upstate New

York responsible for creating Dominic's synthetic blood. Likely the mafia leader knew by now the plant had been destroyed. And when he discovered what Logan did, he would likely come after him again.

"I also made him swear to never come back here again. They will never bother you again."

He bought an insurance policy with Dominic's life when he saved him. Insurance that he would never try to harm Bree again, even if Logan was out of the picture. He could leave her with some comfort knowing she was safe, at least, from Dominic and his mafia.

"You did?" Her voice was quiet.

"I did. And that he wouldn't come after you for the money your father owed him."

She inhaled a deep breath, exhaled it, and then leaned back against the desk. "I suppose I owe you thanks then."

"You know why I did it."

"Do I?"

"You should."

She bit her lip. "I think I do. But I want to hear you say it. Out loud."

Logan took a tentative step toward her. "You know it's because I love you, Bree."

"No." She held up a hand to stop him. "Not like that."

"What do you mean?"

"Don't say it like that. Say it like you mean it."

"I did mean it."

"Say it."

He moved toward her again. Her hand dropped to her side as she looked up at him from her half-seated position. He slid his arms around her, encircling her waist as he pulled her closer.

"I love you, Bree."

A breath shuddered out of her as she blinked owlish eyes. "You do?"

"I do."

"You're not saying it because we're bonded, are you? Or that I made you?"

"No, I'm saying it because it's true. I'm glad you made me." He kissed the tip of her nose. "I'm sorry I stole your revenge but I did it for your own good. I did it to make sure you were safe from them from now on."

"I...I know you did. I'm glad you did. Rafe said I would regret it if I went through with it. Maybe he's right."

He knew she would. Taking another life—vampire, human or otherwise—for any reason would haunt her the rest of her days.

"But I was still mad at you."

"I know. Forgive me?"

"Yes."

"Good." He released her and stepped back, reaching into his pocket. "I have a question to ask you then."

When he first told her the bonding was like marriage in her human realm, he had sensed the wave of disappointment come over her. He knew human customs for marriage and courtship and they had basically skipped to the end. He planned to rectify that. He pulled the small box from his pocket, holding it in his fist so she couldn't see it.

"And what is that?" she asked.

Logan dropped to one knee and popped open the box in one fluid motion. "Marry me?"

Her face drained of color and she gripped the edge of the desk, the nail beds of her fingers turning white. Her eyes were wide as she stared at the two-carat, princess cut diamond ring nestled in the crushed white velvet ring box. He'd had to sweet talk Rafe out of a chunk of money to make it happen. The knight had reluctantly agreed.

"Logan...I thought you said we were married."

"In my world, yes. In yours, no. Isn't is customary for the man to kneel and offer a ring?"

"Well...yes. But I thought—"

"You think too much, Bree. Will you marry me?"

"Yes, Logan. I will."

He rose and took the ring out of the box. She held out her left hand so he could slide it on her finger. She made it sparkle in the fluorescent lighting of the dingy office.

"I also promised you a real date. And I intend to make good on that. But first." He pulled her to him, one arm around her waist, another fisting in her hair. "A kiss to seal the deal."

"Just a kiss?" she asked, her voice low and sultry.

"Minx."

Before she could reply, his mouth overtook hers. He liked kissing her more than anything. Her lips were sweet and full. She tasted like a little piece of heaven. Heaven he could never live without for the rest of his days.

"What about the bar?"

"You can keep the bar if you want." His mouth trailed down her throat.

"I have more questions. Like where will we live?"

"We can live here and there."

"Here and there?"

"New York and the Hidden Lands."

"But—"

He lifted his hand and placed two fingers over her mouth. "Bree, shh. There will be time to figure all that out later. You have a wedding to plan."

"I do?"

"You said you'd marry me. Now you have to make good on that."

"With a real wedding?"

"Isn't that what you want?"

He heard the thought trickle through her mind before she could stop it. It was what she wanted. What every girl wanted since she could dream of her big day. Bree had accepted she would never get that since she and Logan had bonded. Now he was giving her that chance. He was giving her the wedding she'd always wanted.

"Well...yes."

"Then pick a day. And I'll show up in a tux and do whatever you tell me to do."

She smiled. "All right." Her hands landed on either side of his face. "I love you, too, you know."

"I know."

When Logan's mouth landed on hers in a feral kiss, Bree knew what she wanted. What she had to do. What she had always wanted to do. She wanted to make her wicked fantasy come true. She damned the pencil skirt she'd chosen to wear that day because it didn't allow her to wrap her legs around his waist.

She reached behind her and unzipped it.

"Here?" he asked, when he heard the zip.

"Yes." She pulled his shirt up, her hands landing on his chest. "Now."

He grinned as a groan rumbled through his chest. He shoved her skirt down enough for her to shimmy out of it. Her shaking fingers worked on the button of his pants. She tugged until it came free. He batted her hands away with a sudden frenzy to free his erection. She understood—she felt the same way.

His mouth was on hers again as he shoved aside her panties and pushed deeply inside her in one quick thrust. Free of the skirt, she could wrap her legs around him, their mouths colliding in a rush of need and desire. As though they were slaking their thirst for each other.

Her swift orgasm burst through her before she could stop it. And a moment later, his followed. And then everything went still.

But nothing was quiet in her mind. She could hear him again with all his lascivious thoughts. Thoughts of things he wanted to do to her, with her.

"I heard that." Her words came on a pant.

"You can hear me again? In your mind?"

She nodded.

What about now? he asked.

Yes, now, too, she agreed.

"I guess that proves one thing," he said with a grin.

"And what is that?"

"This is the only way to reinforce our bond, to keep you connected to me."

She giggled. "Yes, I think you're right."

Bree wouldn't want it any other way.

❧ Epilogue ❧

Six Months Later

Bree woke in a dreamy haze as sunlight streamed into the bedroom. After a moment of disorientation, she remembered where she was—in Logan's house in the Hidden Lands. They had returned here after the wedding she and Meg planned. Rather than have the event at a fancy hotel or anywhere else, they shut down the bar for a night and had it there followed by a reception. The regulars—supernatural and human—attended. Meg was her maid of honor. Rafe reluctantly agreed to be best man.

She rolled to her back and looked up at the ceiling, her hand resting on the swell of her belly. She was only just now starting to show and could feel the baby moving around as though doing somersaults. He or she was always very active in the morning.

Their life had settled into a natural rhythm. Logan took control of the Council of Five as Chief Magistrate and started to repair the damage Archer left behind. The other clan members and council leaders trusted him, admired him. And she knew it was because of his father's legacy. She wished she'd known him and his mother. All Logan had of them was the house he grew up in and a few pictures.

When they weren't in the Hidden Lands, she was back at the bar. She promoted Meg to assistant manager to help her with the day to day activities while she was away. Bree knew deep down she would eventually have to give it all up, but for now, she wanted to hang on to it. It was all she had left of her own father's legacy.

She found the Hidden Lands were not so different from the human realm. Their technology was as advanced as humans, though some of them preferred the Old World feel of the Hidden Lands as opposed to a city life. There were numerous areas of the Hidden Lands that remained as it had for centuries—wild and untamed. She found she liked that more than the hustle and bustle of the city.

And so did Logan. He was in his element here.

He entered the bedroom with a steaming mug of coffee in one hand and a plate of food in the other. One of the things Logan took pleasure in was plying her with coffee and food. He paused to look her over as she pushed to a sitting position. She could hear his thoughts but she couldn't quite decipher all the fluttering around in his mind. She knew there was something he'd come to tell her.

"What is it?" she asked.

He handed her the mug of coffee and plate. "You know something is bothering me, don't you?"

"Yes, so out with it." She set aside the mug and held the plate, watching him as he prowled the room.

"I found my father's notes on the Blood Stone." He paced the length of the bedroom, his hands shoved deeply in his pockets. "He had them buried in his desk in the study and wrote them in our ancient language. It took me some time to decipher them."

Her stomach twisted with his despondent tone. "What did you find?"

"It is possible for the Hidden Lands to be saved with the Blood Stone. But there's a catch. There are two more relics that have to be found to make it work. A dragon scale and a dragon tooth. But not just any scale or tooth from any dragon. It has to be a particular one from a particular dragon."

Bree's mouth went dry as she stared at him. "What dragon?"

Logan faced her as he took a deep breath. "It's complicated. Among dragon-shifters there are specific breeds—elementals, cold-drakes and fire-drakes. Elementals harness their power from nature and the world around them—earth, wind, fire, water. Cold-drakes, as their name implies, are more like a serpent when they shift and harness only the power of ice and snow. They prefer frozen climates and tend to stick close to them. Fire-drakes are just the opposite. All fire and brimstone. They live in arid, dry regions mostly."

"Mostly?"

"The cold-drakes and fire-drakes have all but died out. Probably due to the changes in climates in the Hidden Lands. It's the same thing threatening us," he said. "One particular clan of cold-drakes, though, moved into the human realm and positioned themselves as a royal family in the small kingdom of Andonia. They had the Blood Stone with them when they left."

"That's where Shi'Ann Jones said it was stolen from," she said, remembering the cop who came to visit.

He nodded. "Yes. There is only one remaining clan of fire-drakes but I haven't found them yet."

"What does this have to do with the other two relics?"

"We need a scale from a fire-drake and a tooth from a cold-drake to make it all work," he said. "Then there's some sort of blood ritual involved. I haven't figured that part out yet."

She swallowed. "What does that mean?"

"It means I have to enlist the help of the cold-drakes and the fire-drakes if I'm to save the Hidden Lands. And since Rafe is still in the human realm, I'll need his help to track them down."

"You think he will?"

"Perhaps. If I promise to release him from exile."

Bree recalled the sadness that had come over his face at Archer's death when he realized he would never be able to return to the Hidden Lands to be put to rest.

"He'd do it for that, I think."

"I'll go see him tomorrow." Logan noticed her plate of untouched food. "Time for breakfast, my lady." He perched on the edge of the bed, shoving away those thoughts of the Hidden Lands and turning to more pleasant things. Like her and the baby. "How are you both this morning?"

She patted her belly. "Active."

He placed his free hand on top of hers just as the baby did a massive kick and then spun. He grinned. "Yes, he is."

"You don't know it's a he," she teased. She hoped it was a girl. When he gave her a sheepish look and didn't answer, she stared at him wide-eyed. "Do you?"

"Your eggs are getting cold."

She set aside the plate and clasped his hands in hers. "Logan, do you know?"

He swallowed hard. "I hope you're not disappointed. I know you wanted a girl."

Bree rested her hands on her active belly and looked down. She was having a boy. Disappointed? Never. She could never be disappointed.

"Could we name him Elijah after your father?"

She sensed a flood of emotions from him. His face softened, his expression changed to one of complete and utter joy.

"If you're sure."

"I'm sure."

When he wrapped his arm around her and kissed her, she knew it was the right thing to do. She couldn't wait to meet her son.

Also by Michelle Miles

Age of Wizards (Epic Fantasy)
In the Tower of the Wizard King
On the Hunt for the Wizard King

**Dragon Protectors
(Paranormal Shifter Romance)**
Desiring the Dragon Lord
Seducing the Dragon Knight
Tempting Her Dragon Bodyguard
Dragon Protectors Book Collection (Books 1-3)

Dream Walker (Urban Fantasy)
Call of the Dark
Blood and Bone
Flame and Fury
Smoke and Ashes
Light of the World
Dream Walker Collection (Books 1-5)

Dream Walker: Origins (Fantasy)
Provenance

Enchanted Realms (Fantasy Romance)
Once Upon a Midnight Clear
Once Upon True Love's Kiss
Once Upon an Enchanted Kiss

Five Towers (YA Fantasy)
The Sorcerer's Daughter

her security detail is ambushed, she's nearly kidnapped, but lands in the arms of the oh-so-sexy Rafe.

Rafe needs Mia to redeem himself and return to his kingdom. Mia needs Rafe to help her secure the Blood Stone and return it to her family. As they become a bonded pair, needing each other more than life itself, will he trade everything he's worked hard for to save her, or will he risk losing her—and his freedom—forever?

Read more at www.michellemiles.net

About the Author

Michelle Miles believes in fairy tales, true love and magic. She is the award-winning author of the epic fantasy, IN THE TOWER OF THE WIZARD KING, as well as the fantasy romance series, REALM OF HONOR, featuring knights and their ladies fair, and the paranormal dragon-shifter romance series, DRAGON PROTECTORS.

In her spare time, she enjoys listening to music, reading, cross-stitching and watching movies. Even though she's a native Texan, she loves castles, dragons, fairies and elves and is an avid Game of Thrones fan. She can be found online at Facebook, Twitter, Instagram, Pinterest, and Goodreads.